COMING OF AGE

THREE DARK NOVELLAS

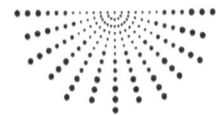

DOUGLAS CLEGG

ALKEMARA
PRESS

CONTENTS

THE ATTRACTION

ALSO BY DOUGLAS CLEGG

STAND-ALONE NOVELS

Afterlife

Breeder

The Children's Hour

Dark of the Eye

Goat Dance

The Halloween Man

The Hour Before Dark

Mr. Darkness

Naomi

Neverland

You Come When I Call You

SHORT NOVELS

The Attraction

The Dark Game (Two Novelettes)

Dinner with the Cannibal Sisters

The Faces

Isis

Mrs. Bluebeard

The Necromancer

The Words

Wild Things

BOX SET BUNDLES

Bad Places (3 Novels)

Coming of Age (3 Dark Novellas)

Dark Rooms (3 Novels)

Criminally Insane: The Series (3 Novels)

Halloween Chillers

Harrow: Three Novels (Books 1-3)

Harrow: Four Novels (Books 1-4)

Lights Out (3 Collection Box Set)

Night Towns (3 Novels)

The Vampyricon Trilogy (3 Novels)

With more new novels, novellas and stories to come.

GET STUFF. STAY CONNECTED.
READ MORE.

Visit DouglasClegg.com

COMING OF AGE

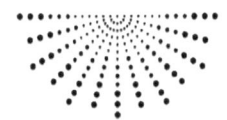

PURITY

For Raul

"Vast, Polyphemus-like, and loathsome, it darted like a stupendous monster of nightmares…" —*H.P. Lovecraft, from "Dagon."*

SUMMER BEGINS

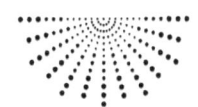

WHY I CALLED YOU HERE

There is no madness but the madness of the gods. There is no purity but the purity of love.

SOMEONE ONCE WROTE that "the most merciful thing in the world, I think, is the inability of the human mind to correlate its contents."

This sentiment describes my feelings perfectly. I correlate too much of my own mind's contents. It's always troubling. I don't live in the chronological moment; I doubt you do, either. I live all at once in the past with only glimpses of the present. I live mostly on that island, when it comes to me, when I think of my life as it formed. I live in darkness now, but the dark brings the memories back. The dark brings it all back. The dark is all I know. I call the dark. It's there that I find the god I met one day when I was just a child. I remember that day; not the days of blood to come. In the end, we were together.

In the beginning, we were not.

HERE ARE the words I will never forget:

"Owen, I'm so sorry. I'm so sorry. I should never have come this summer."

Before that, the gun went off.

Before that, I looked into her eyes.

Before that is when it all began.

Dagon, bring it back to me.

WHO I AM

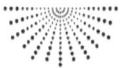

These are the things I know: Outerbridge Island has briny water running beneath its rocks, a subterranean series of narrow channels between the Sound and the Atlantic. You can see the entrances to these channels on the northern side of the island at low tide.

These channels feed into the Great Salt Pond on the westerly side of the island before it empties into the sea. It was said that once upon a time, a Dutch trading ship smashed up against the rocks, and local pirates fed upon the treasures found within the hold of the ship. The treasure, it is said, was buried in the narrow caverns. To add to the chill of this tale, it was also said that the pirates fed upon the flesh of the survivors of the wreck for days.

I've actually swum into the caverns at times. I'm slender enough, and in good enough shape to maneuver in the darkness of the water, but I never found treasure, nor did I emerge in the Great Salt Pond by following the channels within that part of the island. I needed air, after all.

If you want something badly enough, there are ways to get it.

This doesn't mean they are traditional means. It doesn't mean that pain is not involved. It doesn't mean that the cost may not overwhelm the need. It just means there are ways to get what you really want in this world.

If one has a conscience, one can be driven mad. Therefore, a conscience is a key to madness. Everyone is a potential madman. Everyone. The sweetest boy in the world can be driven to the most irrational of acts. The girl who has the world at her feet, likewise, could be pushed toward some act of desperation and tragedy.

And, in many ways, we want the irrational and the tragic and the desperate, because they bring meaning and life back into our existences.

Another fact: My mother prizes three things above all others.

First, the rose garden which my father planted for her before I was born. It runs in spirals along the bluffs and the small hillock behind our cottage. There are fourteen varieties of roses, with hues ranging from pale peach to blood red.

Second, her koi pond, which is really the Montgomerys' koi pond, but it sits on our side of the property. It is largish for a pond, and narrow, nearly a reflecting pool. It was built deep for the harsh winters —the koi can survive a thick layer of ice as long as they can bury themselves down in the silt. My father covers the pool with a plastic tarp to further protect the fish.

And finally, my mother prizes the gun. My maternal

grandfather had a pistol that had been given to him by his mother.

It was a small Colt pistol—what my grandfather called a vest pistol, but which I thought of as a Saturday Night Special. It had mother-of-pearl grips, and a clip that could not be removed from it.

My grandfather had given my mother the pistol in the early years of her marriage to protect herself when my father would beat her. My father never beat my mother, but my grandfather would apparently not believe it. The pistol is useless, I heard my mother once say. Never been fired. I could barely shoot a cat with it, she joked.

Someday, she told me, when she was weepy and bitter about life, she would go to Boston and sell it to a collector and take the money and go far, far away.

When I first discovered my true god and his nature, I took the pistol.

Final fact: Faith plays into all of this. One must have faith that one can do what one sets out to do. One must have the courage of one's convictions. All the world's history teaches us this.

For me, it is that god I discovered. I call it Dagon, although its name is unknown to me. It came from the sea, and I held it captive, briefly.

I am its priest. And Dagon, in a twisted and true way, upholds what I stand for.

One must stand for something.

For me, it is the force of love. The undertow of love. But that sounds romantic, and I'm not a romantic at all. I've been called a lot of things since the day I was born, but never romantic. Schemer. Athlete. Brain. Manipulator.

User. Common. Handsome. Shallow. Arrogant. Mad. Sociopath. Cold eyes. All by my mother.

Jenna Montgomery once told me I had the most beautiful eyes she'd ever seen on a boy.

I had to catch my breath when she told me that.

She said it the same day I made the first sacrifice to the god I'd met.

YEARS AGO, I came upon the god during a storm of late November, a frozen, bitter storm, in which I had gotten caught down at the caverns, taking a dinghy out to look for the famous buried pirate treasure.

I was twelve and lonely, and when I saw the god thrust in between a rock and a hard place, as it were, I knew immediately who and what it was, and how I should please it. I read in my father's bible that Dagon was the god of the Philistines; the Fish-God. I found other books, too, with titles like *The Shadow over Innsmouth* and *Dagon,* that further told of the god and its worshippers and what was needed to feed the god.

Some may say it is just an abominable statue, a cheap and even grotesque trinket of some distant bazaar, brought by sailors or perhaps even the pirates. It is green with age, and made wholly of stone. Its eyes are merely garnet; its tail and fins carved with some exquisite artistry.

But when I bled a seagull over the cold eyes of the little god, while the storm raged around me, I felt a prayer had been answered. I breathed easier then.

BREATHING IS ESSENTIAL TO SURVIVAL, and although this seems like a given, we know—scientifically—that it is not. Most of the problems of life are like that: simple, obvious, graspable, yet shrouded in a secret.

If one can breathe well—through any crisis, and exertion—then one will survive. It is those who stop breathing who have let go of their wills to live. I am what people in this world call a sociopath, although the idea of killing someone has never interested me.

A sociopath is not necessarily a killer, and to assume this is to play a dangerous game. Just as not all famous people are rich, not all sociopaths are Jeffrey Dahmer. If Jeffrey was one at all.

You must know this about me if you're going to understand exactly what went on at Outerbridge Island the summer I turned eighteen, the summer before Jenna Montgomery was to leave me forever.

They say that people like me can't experience love, but I find that a ridiculous statement. I'm fully capable of giving and receiving love, and it is monstrous to suggest otherwise. Even all those years ago I was, and love burned in me just as it did any boy who had fallen.

My mother would take her daily pain pill as I grew up —her pains being life itself and even her child—and tell me that there were two kinds of people in this world, the kind that give and the kind that take, and I knew I was neither, but somewhere in between the rest of the world: I was someone who observed, perhaps too coldly at times. I still observe, and observation has brought me to this place again.

Outerbridge Island, with its rocky ledges and glassy sea, the fog that came suddenly, the sun that tore through clouds like a nuclear explosion, the summers that went for years; the years that passed in a summer.

The storms that came and stayed and never left.

LET me turn it all back to the day I was born, since from what I've read about sociopaths, it's a fairly genetic condition.

My grandmother was probably the carrier of the gene, since she went crazy and ended up in what they called a nursing home over in Massachusetts, but which I found out—later in life, of course—was an impoverished sanitarium, the sort from which nightmares are born.

My mother told me it was my grandfather's fault for driving her to do things—again, not kill, for we have never been murderers—just things that caused people to believe my grandmother was insane.

When I was born, as my mother told me when I was eleven or twelve, I presented a difficult birth. My umbilical cord practically strangled me as I exited her body. She said I was blue in the face for nearly a minute from lack of oxygen before the doctor got me coughing. Then, I spent the first two weeks of my life in the hospital, for I was a month premature and no one thought I would live.

Sometimes I think this is why I'm a sociopath. I've seen documentaries on PBS about baby monkeys who are separated from their mothers for a short time, and this makes them seem without conscience (if that is truly what a sociopath is, although I don't believe it). My mother said she didn't touch me for the first month; she was terrified I'd die, and because she had already lost one child—two years earlier—in some kind of crib death incident, she feared holding her first son, me. My father had to do all the touching and picking up, and even—my mother told me—nursing me felt unnatural and dangerous to her. Instead, my aunt became my wet nurse—she who had, just five months before, given birth to twins and seemed to have milk enough for the entire population of the island.

There were times, when I was older, that I wished my aunt had taken me back with her to her home on the mainland. Times when I hated the island. Hated my mother and father. Hated looking at the Montgomery house—the Montgomery Mansion, the Montgomery Palazzo, the Big Place—staring down at us. But I suppose all this anger came about because of those first few days of life.

These things aren't spoken of much in families—how we each came to be. My mother suffered through bouts of depression, particularly in the winter, and she would stand in front of her bedroom window, looking out across the Sound, her face a shimmering reflection in the thick window glass, and tell me all about myself.

She told me that when I was six weeks old, she realized I had never really cried, at least not the way babies were supposed to. Instead, I would turn red, and my mouth would open, and I'd scream. That's how she'd know I was hungry or needed changing. Because she was so grateful to have a child after she felt God had taken away her first in retribution for youthful transgressions, she tried not to think about what my lack of tears might mean.

As she'd tell this kind of story, I'd shift uncomfortably on her bed, wishing she'd release me from this strange intimacy—the closeness of her depression, the morbid way her mind would pick over my birth and early years.

"I'm so sorry that you turned out this way," she said, once, her hands going up to her face. "I'm happy you're so smart. Not like your father. But this madness that comes over you...."

I remained silent, letting her have her feelings. I didn't understand then to what she referred—I was not mad. I took the ferry to go to school over on the mainland and did quite well in school. The ferry takes an hour and a half in the winter, and only runs twice a day—for school hours, since Outerbridge had no school of its own. Thus, I spent many nights with my Aunt Susan in Rhode Island, and learned more about my mother's mother than I had ever wanted to know. I also managed—through my cousin Davy—to make friends off-island, friends who believed I was like them. And I had a lot of friends as a child.

Although I was not considered handsome at first—at least not by my mother, who found my hair to be too ominous in some way, my eyes too blue and perhaps too sharp, my manner arrogant (even as an eight-year-old, she'd called me that)—I began learning the secret of athletics early and applied myself to molding my body the same way I went about molding my mind. I studied and read and found the boys who seemed to know what they were doing, and I gravitated toward them. I learned what they knew by nature. I was uncoordinated in most sports, until I realized that, as in all things, it was about breathing.

This is one of the secrets of life:

It's all about breathing.

VOICES IN THE DARK:

"It's all right, I know you. I know what we both want."

"Shut up. Just shut up."

"Come here. Come here. Let me help you. It's all right. It feels good."

"No, not like this. No."

"I've been so lonely."

"Oh."

"Wanting this."

"Oh."

"Since the first time I saw you."

"Oh."

HAVE you ever felt that you would do anything to be with someone?

I almost feel sorry for you, if you haven't.

THE PURITY of life is in the secrets—they're simple, they

say everything, they are there for anyone, but we must wake up to the purity first in order to understand the secrets.

My pursuit of physical excellence began early. I tackled solitary athletics since this seemed best for my character. They were also cheaper. My family was poor—have I mentioned that? Not *poor* poor. Not "out in the street with no food" poor, but poor nonetheless.

My mother's first husband had been rich, but had also been a gambler. My mother—I should call her Boston, for that's what my father called her even though her name was Helen—had been the fifth daughter in a wealthy family who had married well, briefly, the first time around. But that man—someone I had never in my life heard of beyond knowing he existed—apparently lost all his and Helen's money, and soon she found my father, a good man (one would suppose) who ended up working as a gardener for rich folk. It paid well enough—like I said, we weren't *poor* poor.

My father probably would've had more money, but he had a sister who was dying—for years—down in Annapolis, Maryland, and he was her only support. So, according to my mother, half of his income went to her upkeep. "She has the longest-lived cancer I've ever heard of," she'd say, sometimes right in front of him.

Of course, this wasn't all there was to it, but if I tell you all the secrets of the world at once, you'll either be dazzled or overwhelmed, and there's no point in making it all explode right now. You'll want to know why breathing is one of the secrets of life.

You know how breathing is voluntary? I've heard that

people with dementia sometimes end up forgetting how to breathe. That's a terrible way to die, although one would suppose that any method of dying would be awful. Well, breathing is the essential component of accomplishing anything.

I observed this early—I was on the school bus, and I noticed a little girl next to me who was terrified of an upcoming test we were about to take. She would, in fact, stop breathing for seconds at a time. I began to count her breaths. I noticed that for every one breath I took, she took four. I suggested to her that she try just concentrating on her breathing.

After a bit of persuasion, she did.

It didn't seem to work.

I held up my father's watch —the one I'd stolen. (Yes, I stole things regularly around the house. I have reasons, none of which you want to know.) I had learned a bit about hypnosis, so I asked her to gaze at the brass back of the watch as it caught sunlight through the bus window.

She asked me if I'd be putting her under. I told her that was up to her. This was, after all, just suggestion, nothing more. I would propose something and hope her mind would accept it. Of course, I was a child. I didn't say it that way. I said it in some little boy way.

She stared at the watch so much her eyes teared up.

I began to slow her breathing. By the time we reached school, she wasn't upset about the test beyond what might be considered a normal concern.

I began asking the other boys—the older ones who were good at softball and running—about the secrets their success. To get them to trust me, I entertained them with my modest ventriloquism skills—I could do birdcalls and the sounds of crickets and even get brief sentences out without moving my lips.

Boys like entertainment, so they opened up and told me about athletics and sports. They all said screwy things, but what I noticed were two solid answers:

Breathing and imagination.

They made sure that they breathed through everything. They also imagined that they would win. This was a huge revelation to me, since I had never felt that I could win anything. I realized that these other boys were winners in athletics because they in fact believed they were—whether from coaches, friends, family or whomever—and because they did not stop breathing. They used their breathing—without even knowing it—to help keep their bodies working.

All right, that may sound simplistic. I believe that the simplest things can lead to the strongest results.

So, I began to work on breathing in a way I hadn't before.

This was not merely inhaling and exhaling, but swimming at the beach in the icy spring and holding my breath underwater. After all, if I were going to be lord of my own breath, I needed to master everything about it, didn't I? I wasn't sure that I'd ever be a great breath-holder, because I never seemed able to go much beyond a minute. I was holding on too much to my fear of dying.

This is one of the first lessons about breathing—if you have breath within your lungs, you will not die. Death comes once there is no more breath.

Again, simple.

Again, true.

"Owen," my mother said, pinning the laundry up outside the cottage that the Montgomerys housed us in. "What in god's name are you doing?"

I had come up after logging in a minute-and-a-half beneath the water, right at the rocky ledge. I had just leaned over and thrust my face underwater. I was eleven at the time. I tried to explain to her the principle behind my experiment, but she did not seem to understand.

However, within a few short months, I had become best friends with the captain of the swim team in seventh grade, and by fall, I was running cross-country. I would never be the best—this was not my goal, after all. I would be a winner. In fact, I knew I would close in on this with each sport or endeavor I tried, because the other kids were lazy. Life and their families made them that way. I did not intend to let a day go by which I could not claim for my own. I was going to own life in a way that neither of my parents ever had. Academics slipped in my middle-school years—but not enough for anyone to notice. I read studiously, and never for enjoyment, but to understand systems of thought that the world was trying to push at us.

I learned quickly that an A+ in school sometimes meant a D- in life, and that equal effort had to be made to excel in both spheres.

When I felt overwhelmed by it all, I practiced my breathing again. Swimming helped, too, when everything around me grew dark and terrible.

Even in December, when the island was desolate and the water cold enough to freeze you to death, I might leap into the sea and stay beneath the water as long as I could stand it. Other icy days, I'd use the Montgomerys' indoor swimming pool for my morning workouts.

THAT WAS the wonderful thing about the Montgomerys' place: they were usually gone all winter unless Mr. and Mrs. Montgomery were fighting, or Mr. Montgomery had gone off with one of his mistresses and Mrs. M was so angry she came to the island for a blisteringly cold February. I used to see Mrs. M in those cold Februarys, and I ran errands in town for her because she spent too much time staring at the walls or sitting along the indoor pool while I did laps.

She enjoyed letting me swim there, and she sometimes even got in and did laps, too.

Once, when I was twelve, Mrs. M told me, "You're turning into quite the handsome boy, Owen Crites."

She was in good shape for a woman of forty, and there were times when I was with her that she reminded me so much of Jenna it was almost like having Jenna there with me.

When I watched her back, as she got out of the pool, bathing cap on, her narrow waist, the way the water beaded upon her skin—it was like seeing Jenna for a moment. This made me happy. Jenna meant a lot to me.

But the pool—dare I describe it now, how I remember it? It was vast. It was Olympic size. I could do real laps there, as opposed to laps at the beach which ended with a summer lifeguard blowing a whistle for me to come to shore before I'd gone out twenty yards. It was off the southern wing of their estate, surrounded with glass, so that it was as if you were swimming outside, as if on the bluffs over the Sound.

You owned the world as you went back and forth, carefully breathing so as not to wear out too fast.

During those winters when the Montgomerys stayed down in Manhattan, my father and mother and I had the run of the house. I could swim naked in the pool and rise to see the reflection of my body in the long mirrors in the small locker room off the pool. By sophomore year in high school I had created—and mastered—a beautiful, strong body. What average looks I had were masked by health and physical near-perfection.

I didn't admire this physique because I believed in beauty.

Beauty is for the lazy.

I admired it because I knew the world admired it. I wanted to own the world.

Wrestling was my winter sport at school, and I did not excel at it, but I held my own. The girls loved me—and the boys, too. I never got too close to them, because I had to spend all my energy creating who the person they wanted to see. The girls all cheered for me during sweaty matches when I brought some great bull of a boy from a competing school down hard to the red mat. Because the psychological aspect to sports can't be emphasized enough, I would—with each match—create some threat to my opponent. Something I could whisper in his ear. This took no small planning as it meant doing research on the boys I might wrestle so I'd know just what button to push to give me a psychological edge.

Dagon helped me. My god took me to books and ideas and *notions* that showed me just what other boys might be most hurt by. Usually, it involved their sense of sexuality.

After all, even *I* knew that showering with other boys, wearing jockstraps, cracking jokes about assorted vulgarities and nicknaming genitalia drew a thin veil across homoeroticism among adolescents.

And who but wrestlers were closest to puncturing that veil?

So, I'd whisper to my opponent something about him, something perhaps his closest friend had told me—his closest friend, drunk, being taken out to a parking lot— his closest friend who, with six beers in him, would finally admit to something that my opponent would be happiest to hide for a thousand years. Sometimes, it was less interesting.

My threat might be, "I know your little sister, Trey. I know all about her leg. I would hate for something to happen to her. I would hate for someone to do something to a little girl so sweet."

You may judge me for this if you like.

It was a competitive edge. This is what we, in athletics, were taught: *find your edge*. Skill alone never wins. I wish it did, but lazy people think that way. Faith is necessary, too. I had found mine. It had grown within me.

Now, my whisperings to opponents ignited rumors about me, but I'd built up a loyal enough following of other boys and girls in school. I became head of the pep squad for the football team—team sports were never my thing, but I knew that I had to somehow attach myself to them. So, when kids from other schools began talking about me saying "crazy, psycho" things, I had friends who were willing to lie down and die for me rather than accept those lies.

I really liked the kids I went to high school with; I liked the teachers. It was easy for me to like them. I think even being poor helped—teachers saw me as an underdog rising. I would tutor children in the local elementary school some afternoons; I took the coach's daughter to the junior prom, just because I was a nice guy and I felt bad that she wasn't pretty enough to get asked by any of the other guys. I was well-liked, and sometimes, that carries you.

But I haven't mentioned much about Jenna yet, have I? In all this talk of myself, she hasn't yet entered—not in the way she should have. She didn't go to my school. She barely existed within my sphere. She was *outer*, her world spun beyond the beyond. How could I even take her to the prom when she only arrived at Outerbridge Island in the summers?

I would count the days until Memorial Day weekend, when the Outerbridge Majesty would arrive in Quonnoquet Haven, heavy with tourists and summer people, and there, on the highest deck, I'd see her with my binoculars and then lie back in the muddy grass to look up at the pale sky and think: Please remember what we promised. Remember everything and don't leave anything out. Remember why I came to you and why you let me and why it would make everything be the way it was supposed to, and why you're the reason for my every breath.

That's what had happened when I was twelve and

dedicated my soul to the god of dark places. By the time I was seventeen, I was a dedicated servant to the one I worshipped. And the only thing I asked of this divinity was:

Give me Jenna.

I'LL TELL you what really happened the summer I discovered purity—*genuine purity*—in the shit of human existence.

I can see myself as I was then, young, even pretty in a way with my thick hair falling to either side of my face, my eyes sharp, yes, but expectant. My polo shirt a preppie affectation—my mother never wanted me to look like the other islanders, she wanted something better for me, as did I. Khakis, no socks, catalog-ordered moccasins or village-made leather sandals—my face burning from the beginnings of summer sun, my heart racing.

It's no longer me as I am. It's that boy, this boy who is almost eighteen, maybe a man at this point, a boy who moves in the direction from "want" to "have."

I, he, you, it doesn't matter what I call that boy-man, he just exists in this globe of eternal summer. I can feel his breath and smell dime-store cologne on him. When he smiles I can see the cap on his front tooth that cost his father a pretty penny after he fell and chipped it in sixth grade while running.

I sense a dense fog lifting between this day and that one.

He watches, this magnificent Owen Crites, for her.

A WINDOW VIEW

Owen Crites looked to summer for one thing, and one thing only. It would be the arrival of Jenna Montgomery, and that would mean his misery, his feelings of loneliness would vanish. He could nearly forget himself.

Where is she? he wondered, remembering the first time he knew she belonged with him.

"Hı," he said to her when they were both six.

"Hi," she replied. But she hadn't needed to. She was all ringlets and ribbons and party dress.

"Owen," he said.

"I know. Hank's your daddy."

The fact that she called his father by his first name shocked Owen. No other child called a parent by the first name. It was taboo. And to call his father "Hank" and not "Henry" seemed far too familiar.

"I know where you live," she added, an afterthought.

"Down the hill," he said.

"In my yard," she said. "You're near my goldfish pond."

"Koi," he corrected her.

"And all the roses my mommy loves," she said, and then took him by the hand and brought him into her world—the birthday party, the beautiful children from New York, the pony rides on the bluffs, the smoked turkey sandwiches, the games of pin-the-tail, and the dance.

He had been woefully underdressed in a torn pair of jeans and a T-shirt. The other boys all wore white shirts and little ties; their hair glistened with gel. The girls were in puffy dresses and glittery shoes. He had no gift for her then. It had panicked him midway through the party.

Owen took a gift off the pile from among those she hadn't yet opened. He threw away the other child's card. On the wrapping paper, he scrawled "*Happy Birthday from Owen.*"

As it turned out, the gift was a small hand puppet, and Owen took it from Jenna and began doing something that he didn't even know he could do. He threw his voice, so it sounded as if the puppet was speaking without Owen's lips moving. Even Mrs. M commented to Owen's mother about her son's delightful talent.

Owen received punishment for presenting the gift as his own, but he didn't mind.

Punishment was the result of knowledge. Smart people punished themselves, his older self knew. All people with brains received punishment.

From then on, Jenna Montgomery became everything

to him. In all those years from child to boy to man, he never experienced a night without thinking of her.

His teenage years nearly past, Owen waited for her, watching the glinting sea for the ferry on the Thursday before Memorial Day weekend.

HIS EYES TURNED to slits against the western sun; it was the last ferry of the day, and he couldn't find her or her parents among those on the deck.

Perhaps she wouldn't be coming until after the holiday —it had happened before. He didn't want to believe it because he never liked to consider the options that people had. His own life felt without options. He had created within himself the person who could most handle his life. He had worked his body, developed the grace of an athlete, he had tried to keep his face pleasant—and when the anxieties of his family or of studies became unbearable, he would go to the mirror and practice relaxing his facial features until he was sure he looked pleasant again. He did not want to seem anxious, even if he was. He wanted to give nothing away to those around him.

He ran down to the docks to see if she might be somewhere else on the ferry—perhaps she was sick and wanted to stay below. Perhaps she was taking a nap in the back seat of her family's Range Rover. Perhaps, perhaps, he repeated to himself as he sloughed off inertia, and jogged down to the paved road near the marina.

The summer people were like ticks—they attached themselves to every aspect of the island, they drank all the beer, they ate the best the local cooks had to offer, they had all the accidents—more people would die from boating or swimming mishaps in three months than would die in six years during other seasons.

They were careless, they were bloodsucking, they were here to forget the venal world from which they came. They, he thought. *They.* They debarked the ferry, bicyclists, clownish men and women in golfing outfits, or overly gilded women with poodles and wolfhounds and shih tzus, followed by weary overworked doctor-husbands; the college crowd, too, had begun filling up the local bars and the beach, and all these he hated with a passion. He had spent his life watching them come and be carefree in the summer.

He had watched them spend more money some nights than his father could make in a month.

Dagon, he prayed, Dagon, hear me. Cast them down. Raise me up.

He ached for what they had. The lives they possessed. The freedom from this island. From the world he had mastered.

He read books on Manhattan; he learned about Jenna's family, how her great-great-grandfather had worked on railroads and then had gone on to own them, and how her great-grandfather had lost that fortune; how her grandfather had gotten into radio and television and magazines, owning several, selling them, building up a small but substantial media empire; how her mother had continued that work, married a great media magnate, divorced, married again, had Jenna and remained with Mr. M although the marriage ran hot and cold.

The story of Jenna's family was the story of all the summer people, and though they lived simply on the island for the three months, though they rode cheap bikes around the Great Salt Pond, though they dressed casually even for the one restaurant in Old Town Harbor (the Salty Dog), they were all over-moneyed as his father often said.

His father spoke of money as evil; his mother spoke of it as if it were a lost child.

Owen felt money was something like fire—to be feared and mastered. It was what other people were given. It was what he would be granted. And these people tromping off the ferry had it. They lived it. They did not dream of getting off this island. They dreamed of things beyond what Owen could imagine.

JENNA DIDN'T ARRIVE at the harbor that day. He walked the long, narrow wooden staircase from the beach up to the bluffs, and ran along the fringe of pines to the dirt path that went further up the rolling cliffs. He didn't look back down to the water until he was at their property.

At the house, he went and sat in one of the wrought-iron lawn chairs and leaned back to gaze up at the sky.

"Owen?"

He sat up, looking around. He rose from the chair, practically knocking it over, and there she was—at the third-story attic window.

No, it was Mrs. M. Her auburn hair was swept back from her face, damp from the swimming pool; her robe fastened none too tight.

"Owen? It's good to see you."

"Yeah, Mrs. M, me too. I didn't think you had got here just yet."

"Oh, my husband still hasn't left his desk yet. I've been here since Wednesday. Good to be back. I despise the city."

"Survive winter okay?"

"Superbly," she said, but in a way that meant its opposite. Mrs. M was a woman full of irony; he had known it for years. Mrs. M. embodied the house: beautiful, classic, and rich.

"Do you want coffee?" she asked.

"I SAW YOU WAITING FOR HER," Mrs. M said.

They were in the sunroom off the kitchen. Owen had just finished his first cup of cinnamon coffee. He got up to pour himself another, but Mrs. M interceded. She had a fresh cup, with cream, all ready for him. He sat down at the table again.

She took the chair across from him. He saw her knee emerge from her robe. The hint of breast, like a reward.

Mrs. M was in many ways more beautiful than her daughter; but still, his heart belonged to Jenna.

He did what he could to look at her face, but something in her eyes bothered him. He looked, instead, at her silken arms.

"You're in love with my daughter. No, that's fine. I've known it since you were both young. Do you think it will lead anywhere?"

"Lead?" He said the word innocently, but she must've seen through him. "I don't know."

"Yes, you do. You're smart. But, do you think she's right for you?"

"I haven't…I haven't considered…" he stammered.

"You're a remarkable young man," Mrs. M said. "She doesn't deserve you."

Then, she put down her own untouched coffee and got up, drawing her robe together. "She gets in tonight. After midnight."

"How? The ferry—"

"She has her ways," Mrs. M said. She brushed something from the edge of her eye and combed her hands through her hair like a mermaid would. "Fancy a swim?"

"Not today," he said.

"Come on, just a nice long swim. Haven't you been practicing all winter?"

He nodded.

"I thought so. You ripple now. You don't move, you ripple. You're in better shape than he is," Mrs. M said, and then went to get her bathing suit.

COME MIDNIGHT, he saw the shroud of a blue and white sailboat press beneath the lights of the harbor. He sat up on the bluffs and watched as she docked; the sail came down. No one stepped off the boat at the jetty. Was it her? Was this what Mrs. M had meant?

He fell asleep in the cool wet grass and awoke at dawn. And he knew.

Jenna Montgomery had found another.

IN THE AFTERNOON, AT THE MONTGOMERYS', Owen met his rival.

"Jimmy," the guy said, his face gleaming, tanned, teeth so thoroughbred he could've raced in Saratoga, his eyes squinty, his nose small, his hair honey-blond from too much sun, and his handshake strong and sure and arrogant. He looked rich without ever having to say it. He smelled rich. He probably tasted rich.

"Good to meet you, Crites."

"Owen."

"You're not an Owen or a Crites," Jimmy said. "You're a Mooncalf."

"Mooncalf?" Jenna laughed, looking at Owen and then back at Jimmy. "That sounds ghastly."

She wore a bikini, but had a long towel draped about her waist that ran all the way to her ankles. Her hair was wet and shining from a morning swim.

For a moment, Owen imagined how it would feel to untie the bikini top and press his face against her breasts. For a moment, the image was in his mind; then, gone.

All Owen could think was: they'd slept together on the boat. Jenna and this Jimmy character. Jimmy had done it with Jenna. Done it. A sacred act if it was love. A debased ritual, if it was lust and emptiness. Which it had to be. He tried not to imagine Jimmy drawing her legs apart, or the scent of passion that clung to them, the sweat and fever, as they joined together. Tried not to imagine the thrusts.

"Mooncalf reminds me of upstate New York, or Pennsylvania," Jenna said with no little disgust. "Cows and chickens. Amish in carriages. Birthings and midwives. Owen can't be a Mooncalf."

Jim snorted. "No, it's a beautiful name. Mooncalf."

Owen remained silent, still numb from meeting the interloper.

"Well, if he's a Mooncalf then what am I?"

"Kitten." Jimmy laughed.

"If I'm Kitten, then you're Cat."

"All right, then I'm Cat. Now, what shall we call this island?"

"Outerbridge," Owen said. "Call it Outerbridge."

"That's not the game." Jimmy grinned, and damn if his smile wasn't dazzling. Anyone would fall in love with this guy, anyone, man, woman, or dog, he was so damn attractive and warm, it made Owen want to walk away and forget about Jenna completely. "The game is everything, Mooncalf. It doesn't matter what things are. You shape them into the way you want them. That's how you gain mastery."

"Mastery's the thing," Owen said, faking a sort of blissful—and very nearly nonchalant—take on all of it. I'll beat you, he thought as he watched his rival, this Apollonian boy with his golden hair and squinty green eyes; his arrogance felt absolutely seductive.

I will beat you, Owen made the oath then and there.

He glanced briefly up at the unfettered sun and prayed

to God that if nothing else went his way in this life, he would beat down this Jimmy.

Then, Owen reached a hand out and gave Jimmy's shoulder a friendly squeeze. "Just not big on games, I guess."

Jenna laughed. "Owen, the game is called Paradise. You rename everything to your liking. Jimmy invented it. Isn't it…marvelous?"

She pecked the bastard on his ear.

Owen noted: the kiss went to his earlobe, and Jimmy barely had an earlobe. His ear was smooth and rounded and touched down right behind one of his several dimples.

Jimmy laughed, shrugging, grabbing her around the waist and pulling her close to him.

"Let's call the island Sea Biscuit."

"No," Jenna groaned. "That's terrible. Terrible. Owen, you name it."

"Outerbridge," Owen said.

It was noon, and they were at the jetty. The sailboat bobbed gently with the current, and Owen finally took his baseball cap off.

"There now," Jimmy said, approvingly. "You look less like a little boy and more like a man. The Mooncalf has such pretty hair for a moody guy."

He reached over and scruffed his hand through Owen's hair. His fingers felt electric.

"I know the name for this island. I know. It's called Bermuda. We're in Bermuda." He laughed, leaning into Jenna, kissing her just behind her ear.

No, Owen thought.

You're in the realm of Dagon.

A RESTLESS NIGHT came to him, and then another and another. He lay on his single bed, sheets pulled back, and a fever such as he had never before felt washed over him.

Whosoever has loved the way I love Jenna Montgomery, he whispered to the stars through his bedroom window, has known sacrifice and torture and days and nights of endless wanting, thirst without satisfaction, hunger without morsel. Whosoever has wept within themselves for what they could not reach, could not touch, has felt what I feel.

Whosoever has spent his life working his body, mind, and soul to its absolute limit to become the extreme candidate for the love of a beautiful and angelic girl as I have for her, as I have given myself to the shape that she would long for...

That man would not rest were a rival to steal the prize from him.

Dagon, he whispered soundlessly. *Dagon. My god. Bring her to me.*

Eventually, Owen Crites slept better imagining the world under the sea where the people who were part of the Dagon realm dwelt, with their vast and imperious citadels, their large cold eyes and wet shapeless forms. He imagined the great sacrifice he would throw to them for their entertainment.

"How ARE you going to waste your last summer?"

Owen's mother asked as she switched off the faucet, plunging her hands back into the soapy water. "Now, don't blot, Owen, dry. There's a difference."

She passed him the first dish, which he sprayed down and then wiped with the green-and-white hand towel. The kitchen in the caretaker's house was as narrow as one of the closets in the big house; but the window looked out on a small sunken garden, behind which the pine trees stuck out like crooked teeth.

"Don't blot," his mother repeated.

Owen began stacking the dry plates carefully.

"I need a job."

"You work for your father."

"Not this summer," he replied. "Hank'll do without me."

"Hank?" his mother said, nearly laughing. "Hank? Next you'll be calling me Trudy." Then, her mood darkened. "Show some respect."

His mother reached down to pull the plug on the drain. She reached back to her hairpins, pulling them out so that her gray-streaked hair fell along her shoulders. She smoothed it back, and turned to watch him dry the rest of the plates and bowls from supper. "I know what you're thinking."

He glanced at her for the barest moment.

"You're thinking that you'll work down where she goes at night. The restaurant. The dock. You'll be there for the dances. I've seen the boys working at those places. They live here all year round. But in the summer, sometimes they get the rich girls. But those girls don't care about them. The boys are just part of summer to those girls. Just like the beach. Just like a walk."

He remained silent, and kept his eyes on each bowl as he carefully wiped the towel through them.

"I grew up in her world. I know what she'd have to give up. Don't ask her to do it. Not if you care about her," his mother said.

Then, she nearly snickered.

"What's funny?" he asked.

"I remember your father when he wasn't much older than you. I remember him so well," she said. "He had big dreams. He's working on the pump now. The pump and the well. Today he worked on the azaleas and the rosebushes. Tomorrow, he'll probably check the pool. If I had only known. Owen, you might as well go find that pirate treasure as think a girl like that will be interested in you beyond a summer fling."

Owen dropped the towel on top of the cutting board, and turned to walk away.

"I know what you get up to," his mother called to him, but he had already stepped out of the house, letting the screen door swing lazily shut. "You're nearly a man, Owen. You need to grow out of all your imaginings now."

Her voice, behind him, was part of another layer of existence. The smell of fresh grass mingled with the slight scent of the roses which were just blooming in spirals and curves up on the bluffs. He walked to the edge of the hill, feeling the late sun stroke him like a warm hand.

At the rim of the koi pond, he knelt down and looked at his reflection in the green water. Soon, the patchwork fish came to the surface. He reached his hand into the murkiness, shivering with the chill, and found the god lying where he'd left it, behind the lava rocks.

He felt the edge of the god's face.

IN A SCHOOL NOTEBOOK, Owen wrote:

Things Jenna likes.

1. She loves swing dancing.

2. She likes expensive perfume. The kind older women wear. Not like other girls.

3. She likes sandals.

4. She likes to let a boy open a door for her.

5. She likes clothes from Manhattan.

6. She likes to be complimented on how smart she is.

7. She likes someone who listens to her.

8. She likes holding hands.

Things Jenna hates:

1. She hates heavy metal rock.

2. She hates boys who look at her breasts.

3. She hates having to wait for anything. Ever.

4. She hates most movies. She reminds me of movie stars though.

5. She hates when animals get hurt.

6. She hates being treated like a piece of meat.

7. She hates boys who want to go all the way because she told me three years ago that she's going to wait for the right one.

8. She hates having to do things she hates.

HE WAITED a week before going back up to the Montgomery place, and even then, it was after eleven, and the house was dark and silent except for the kitchen, where Mrs. M always kept a light on.

At first, he intended to stand beneath Jenna's bedroom window and maybe toss a pebble at it to get her attention.

He noticed that the window—on the third story—was open, and he decided he'd call to her.

Then, he noticed that one of the guest room windows was open, too.

That would be Jimmy's.

The bastard.

Owen glanced along the trellis and gutters, and decided he'd try that route first. He climbed the trellis with the agility of a monkey, although it threatened to pull away if he didn't balance his weight just right. It wasn't much different from the rope climb in gym.

When he worried that he wouldn't make it to the third-story roof, he remembered the breathing trick and began inhaling and exhaling carefully. That was where the balance was: in the breathing.

Then, he grabbed the rain gutter, and scaled the slant of the roof. He crawled along it, slowly, cautiously, and went to look in on Jenna while she slept.

He felt himself grow hard, imagining how he could hold her while she slept, imagining how he would smell her hair.

When he looked through the open window, he saw the other boy there, Jimmy, in bed with her, holding her, moving against her. Owen caught his breath and held it for what felt like the longest time.

He could hold his breath underwater for a few minutes. He held it while watching Jimmy press himself into her like a hummingbird jabbing at a flower but not as pretty. Just dark and murky with Jimmy's body rising and falling as he plunged, not gently the way she would want it, but like a jackal tearing apart some carcass.

A MORNING SWIM

"*The Salty Dog,*" Owen said, lifting himself from the swimming pool. "Waiting tables. Since Memorial Day weekend. Lifting weights, too."

"That must be delightful," Mrs. M said.

She stood near the changing rooms, swathed in a sheer robe beneath which her green bathing suit shimmered, dark glasses covering her eyes. She looked like a movie star. She had a cigarette in her hand, which she waved dramatically.

"I imagine you meet lots of others your age at that dive."

"Some."

"You're still very young," she said, and then caught her breath for a moment. "I'm sorry. I didn't mean that in a negative way. I meant it as...as...you're so innocent compared to the boys at that school Jenna goes to. They've already begun those patterns they'll have for life."

She exhaled a lungful of smoke. *She's like a beautiful dragon*, he thought. *A jade dragon with sparkling eyes.*

Owen drew himself up over the pool's edge. He exhaled deeply, coughing.

"My smoking bother you?"

"No," he said, swiveling to sit down more comfortably, his legs still in the water. "Just holding my breath. Trying, anyway."

"Trying to reach some goal? Underwater?" She took her sunglasses off, and dropped them carelessly on the tiles.

He nodded. "To beat the *Guinness Book of World Records*. This guy, he held his breath. Thirteen minutes."

"That's impossible." She walked casually over to him. He could see her sapphire bathing suit top, and her breasts cupped within it as her robe fell open. She stepped out of her sandals.

For a moment, he imagined what she would look like with her suit ripped from chin to thigh, with him pressing into her—no, not him, Jimmy, the way he had torn into Jenna.

Mrs. M, a smile on her face, could not read his thoughts, he hoped.

"No one can hold his breath that long," she said. "It must've been a cheat."

"If you believe in something, maybe you can do impossible stuff, Mrs. M."

"That's magical thinking, sweetie. And Mrs. M, good lord." She laughed, dropping her robe completely. She shimmered. "You're a man now. You'll have to start calling people by their first names, Owen. I feel like a school-marm when you call me that. Is that what you want me to feel like? A haggish old schoolmarm? I'm forty, not seventy. Catherine. Or Cathy."

"Oh, yeah, okay," he said, grinning. "Cathy."

As she walked along the edge of the pool to the far end, she pulled her hair back and tucked it into her white bathing cap. She lifted her arm in a certain way to him, like a salute. Then, she dove into the pool, graceful as a mermaid.

He watched her do laps while he caught his breath.

WHEN HE WENT to shower off, Owen saw the other boy's towel hanging from the bathroom stall.

Steam began to fill the changing room. Owen pulled his wet trunks down, and tossed them on a chair. He grabbed one of the long white towels that the Montgomerys' maid kept neatly rolled in the cabinet over the toilet. Then, he walked the narrow hallway to the large shower.

All three shower heads were running, and Jimmy stood there rubbing soap along his arms, his face frothy with white soap foam.

Owen ignored him, and—stepping beneath the spray—grabbed a bar of soap from the shelf.

"Mooncalf," Jimmy said, as the foam rinsed from his face. His hair stuck up high on his head. The smell of soap was overpowering. "Haven't seen you in a while."

"I know," Owen said, his voice husky.

He didn't feel the way he did in school with the other

boys, not with this Jimmy, this eighteen-year-old who he had watched deflower Jenna. He felt disgusted.

"Been busy."

He turned his back on Jimmy for the rest of the shower, hoping the other boy would leave to go swim in the pool. But Jimmy toweled off, and began dressing just as Owen turned off the water. He slipped his shorts on, and reached for his T-shirt.

"You've been working out a lot. Me, too. I run every morning. I play tennis."

"Swim," Owen said. He walked back to the toilet to take a leak.

"Swim?"

"I swim."

"Ah, a complete sentence out of the Mooncalf." Jimmy chuckled. "That's the first thing I noticed about you, you know."

Owen said nothing; flushed the toilet. Sat down on one of the chairs, and reached for his shirt.

"You talk in bits of sentences. Well, that and your hair."

Owen twisted back to look at him, his T-shirt half over his head.

"My hair?"

"You've got pretty hair. It's soft, too. Most guys' hair is like bristles."

"Weirdo," Owen said. "Sleep in any of the guest rooms much?"

He pulled the shirt down, and then went to grab his socks. Jimmy followed him, sitting across on a short bench.

"I don't even know what the guest rooms look like. I sleep with Jenna. That bother you?"

"No. It's weird her parents don't care."

"Her mother doesn't. Her father's still down in the city. And anyway," he said, shrugging, "you seem to know a lot about where I sleep. I'm hoping you don't sneak around and look through windows or anything."

Owen averted his eyes, glancing down at his feet.

"Hope it doesn't bother you, Mooncalf," Jimmy said. "When we first met, I thought you might be hot for Jenna."

"We're friends. That's all."

"Boys can't just be friends with girls. We always want something else."

"Okay," Owen said. He laughed, but it was fake. It echoed off the turquoise tile and sounded less genuine as it went. He looked at Jimmy, who was watching him the way Owen's father would when trying to figure him out.

"You know, Mooncalf, you comb your hair to the left a little more—make the part slightly higher—and you'd look top drawer. You really would. Your chin's strong, your body's fit. You need to get rid of these," Jimmy pointed at Owen's T-shirt, "and start wearing some oxford cloths, button-downs. With sleeves. Short sleeves are for kids. It would show your best side. And maybe some khakis. When you grin, don't show all your teeth."

"Bite me."

Jimmy laughed and reached out, pressing his hand against Owen's shoulder in what could only be a casual and friendly—even brotherly—gesture.

"Good. Some spirit. I'm just trying to help. You look

good, but you look too island. You need a little charm. All guys do. Swimming only goes so far, after all." Jimmy, ever annoying, kept up the jabber. "I'm not much of a swimmer. I sail, but the idea of water, well, let's just say I do a passable dog paddle. But you've got those biceps. Amazing shoulders for such a Mooncalf runt. Pretty good. How much you bench?"

"Who cares?"

A brief silence.

Then, "I do."

"Well, not all that much," Owen said. "I just stack the weights on and push. I don't notice how much."

"Don't notice? My god, sport, you mean to say your goal isn't the weights?"

Owen shrugged. "I never think about it. I just want to be powerful. I mean strong."

"You said powerful."

"Same thing."

Another brief silence.

"You ever up for tennis?" Jimmy asked.

"Not really."

"I can teach you if you like. It'd be fun to a doubles match one day. Early, before it's too hot. You, me, Jenna, and maybe you could find a friend to bring. It's always fun to play doubles," Jimmy said.

Owen noticed the combination of arrogance and nonchalance, as if none of this mattered.

Jimmy probably screwed Jenna on a nightly basis. But he never thought about Owen, or Owen and Jenna. He probably lived in the moment. Completely.

"Saturday should be a ton of fun," Jimmy said, wiping

the last of the spray from his shoulders as he pushed his feet into the cheapest sneakers that Owen had ever seen. "You bringing a date?"

Owen glanced up. "Her birthday?"

"Yeah, you know, the whole crowd's coming from the Cape, and then we'll just do tequila shots till dawn. You got a girl off-island?"

Owen began to lie, just to fill that emptiness between them. Yes, he had a girl. Yes, he was excited about Jenna's birthday party, even though he had not been invited to it. Yes, he was considering his options as to which colleges he was looking into—Middlebury looked promising, he didn't think he had quite the grades for Harvard, but his uncle had been a dean at Middlebury, and yes, they could all go skiing in the winter up there on some distant holiday.

The whole time Owen was talking, Jimmy reached into his shaving kit. He went over to shave at the mirror and applied some kind of lotion to his face. He finished it off with a spritz of the most obnoxious cologne that Owen had ever smelled. While they small-talked it, Owen knew, standing there in the diminishing steam of the changing room, he *knew*.

Just by standing there with Jimmy in the shimmering mist.

Jimmy had a weakness.

Owen began spending a lot of time, after that, thinking about that weakness.

Thinking about how he could get Jenna back.

OWEN'S SHIFT at the Salty Dog began at three and lasted until eleven, six days a week. He emerged sweaty and stinking of grease, because half his job was cleaning out the fryers and grease pits at the end of the night, and when he got off shift in early July—it was nearly two a.m.—he went down to the jetty to stare out at the early morning mist of the Sound, smoke some cigarettes, and chill.

He didn't turn around when he heard the footsteps coming up behind him.

"Mooncalf."

"Hey Jimmy."

"Got a cig?"

"Take one." Owen tossed a cigarette back.

"Thanks. I guess you want to be alone."

"Didn't know you smoked."

"I don't. Not when anyone looks, anyway."

"That's nice. Anything else you do when no one's looking?"

"If I told, you'd know my secrets."

"How's Jenna?"

"She's okay. She fell asleep early. I just needed to wander a little. How's the job?"

"Good. You can smell it on me. You wander late. It's almost morning."

"In Manhattan, I wander at all hours. I like this time of night. You meet all kinds of interesting people. I kind of miss work. I used to work summers in one of my dad's stores. It was fun sometimes."

"Seems like more fun to run around the island all summer. Like you two."

"It gets old. I take that back. Yeah, it's fun. I guess you

want to be left alone."

"You guessed right," Owen said, cricking his neck to the left a bit.

"Your neck hurt?"

"It gets stiff. Leaning over a mop half the time. On my knees cleaning out all kinds of shit."

"Here," Jimmy said, and Owen felt hands at the back of his neck, gently massaging. "Better?"

Owen let him continue. "This fog depresses me."

"I think it's peaceful."

"You would."

"Mooncalf, you hate me, don't you?"

"Not really."

"How does this feel?" Jimmy pressed his thumbs into Owen's shoulders.

"Oh yeah," Owen said. "Right there."

BEFORE DAWN, he had gone to the pond. He knelt beside it, and reached down among the algae and slimy rocks until he found it.

He drew the statue up, and set it down on the wet grass.

"I guess you're just made up," he said aloud. "I guess I'm just a screwed-up guy who made you up. Maybe when I was twelve I was warped. But you're just some cheap souvenir someone lost. No one believes in gods."

Still, the itchy thought touched him somewhere between his eyes and scalp—he could practically feel the fire crawling on him.

But if you're not.

If you're real.

I'll do what needs to be done.

Mrs. M, in her own words:

Here's what I thought of it all: my daughter Jenna had been trouble from the day she was born. She was pretty and plain at the same time, and I say that as a loving mother. She inherited her father's face, not much of mine, although I guess she got my eyes.

Lucky her—my least favorite feature, since my own mother always told me I had sad eyes. When Jenna was four years old, she told me that no man was going to do to her what her daddy did to me. Definitely wise beyond her years, but just not special enough to handle what life would deliver to her, that's for damn sure.

It was her trust fund. It made her trouble. Look, there's something that everyone pussyfoots around but no one ever talks about. That's money. Pure and simple.

Money.

When a girl has some, she can be elevated to the status of goddess.

The most ordinary—even homely—creature can become ravishing with just a portfolio or a trust fund.

That island—in summer—is full of trust fund widows who should by all rights be considered blemishes, but instead are constantly sought out for parties and gatherings and literary events.

For Jenna, there's always been money. And I've

watched it feed her in a way that can't be healthy; but what could I do? She has access to money. Lots of money. Money clothes her. She was ruined because of it, basically.

She could never learn how to survive. She could never learn how to rely on herself and her own character to get through a challenging situation. She could always buy her way out of things.

This isn't true of me. I was raised solidly middle-class. My father had died when I was six, and my mother didn't have too many options, not back then.

In many ways, I feel for Owen because of that. Who wouldn't? His life is a lot like mine was as a child. Yes, there was some inheritance later for me, but when you spend most of your childhood wanting things you never really get over it.

And money becomes a prison, too. When you know what it's like to live without it, and when it's within your grasp, then you know what it's like to not have it.

So, you cling to it. Pure and simple. You hang on for dear life.

I suppose people will say things about my marriage to Frank that reflect this, but my marriage is a different kettle of fish. We've got our way of living, and yes, you can criticize it all you want, but it works for us nine times out of ten. Those times when it doesn't quite work, well, we have places to go where he can live his life and I can live mine, and the breather is well-needed. On both our parts.

I'm not the easiest woman in the world to live with. And he's no saint.

I sat down with my little girl when she was just learning about sex, and I told her that men have different ways of dealing with love, and usually it's through the one part of their body that seems to cause others the most damage.

"But it's just his body," I told her.

She cried over all of this. She cried when she found out her father had another woman. A mistress.

But you have to cry at first, don't you?

To get all those little fairy tales out of your head about how life gets lived, about how there are a few good men, how some men don't cheat. And it's not true.

All men cheat, and all women marry cheaters, and to not look at that square in the face is like not looking at the good side of marriage, too.

So she cried off and on for a few years, and I held her sometimes; I was cold to her at times—I knew she needed to work this idea out in her mind.

When she fell in love for the first time, she told me she was grateful for what she'd had to go through with her father.

"I don't know why men do what they do," she told me.

"If you did, you'd have solved the greatest mystery of life," I said to her. Or something like that.

But for my money, she should've avoided that Jimmy McTeague. He was bad news. I know every little deb and sorority girl east of the Mississippi thought he was just the end of the world, but they were such goofy little virgins it was hard to have patience with them.

Jimmy McTeague is the devil incarnate. I know that's an over-the-top way of putting it. He wasn't evil, but he was cold. I knew a little about his family, and none of it was very good. His father had some bad business deals going, and even if he had all the stores, Frank told me some things that alarmed me.

With Jimmy, I felt it the first day I met him, which was sometime before summer. Perhaps Easter break?

She brought him by the house in Greenwich, and the first thing out of his mouth was, "Hello, Catherine. I've heard so much about you, I almost feel like we've had an affair."

He thought that kind of thing was funny, that off-the-cuff jokiness. Within minutes, he'd given me some nickname, which of course he had to repeat five or ten times to truly annoy me, and within an hour of chatting with him, I knew more about that boy than I cared to know.

He is dangerous.

And so yes, I think it all has more to do with Jimmy McTeague than with anybody.

At her birthday party in late July, he told me that he thought the world was meant to be owned by people like him.

I believe those were his exact words.

Yes, he had money.

Yes, he was extremely good-looking for a boy his age. Extremely. Only a fool wouldn't notice that.

But he had no spirit. What he had was pure badness. He was absolutely pure in his badness.

I once had a dog like that. Beautiful. Completely bad. Jimmy McTeague's like that. I really began to hate that boy at Jenna's birthday party.

A BIRTHDAY PARTY

I n the mirror, Owen combed his hair, parting it and fluffing it, not to the middle of his forehead, but certainly an inch above his usual. He also brushed it back so it rose even higher. The summer blond streaks looked better this way. He rubbed some gel into it, and made sure the part was clean.

He smiled as naturally as he could. No, that wasn't right. He let his lips pull back slightly. He squinted his eyes the way that Jimmy did. It looked rich to do it. Like the sun was always on his face, even on a cloudy day.

Then, he rubbed some of his mother's lotion on his face. It brought a shine to his cheeks and nose. He wasn't sure if he liked it, but it seemed to be what the rich boys had: that shine.

Hanging on the bathroom door: the crisp J.Crew shirt, pale blue, the tan chinos.

He dressed, and then returned to his bedroom to get the gift he'd wrapped that morning.

"You're not going to that party," his mother said,

glancing at his father. Both sat in the small living room in the dark, the television providing the only source of light. Their faces flickered.

His father laughed. "Oh, he'll have fun. The kids are really going to mix it up."

"Yeah. It'll be fun."

"You're not one of them," his mother said. "You can pretend. You always pretend."

Then, she turned to his father, patting his shoulder. "Well?"

"Leave it alone, Boston," his father said. "It's the kid's party. You used to go to parties."

"What's that you've got there?" his mother asked. She got up from the couch, setting her beer down on the coffee table. His father reached over, turning on the standing lamp. Light came up. His mother looked gray despite the fact that she colored her hair. Even her skin seemed gray. His father looked like a wisp of smoke. It was all Owen could do to keep them from vanishing within the room.

Owen looked down at the box in his hands.

"It's her birthday."

"You bought her something?" his mother asked, a grin spreading like blood on her face.

He could imagine her dead, her skull cracked open like an egg.

"You bought the Montgomery girl something? Working for tips at the Salty Dog, and you bought the richest girl in the world something?" She shook her head gently. "Owen, you're always trying to impress someone with what you don't have." She said this sweetly.

He almost felt bad for what he'd done. He almost felt bad for what he'd stolen from his mother to put in the box.

He almost felt bad for what he was giving Jenna.

Almost.

THE PARTY WAS in full swing by ten at night. Every Nancy, every Skip, every Jess and Sloan—all were there, poolside.

The great curtains were drawn back, and the glass doors had been removed for the party. White tents had been erected along the yard; lanterns of every conceivable hue were strung along the walkway to the Montgomery place, and balloons flew with some regularity from the backyard. The smell of cigarettes and perfume and gin and beer and money were there, too.

Watching it, you'd have seen nearly fifty teenagers dancing, laughing, shouting, a tall blonde girl with flowing hair and limbs soaked from having been thrown into the swimming pool, the fat drunk frat boy vomiting over by the birdbath, half a dozen homely young women shining under the spotlight of boys' gazes—for lust and money and breeding and privilege all attract beyond mere looks.

The Sound sparkled with moonlight, and summer was at its peak; the sun had only just gone down an hour before, and the smell of salt sea air mingled with the foam of mermaids' souls, lost from true love.

All these things Owen thought.

"DID you see Jimmy at the nationals? God, I hear he's going to be at Wimbledon someday. Soon."

"If he's at Harvard—"

"When he's at Harvard, I'm going to call him Jimmy McTeague of the Ivy League. Isn't that cute?"

"I think what's cute is his father. Have you ever met him?"

"Well, I've been in the store."

"Sports superstores never interested me. It seems crass to sell that kind of thing."

"I read in Forbes that his dad is worth several billion."

"Dead or alive?"

"Dead; then Jimmy's worth that."

"Jimmy McTeague is shallow. He is. He's not smart either," one deb said, her party dress ruined because someone spilled a Bloody Mary down the front. "He's pretty but he's dumb. And my uncle went to Yale with his father, and let me tell you, that man was nearly kicked out for cheating and once that kind of thing happens, you never know."

Owen stood back, beyond the lights that had been set up along the tents, and watched them all.

The small gift in its box, in his trembling hands.

"Smooth. Just be smooth," he whispered to himself.

He wanted to make sure Jenna saw the gift. Saw what it meant.

Jimmy McTeague held onto a bourbon and water as if for dear life, laughed with his jock friends, eyed the other girls but mainly when they were with their boyfriends, and he thanked Mrs. Montgomery for the excellent whiskey.

"People who have whiskey like this should own the world," and even as he said it, he didn't know what it meant.

When he saw Owen standing just at the edge of the party, he raised his glass and shouted, "Yo, Mooncalf, get your ass over here!"

Jenna Montgomery, in her own words:

Here are things I've read somewhere or heard about and I really believe: The happiest people don't necessarily have the best of everything; they just make the most of everything that comes their way. Happiness only happens for those who have something to lose and cry over and those who get hurt, for only then can they can really appreciate things.

And maybe they deserve all the good things, too.

I think that, anyway.

Okay, before you think I'm just some rich bitch who gets sentimental and gooey over greeting cards and romance novels, the reason I think about those things is because when you are beautiful and you have money, it's those simple things you have to remember.

And I was pretty happy for the most part, right up until summer. But it's not like I never had sad things happen. Or didn't cry. Or didn't feel pain. That's all on the inside. You don't show it because people don't like people who cry over things.

This whole summer issue probably began because Daddy didn't want me to open Montgomery Hill on Memorial Day like we always did. Mom was already up there, a week or two early, and I'd only just come home from finals.

I have gone to Outerbridge Island since I was about four, and I never miss a summer there. It's what I look forward to after a tough year in school, and since I would turn eighteen over the summer and I had just finished school—but I'd be entering college in September—I really wanted to enjoy what time I had left to just be a kid.

Daddy was in one of his moods, though, and I suspect that woman he knows was part of it. Mom told me all about that woman when she gave me the speech about sex and life and marriage when I was fourteen.

"Men have problems with their bodies," she said, looking only a little embarrassed. "They all cheat. It's just something we put up with if we can. It's nothing about love. Don't even think that. It's just their biology. They have their good sides and their bad sides. And there are plenty of bad women, too," she added. "Like *that woman*."

That woman lived in Brooklyn, in a brownstone that my father had bought for her in the 1970s. I took the subway out to it once, and stood on the steps in front, looking through the windows. That woman had a nice chandelier and some paintings on the walls, but it was a fairly plain house in Park Slope. I sort of think I saw a little of her, too, walking up the street. She wasn't even pretty, which was sort of what amazed me. She wasn't like my mother. She was tall, with big feet, and red hair that needed some kind of style. Her face was nothing like my mother's, nothing like the women I knew, she looked Irish, I guess, she looked sort of round and plain.

I don't really know if it was that woman I saw, but I suspect it was.

So, just after high school graduation, I was all ready to go to the island, but Daddy was moody and told me I needed to stay because of Jimmy, who was supposed to have been in town.

All right, Jimmy McTeague.

He's a tennis player who goes to Wimbledon every year, he's practically a national champion, and his father owns McTeague Sports, the chain, although I never understand why they don't have stores in Manhattan.

I met Jimmy when he was at Exeter, at some dance, and I was just thinking he was cute. Marnie called him the Leech for some reason which I didn't quite understand, but I knew there was something interesting about him. He lived a different life than me, and I never really saw myself with that Midwestern jock-type. He was always sweating, too, which I guess goes with the whole athletic thing, but it's not something that's pleasant to be around an hour after a match.

Still, by the time I was seventeen, I really liked Jimmy. And no, I had no thoughts of marriage or anything like that. We hadn't actually even been intimate or anything, just held hands a lot and went to dances and out to dinner.

When I debuted, Jimmy shared the drudgery of that awful debutante season by being my escort; when I was really pissed off over not getting into my top college choice, Jimmy actually flew in from the West Coast—where he had some important tennis match—and took me out to dinner. Then, the night after I would normally go to the island, Jimmy told me we could sail there in this little boat he kept in Greenwich at the club.

That first night on the boat, I became a woman. Well, that's what he said. Sort of annoying that he said it. Not like I was a little girl ten minutes before. But boys are annoying sometimes.

Maybe I shouldn't have had the wine. Or maybe I'm glad I did.

We drank too many glasses of Chardonnay and one thing led to another.

Jimmy was never very aggressive before that. He was kind of shy that way. So I pretty much had to seduce him, but once we both closed our eyes and let our bodies take over, we knew how to make love.

And it really was love. It really was. I felt it.

At least it was that first time.

We spent that first night on the boat. We got into the harbor at about twelve or one in the morning and just slept together in the little bed. He snored sweetly. Not a hacking or sawing snore, but like a puppy dreaming. He did say something funny to me in the morning, something that struck me as odd, something about how maybe we could think about the future more now that we'd "mated."

I laughed at him when he said "mated." Sounded a hundred years old to say that. Or like we were animals in a zoo. I wondered if he couldn't say the more basic terms for sex.

He got a little angry when I laughed.

All right, I knew that maybe there would be trouble with Owen when I saw him on the jetty when we got off the boat the next morning. He looked like he'd been waiting there all night.

Like he'd been watching us.

The little turd.

He really was.

I care a lot for him, of course. We've known each other since we were both kids. He's the son of the gardener. His mother sometimes helps out with parties and laundry and other things.

He's cute, which helps, too, because although I have nothing against boys that aren't very good-looking, there's something about a good-looking one that just makes you want him around all the time.

So I'm barely dressed, some tacky beach towel around me basically, and there's Owen at the shore seeing both of us coming up from the boat and the first thing he says to me is, "What happened?"

I felt all nervous and even giggly, like I needed a cigarette. I told him I didn't want to see my mother for a day or two.

And then Jimmy just took over, like he always does. He has this way with guys—he always gets them on his side. Jimmy gave him a nickname and acted like Owen was Jimmy's kid brother and they just seemed to get along fine. It was like they'd known each other all their lives, in about five minutes. Owen seemed to like all the ribbing and you know, that sort of adolescent boy-talk they do. You know that. That way boys have of getting together and sort of sparring, and talking, and noticing each other's hair, or how one of them is sad, and they either peck it to death or get all brotherly. I saw it with Jimmy and his best friends at Exeter, too. The way they played like puppies. That's just what it was like—like watching two golden retrievers wrestle over a bone.

I didn't see Owen much during June. I guess he got the job down in town. Sometimes I saw him when we went to the Salty Dog, but he never waited on our table.

Jimmy was virtually attached at the hip with me, which can get annoying no matter how much you care for a guy. I used to try and lose him in the mornings after he'd go off to play his beloved tennis with one of the local pros or with my mother. My mother is excellent at sports, which are pretty much not my thing. I like golf a little, and sometimes I like to swim, but the whole girl-jock thing is beyond me.

So Jimmy would slip out of bed and I'd get dressed and go down to visit Marci and Elaine, or maybe Elaine's brother, Cooper, down island.

Sometimes we'd take whole afternoons just having brunch, or wandering the Cove by Big Salt Pond.

Jimmy would get all pissed off at me. He was a little jealous. Well, a little more than jealous.

He thought that since he was the first guy I'd slept with, he somehow should've had more ownership of me. Or maybe I should've been more attached to him. I mean, I *was* attached. And he was *technically* the first guy I'd slept with, although I let Ricky Hofstedter press his fingers up there sophomore year, and then there was that time that I got drunk at Hollis Ownby's party and wound up making out with Harvey Somebody. He *was* a Somebody. I just can't remember his last name.

But Jimmy had all these needs and some days, particularly in June and early July, I just wanted to chill and hang out with some friends without worrying about whether I was paying attention to Jimmy and all his issues.

I didn't think of Owen much, except sometimes I remembered how fun he was when I was younger and exploring the beaches; or how I'd take him out in one of my dad's small boats while he'd tell me all about his future plans. How he was going to start investing in stocks. I'd ask him how? And he'd look at me funny, and laugh. Then, he'd tell me how his mother's father had been well off and then when he turned twenty-one, he'd come into some trust fund.

I knew he was lying but I sort of liked his lies. They made the days go by. Sometimes the summer seemed short when I was around him, and by the time I got back to school in the fall, I felt renewed. I owed a lot of that to Owen.

But this summer, I've been distant from everybody. Part of it is Jimmy. And yes, it's sexual, I guess. But since I'm paying you by the hour, I'd guess that you're okay with me telling you, right?

Well, Jimmy seems to not be all that aggressive in bed anymore. I know that must sound weird since I'm not terribly experienced in that arena, either, but I've watched movies, I've read books, and I talk with my girlfriends about this stuff. This isn't like twenty years ago when no one ever talked about sex. My friends all say their boyfriends seem to put the moves on them constantly.

With Jimmy, I have to literally reach down and grab him. And then, he just sort of, you know, touches me here and there and then he—well, you know—and then it's over and sort of unpleasant even though it's not ghastly or anything. It's just not what I expected.

And then there was that fiasco with my birthday party. Christ, it was embarrassing. Mind if I light up? I'm hungry for nicotine at the moment.

Ah, that's better. I know everyone has to give up smoking at some point in their lives, but how nice to not have to give it up just yet.

So, the 17th was my big party, and I didn't even want Owen there—he didn't fit in with Jimmy's friends. Most of my friends found him a little cold.

Plus, there was the whole problem of his mother, who's a force to be reckoned with. She's always looking at me like I'm the Whore of Babylon. She was helping us set up the party but she kept giving me that look.

You know that look.

That mother look.

But when Owen showed his face I was happy to see him. It was sort of a relief to finally because he definitely is nice to me no matter what. And I barely saw him this summer. Well, I saw him when he went swimming.

In our pool of course. In *our* pool. A whole ocean out there and he has to be in our pool.

I called him Leech (funny that he and Jimmy both have been called that, huh?) when he wasn't around because he really is such a leech. I mean it in a funny nice way, not some awful way. I once slipped off a rock into one of the little ponds on the property, and my legs were covered with leeches. They don't hurt. You'd be surprised at that, wouldn't you? You'd think something that sucks your blood would hurt, but they don't. It's just the fact they're there that makes them bothersome.

So it was my little joke: calling Owen "Leech." I care a lot for Owen, actually. We grew up together practically. My island boy. My father laughs whenever I call Owen a leech behind his back but my mother, well, she doesn't understand that kind of humor. That ironic kind of humor. I mean it as an affectionate term.

Sort of like the way Jimmy calls him Mooncalf. It's a name.

I guess it distances me from him or something. But it does get annoying when someone is always borrowing things or using your things or assuming things just because his father works in the garden. I like them. They're like family. I feel a lot for Owen, but really, he should've gotten over that Leech thing years ago.

I can hear my mother's voice in my head: "That's cruel, Jenna."

I get accused of cruelty all the time. Not physical cruelty. My mother means it's cruel to fault poor people for using our things.

My mother has this thing for Owen. Well, for all young men. She won't acknowledge it, and she thinks Daddy's the bad one, but I know she likes the boys who hang around me. And no, I'm not jealous of her. Why should I be? She's old. Her time has come and gone. My time is only just beginning.

Anyway, school boys do not want forty-year-old women. It's embarrassing, really. Even at the party, Mom is sauntering around in that green getup she has that looks too glitzy for the island. We all go casual here, so she looked too done up. *Too* too, as Missy Capshaw says. She's *too* too.

Missy came down from the Vineyard for the party. Shottsy had his cousin Alec with him, and pretty much the whole gang showed up except for the Faulkners who all went to Maine for the summer.

I guess a bunch of my other friends came, and then six or seven of Jimmy's, and then Owen with his shirt that was so new it still had the wrinkles from the cardboard box. Shottsy made a big point of letting everyone know that part of the plastic liner was still under the collar.

Owen brought me this nice little gift. I mean that in an ironical way.

That's really the issue here. What he brought.

I was enjoying some margaritas and just getting sort of high and Marnie regaled me with that story again, the one about her brother's professor and how he and two female students had gone off to Fenwick together and then got caught in the worst way, the very worst way possible.

That's when I saw what Owen was doing.

I saw that he had already cast a spell. Some kind of spell. Just like a witch.

Over Jimmy.

I saw Jimmy put his hand in Owen's hair. I noticed how they laughed together over a private joke.

I know it must seem irrational and paranoid, but the first thing I thought was:

That island bastard is trying to steal my boyfriend.

You can imagine how I felt. I mean, I thought it was ludicrous. It wasn't like Skippy Marshall and that Donovan character from Harrogate School—they were both obvious homosexuals. We all knew about it since they got into the drama club and developed the perfect butts in the workout room doing squats.

This was different. I thought it was absolutely ludicrous. But I became livid as I watched them. Absolutely *livid*.

Working on my third or fourth margarita, I cast sidelong glances over at the two of them. Missy kept talking and Alec kept eyeing my breasts like the stupid jerk he could be. I had my little circle, but they knew something was up, too. They knew that Jimmy did not fawn on me, and I didn't really enjoy that.

I suppose if I had not been drinking, I wouldn't have caused a scene.

But I kept my eye on the two of them, and I saw the touches.

Yes, that's right. *Queerish little touches.* Not the kind that boys do. Not normally.

Owen touched Jimmy's elbow, and Jimmy looked at Owen's hand. They laughed. Whenever one of them could, he took his fist and gently patted the other on the chest.

Like old chums? Yes, sure, maybe. Certainly that's what I'd like to believe, but in fact, I saw Jimmy show him more genuine attention, not that needy attention he showed me, but the kind of attention every girl wants but never gets from a boy.

That adoration kind of attention.

And Owen *milked* it.

I asked Marnie later on. She said I was imagining things, that Jimmy had been bedding girls since eighth grade, that it was just that boy thing. That's what she said: "That prep-school boy thing where they get together and they touch each other and they tell dirty jokes and they check each other out. It's because they both want you. They need to figure out the competition."

But I don't know.

I stood there, feeling embarrassed and humiliated, and at *my* party.

At my *own* party.

Finally I couldn't stand it.

Jimmy leaned forward and whispered something to him. It was like slow motion. I can remember it now like it's happening right in front of my face over and over again.

I saw his lips move as he whispered. Owen leaned into him. Jimmy's hand rested on Owen's shoulder. Maybe I was hallucinating or maybe I saw what I saw, but I think Jimmy McTeague placed the barest whisper of a kiss on Owen's ear, at my party, with me watching, with me having to bear witness to it.

God, it's so gothic. It's so…*Provincetown*.

It really hit me hard. I began crying, without knowing I was doing it, weeping, just standing there.

Alec took my hand and said, "Aw, princess, what's up?"

I shook myself free of that crowd and walked right

over to those two horrible boys, that horrible Jimmy McTeague.

"If you embarrass me here, I will destroy you," I whispered.

And then, of course, I had to go back to my party. I *had* to. I was obligated to all my friends. I was not going to let the boy who'd been sleeping with me for nearly two months humiliate me in front of everyone.

It wasn't until the next morning that I opened the gift that Owen had given me. That's pretty much why I freaked out with my usual panache.

I didn't want to see Owen again.

Ever.

But I knew Jimmy would still be mine no matter what we both went through together.

After all, remember these things: The happiest people don't necessarily have everything. They just make the most of everything that comes their way. Sometimes good things come out of a good cry. You can't base how you'll feel about tomorrow on what today brings.

When I think of all I've had to deal with, particularly with Jimmy, these sentimental thoughts bring me comfort. Even if they're off some greeting card somewhere.

Oh yeah, what Owen gave me for my birthday.

It was a gun. A crap-ass gun at that. It was tiny. It had some pearly kind of handle and the safety looked like it had rusted out.

I doubted that it even worked.

I thought it was a joke at first, but I guess not.

It looks like something you'd buy from some little old lady in Brooklyn, some little old lady with a thousand cats and one of those old fox furs who chain-smokes and lives in a studio she's had since the 1950s.

Still, it was a gun, and I have to admit, that's the creepiest thing he could've given me.

He scares me a little.

I mean, what kind of psycho gift is that?

AFTER A PARTY

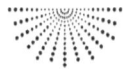

J immy grabbed Owen's elbow, laughing, the smell of
beer and tequila mixed in the air.

Owen giggled, too, and said, "Let's go to the
jetty. It's beautiful there. You can see the North Star."

"You know the North Star?"

"Yeah. I know all the stars. I'm an islander. I know the
Dippers and Scorpio, too."

"You're such a Mooncalf with all the stars in your
pocket," Jimmy said, his grin big and goofy and not that
of the controlled jock he'd once seemed. "God I wish I
knew the stars like you. I want to just—just—look at the
stars and know which ones they are, and where the earth is
in relation to them. You can show me all of them. We can
go out night sailing sometime. I would love that, wouldn't
you? You can really see the constellations when you get
away from all this. You could tell me all of them, all their
stories, all night."

The party spun around them, and Owen sensed that
Jenna glared at his every move.

She'll understand, he thought. *Eventually.*

"Maybe Jenna can come, too."

"Why? She can be a bitch," Jimmy whispered. "She and her friends and half these people here. All these quote-unquote friends of mine, of hers, who are they? Damn it, who are they? And Jenna. Christ. Jenna. She doesn't know me. She doesn't know you."

"So just you and me," Owen said. "Want to go down to the jetty? We can see the stars there, too."

"God yeah, show me the stars," Jimmy said, and he kept saying it over and over again as they stumbled their way down the path along the bluffs.

Every now and then Owen stopped and let Jimmy take his hand.

Jimmy's hand was warm, and above them, the sounds of the party faded, and the smell of pine and sea mingled.

The moon cut a path for them all the way to the jetty.

By the time they got there, Jimmy had already grabbed Owen and pulled him close until their chests pressed together, their thighs met.

Jimmy brought his lips to Owen's mouth.

VOICES IN THE DARK:

"It's all right, I know you. I know what we both want."

"Shut up. Just shut up."

"Come here. Come here. Let me help you. It's all right. It feels good."

"No, not like this. No."

"I've been so lonely."

"Oh."

"Wanting this."

"Oh."

"Since the first time I saw you."

"Oh."

"Does this feel good?"

"Ah."

"Will you let me take you?"

"Oh."

"Ask me."

"Oh."

"Ask me."

"Owen, take me? Owen? Take me."

OWEN

I had found my way to Jenna. It wasn't much different than kissing a girl. Once I allowed Jimmy to feel as if he needed to seduce me, that I might be the unwilling partner, it was easy to hold his attention because he liked resistance. I could feel it as he held me. He wanted me to try and pull away.

He told me to close my eyes and pretend he was a girl, to just let him do things to me, to just keep the image of a beautiful girl in my mind while he did things.

Jenna's was the only face I saw.

I knew that once I had Jimmy McTeague of the Ivy League in my arms, once I had pushed myself into him, owned him, dominated him…Jenna would be mine.

I look at the boy that I was then:

Owen Crites. Mooncalf. He mounts the rich boy and drives his point home.

And no, I'm not gay.

I got no thrill from what I did to Jimmy McTeague, how I made him feel tenderness and acceptance and release that night.

It felt less like sex to me than stabbing someone over and over while they curled around you.

I caressed him as no one ever had, to the point that he wept against my chest.

It was purely because I thought of Jenna. My love for her.

Love is purity.

My next decision, as I lay there with that puppy whimpering his soul into my ear, was just how I was going to murder him.

THE LAST OF SUMMER

JIMMY MCTEAGUE KEEPS A DIARY

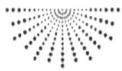

Dear Diary, as they say:

1. Need to train better. Wake up an hour earlier every morning. Run two miles. Then practice. Then row.

2. July was a waste. Feeling like I'm getting lazy. More strength training. Check out the sucky gym in town.

3. Jenna's a bitch. She thinks she knows. She doesn't know. She'll never really know.

4. Need to get back with Jenna. Need to figure this out.

5. I can't resist him. It's awful what we're doing. But I know I can stop. I know if I just stick with the program I can stop. I think he's evil.

6. What we did was wrong. I know that. What Jenna and I can build is right.

7. Call the Padre and Madre for more money.

8. Become a better person. Quit all the lying. Lying is bad. There's no reason. If you feel the way you feel, let it all out. Don't keep holding it in. Doesn't matter what

Dad thinks. Doesn't matter if you know what you need from life. You can let it out. Other people do. Other people need those things, too.

9. Maybe it's not real. Maybe it's just sex. Maybe I shouldn't let it happen. But now all I think about is him.

10. Jenna and Mooncalf.

11. Mooncalf.

12. He told me something really smart. Just shows that you don't need all these prep schools and universities to be smart. He said, "Love is purity." It is so true. It's something I couldn't say out loud. But it's so true. But there's more to life than love. You can't survive on love. You can't have the important things in life just because of love. No one pays for three houses and European vacations and clothes from Italy and Rolls-Royces with love.

MY NAME'S JIMMY MCTEAGUE. It's safe to assume you know that because you are me sitting here reading my diary. Since, after all, no one else is going to read this if I can help it.

It's also probably safe to assume that you'll burn these pages someday to make sure no one else reads them. But for now, writing it down seems right. My favorite movie is probably still the *Little Mermaid*, which I saw when I was nine years old, and I still watch it once a year at least. Why? Because it's about sacrifice for what you want. I've always sort of believed in that. My dad doesn't understand why I watch a cartoon to inspire me. Sometimes I watch it before a match because it gets me going. I don't see why being smart and grown up has anything to do with abandoning the things you believed in when you were a kid.

I've wanted to keep a diary since I was about nine, about the same time as I saw that movie, but I didn't start till I was twelve and then I threw it all out. So after another brief attempt at sixteen, I've decided now that I'm about to enter Harvard, it's time for me to keep one. I'm not only about tennis, anyway. I get tired of that dumb jock image. My SATs were through the roof. I get good grades and I'm totally wrapped up in Medieval history, which I figure I might pursue even after I graduate. If I graduate. If I make it through. If all the bad things that I've found out about don't happen in the meantime, and it all ends.

This part of the diary is about my summer. Jenna and I were having a great year together, although I wasn't always there for her, I suppose, because of the matches I had in England and out in California, and then she spent spring break in Aruba, so that last week in May was really our first full week together, which is why I took the *Karenina* out of the yacht club and we sailed lazily up and down the coast for a few days.

I was so pissed off at Dad over a lot of things. First and foremost was the talk he gave me, about how I needed to uphold the family and how I needed to look at life differently, not as a kid but as someone who had responsibilities and wanted to live a certain way with certain kinds of people.

I didn't forget about Chip, but I guess that's one of those things I have to put aside. My dad says so anyway.

Chip was annoying anyway, and the time we spent

together wasn't very meaningful because the whole time I kept thinking to myself: where will this go? Two guys can't marry. I'll lose everything.

And Chip was all about loins, anyway. And he wanted me all the time. I like a bit of chase. I don't want someone who always wants me. What's the fun in that?

I shouldn't even write about it here. What if someone finds out? I'm not really gay anyway, I just get in these situations. I suppose I fall in love with people. And of course, the animal needs. They take over, don't they? Everyone's like that. You see someone pretty and you just want them.

Chip turned out bad. All that mess about fighting and arguing and him claiming I broke his arm when I didn't break it and if he fell it was his fault anyway for standing in my way and not letting me pass. He did that sort of blackmail thing too, but I showed him I wasn't going to put up with that kind of shit.

I fell for Jenna pretty hard.

I mean, who wouldn't?

She's gorgeous and full of life and her brain is just amazing.

And the money. To pretend it's not there is like not noticing her bra size.

All the guys seem to want her. I really had to fight off that bulldog with the Ferrari from Choate, but it wasn't too hard to dazzle her on the courts. She's a big fan of tennis, which helps, and that night we went for a walk back in the city really turned things around for me.

I mean, we were walking down Fifth Avenue, and she was talking about what she wanted from life, all the wonderful things, to see the world and experience the best of everything and how her trust fund was huge and she intended to always have the life her parents had…and my mind was turning a hundred little things around. I was walking with her under cloudy skies and I was thinking about how this was right.

Being with Chip was wrong because it was based on that one thing, that physical thing, the urge I had that took me over when he was under me.

I thought, all right, I know where this will go with Jenna. We'll marry, we'll have children, we'll build something really solid.

She has all this family land and properties and I'm really good at handling investments, so we'll be perfect together. She'll look right for business, too. And she wants kids really badly. So badly that she's not all that interested in college.

I suspect she wants to just get out from under her parents and be on her own and make her own life.

She has millions from her grandmother and it's earning more millions every year, she said, so why should she have to go through college? She wanted to do some magazine work, one of those high fashion magazines and her family has huge pull in that area and she was smart enough.

It hardly bears comparison with a night spent on a dirty mattress in the back of some studio apartment in Chelsea with Chip, who fell on hard times after prep school.

That sleaziness he had, like an air, like marijuana smoke in the back of a bus—that's what his place was like.

He was slumming; degrading himself. His parents had cut him off, and he was willing to live like that. Hardly any furniture, a job that barely paid him per month what a reasonable man can live on. And still, he was willing to live like that for the sake of the feeling in his dick.

I am never going to let that happen to me. I am never going to let people know how I am on the inside if I can help it. I got so mad at Chip I guess I ended up roughing him up a little, but he kept trying to ruin things, and I just won't let anyone do that. My dad is ruining things as it is, and pretty soon other people are going to know how he's ruining things, and I do not intend to be in that spot with him.

I remember clasping Jenna's hand while I listened to her go on about the life she intended for herself. So I knew that if I just kept my eyes on her, it would all go in the right direction. When we made love for the first time, it even felt right. She was overheated on the inside, it was like lava or something, it felt so natural.

I thought it would all turn out all right.

Until I met Mooncalf.

I tried to fight it, too. I looked at him and tried. I tried not to look at his body. So well developed. The way he spoke, almost sullenly. The fit of his khakis. The smile when it comes up, finally. Even his toes sticking out from his sandals.

Don't ever say someone can't fall in love through the eyes, because those blue eyes of his just grabbed me and held me the first time we met.

I didn't want him then, but I knew this guy had it in him to take me over.

And I suppose he already did that.

There's even a dangerousness to him I enjoy. I find myself looking over Jenna's shoulder, when we're at the beach, or bicycling, hoping he's there, just out of reach.

And then, the party. It was like waking up for the first time. It was like knowing that I'd been telling myself lies for years. That I'd been foolish and wrong. Now, all I think about is Mooncalf and I wish we were in a different world, not one of secrets and half-truths, but one where we could just be together. I know he feels the same.

I'm pretty much sleeping on the boat now. I can't stay with Jenna.

Not in her room.

And her dad gives me those looks, which aren't pleasant, either. Jenna's been cold. Can't blame her.

I know somehow it will all turn out okay. I know it will because I know life is not meant to be bad or confusing. If we can all just get through this summer, it'll somehow work out because life is supposed to work out.

Sometimes, I get so lonely I want to just hold someone. Even Jenna.

As a friend.

I want to see Mooncalf again, but he's been avoiding me since the party. I've had two weeks now, seeing Jenna and her family, playing a little golf, some tennis, taking the boat out when I can. Jenna's been good about this even if she's turned icy. She seems to handle my silences well. She really is a friend. I'm glad we can be this close and that she can be so understanding. Most of the time, she seems to act as if the night of her party never happened, as if I didn't go off with him.

She won't really understand what it means, anyway. She'll think she'll know, but I'll let her know it was nothing.

I'll get her thinking about us again, which is what she really wants, anyway.

A HURRICANE APPROACHES

There he is again:
I see him. That boy Owen. He's been running along the beach, swimming too much for his own good, working on his oxygen intake because breathing is the key. He has felt an unexpected strength grow within him to match his body's power.

THE WEEKS after the party went in a blur of moments and flashes in Owen's brain—the sky clouded and then became unbearably sunny, the humidity soared and then dropped and then soared again; a tropical storm to the south had been upgraded to a hurricane but it would not strike so far north as Outerbridge.

One night, Owen lay in bed convinced he'd heard a gun go off somewhere on the island.

August was like that sometimes.

"OWEN. WHY?"

"Why *what?*" he asked, shielding his eyes from the sun.

Jenna had emerged from the wooden deck all wrapped in a big yellow towel; to him it was as magnificent as a summer dress.

The smell of the pool was intoxicating. He had just finished his morning laps and felt clean and strong.

He wanted to kiss her. He thought of what it would be like to touch her. They stood so close.

"What kind of birthday present was that?"

"It's just a pistol. An antique."

"Why?"

"I thought you'd want it. I thought you'd like it."

"I'm not a fan of guns."

"No one is. But it has that inlay. It seems feminine."

"You must be out of your mind. To give me that as a gift. On my birthday."

"It was my grandfather's."

"Well, I'm giving it back. God, I don't want it in the house, let alone in my hand."

"You need protection."

"From what?"

"Jimmy," Owen said. He sucked a breath in briefly. It was time to let it begin.

He felt a curious shiver sweep through his body, as if he were on the verge of some delightful pleasure.

"He told me…"

"Told you what? What did he say? Was it about me?"

He wanted to make sure that she was completely focused on him. On his lips as he spoke.

"No, it's nothing. I just think you should keep the gun."

"No, he said something," she nearly snarled. "Tell me."

"I'm sure he didn't mean it," Owen said.

"It made you think I needed a gun?" Her face went blank. She looked down at her feet for a moment. Then, she glanced up and looked him in the eye. "What's been going on between you two?"

"Nothing," Owen whispered.

"Owen, what's going on?" she said.

He took a deep breath before speaking again.

"Jenna, I want you to be safe. That's all. Look, I know you don't care for me, and that's fine. I can't make you like me. And I know I can't make you…care for me…in a way I happen to care for you. No one is magician enough for that. I've thought about you since we were both little kids. I've always considered you someone special."

"*What?*" she asked in a voice that was barely more than a mouse squeak.

"I know that you'll go on to some really great college and you'll meet lots of guys like Jimmy and you'll come back to the island during the summer and be friendly with me but you'll see me as the townie who paints houses for a living, or maybe works on boats. And you'll have a different life."

"What is this all getting to—" Jenna gasped, and then her eyes lit up. "You lost the island accent. You talk like one of us now."

She said it as if it was one of the most dreadful things imaginable.

"That isn't true," Owen said. He glanced away, looking to the house and the beginnings of the roses his father so lovingly tended.

"This makes no sense. I don't want that gun."

"I know I'm nothing to you, Jenna. But please just consider keeping the gun as some kind of protection. Jimmy is not who he seems. I've seen a side of him…well, I've heard him say things…I just think you need to have that gun just in case."

He turned and walked away, his body barely dry from the swimming pool.

She called after him.

He walked from the pool to the back lawn and disappeared down the path.

ANOTHER MORNING, he helped Mr. M with his golf clubs and luggage, driving the truck up from the ferry. Mr. M had almost missed summer on the island.

"Business takes a man over," he told Owen on the way up the hill to the house. Mr. M was the biggest man Owen had ever seen—like a bear, but slick, too, and shiny. He had on dark glasses and a rumpled blue oxford cloth shirt. His skin was like pink snow as if he never allowed himself more than a minute or two per day in sunlight.

When Owen got to the door with the last of the bags, Mrs. M (he had to start thinking of her as Cathy if he was going to ever grow up) kissed her husband lightly on the nose.

"How's the summer?"

"Quiet," Mrs. M said.

"Where's that boy?"

"Which?"

"McTeague," Mr. M said.

"I think it's over. She's gone to Dr. Vaughan three times in two weeks. That's a record for her," Mrs. M said, and then turned to Owen. "Sweetie, would you mind picking up the mail for me?"

Owen nodded, feeling far too obedient, his heart beating too fast, too much within his frame, as if his muscles were about to twist and untangle; he was afraid for a moment that he had not heard what he thought he'd heard.

OWEN SAT by the koi pond, absorbing the last of an afternoon sun on one of his days off—the weather had gone back and forth, between brief bouts of showers and then sudden sunbursts. He was about to reach for Dagon beneath the placid green water, when he noticed a shadow reflection move across the water.

He didn't turn, but knew that Jimmy had come up behind him.

"Aren't you ever going to talk to me again?"

Owen shrugged.

"I thought...I thought we could...we could at least be friends," Jimmy said. "I think about you. All the time."

"Don't come here again." Owen measured his words carefully.

The shadow withdrew and Owen had the sun to himself again.

OWEN LAY back in the grass and closed his eyes.

As the violet darkness of his inner mind grew, he began to see the shadow sea of Dagon's realm. From the dusky waves, a form emerged, a magnificent sea god, its eyes round and without mind, like those of a shark, its body slick as oil with thousands of fins sprouting along its back; and as it grew, Owen knew what the god asked of him.

"I SAID PEEL THE POTATOES," his mother said, but he could see the look in her eyes. She wouldn't look directly at him. His mother was afraid of him. A little. Just a little fear.

That was good.

"Don't use that tone of voice with me," Owen said almost politely, as he lifted the first potato and brought it to the small sharp knife.

"Something's missing in the house," she said, but his mother had begun saying strange things the past few weeks—sentences that didn't go together, phrases that meant something only in her mind.

"You probably misplaced whatever it is," he told her

almost nonchalantly. "You've always been like that, haven't you?"

WHEN STORMS COME TO OUTERBRIDGE, they usually have lost most of their power, they usually have been downgraded from hurricanes when they hit Bermuda to tropical storms when they reach Long Island, and by the time they make it past Block Island and start heading to the Avalons, it's usually high winds and warm rains but not much damage. The islanders who are over sixty remember the storm of '53 that "took the hats off houses," as they said, and generally made a mess of the summer homes.

The storm that arrived the last week of August was not a terror, nor did it threaten to take the hats off houses. It was a warm palace of rain and wind and it changed the geometry of the island with its shifts and movements.

The sky became a hardened gray and the rain constant while the koi pond overflowed. Owen ran outside with his father, newspapers curled over their heads, to try and save the fish as they flip-flopped along the mud and grass, their patchwork colors seeming to melt beneath the downpour.

OWEN WAS on his way to work, using his father's truck to get to the Salty Dog, when he saw the figure standing in the pouring rain of afternoon down by the docks. Owen pulled the truck to the edge of the road and parked. He got out in the rain, opening his dark umbrella. The smell of fish was overpowering—it was a stink he was used to, but with the storm it was worse.

Jimmy looked otherworldly: he wore a shiny parka, and his face was pale beneath it. He nearly galloped over to Owen, and reached out to touch him on the shoulder, but Owen pulled back.

Owen slammed the truck door shut.

"I'm going to work," Owen said.

"Mooncalf?"

"Leave me alone."

"I thought you—"

"You thought wrong."

"I've been waiting for you. At the boat. Every night, I watch you leave the restaurant and walk home. Every night I wish you'd come to me."

"You disgust me."

"Stop it. I know that's not true." Jimmy's shoulders began heaving.

The sound of the rain became thunderous and sheets and blocks of it seemed to dump right down around them.

"God. God!" Jimmy cried out, his arms going up to the sky like some clown, like some revival preacher clown; the rain pouring against his face. A thunderclap hid the sound of his bleating. "If only you knew! If only you could grow up inside me! Knowing how I've been pushed and pulled, first my father forcing me into tennis and basket-ball and soccer since I was six years old, the camps I've gone to every summer, and these schools I go to, and what it all means when *inside*…inside, Owen…you know some-thing about yourself that's like a doorway into a different world. Something that's like...I don't know...like a doorway out of this torture place and into this garden."

Jimmy's arms came down, and now he hung his head. The rain obliterated everything else and it was just the two of them left surrounded by a slate gray world.

"When I was a little kid I had this garden that I helped create," Jimmy said, still shouting but looking down at his shoes as he stepped closer towards Owen. "It had vegetables and flowers in it, nothing pretty and nothing special, but it was mine. My dad dug it up in the middle of the night. He dug it up and told me that no son of his was going to be a goddamn gardener."

Owen leaned forward into Jimmy, putting his hand on the side of his face and looking at the weeping boy, the rich boy who had nothing, all that wealth washing away in the storm.

"That's what this feels like," Jimmy said through heaving sobs, his voice growing smaller and smaller the closer Owen got. "Like someone is trying to dig up the garden I need to grow. And you know you need to go to that garden, but every single person, from your mother to your father to your coaches to your teachers to your friends to even strangers—every single human being—wants you to keep away from the one garden where you know you can just help things grow and where you'll feel calm for once in your life...where you feel that what you have known inside your body, inside your heart, inside your mind, is the way God and nature and whatever it is that moves things within any human being—meant for you to be."

Owen gasped when Jimmy finished.

"Jim, Jimmy, Christ, I know," Owen said, feeling as if he'd rehearsed the lines. He attempted a feeble smile. Part of him felt removed within his body. He was watching himself—Owen—react, seem gentle, seem kind. "It's just like that for me, too."

The rain began to let up as they stood there, Owen's hand feeling the heat of Jimmy's face as he cupped it. A vague sliver of sunlight broke free of clouds to the east.

Owen looked around at the tourists coming off the ferry, their black and clear and red and green umbrellas all blossoming above their heads, and there, beyond the crab shack were six of the island guys he'd grown up with.

"Look, we can't do this here," he said. "Get in the truck."

OWEN DROVE in silence through a rain-shattered world—and followed the slick black island roads until they were nearly to the Great Salt Pond. Jimmy seemed content with the quiet of the drive. When Owen glanced over, he noticed that Jimmy pressed his forehead against the window beside him, reminding him somehow of a puppy.

Finally, they came to the end-of-road break that looked out over the enormous pond.

When he'd turned off the ignition, Owen reached over and took Jimmy's hand.

"I know it's difficult," Jimmy said. "I'm not like this either. Not really. There are things I want out of life. Things that have nothing to do with this. But right now. Christ, right now, this is it."

"Other people can do this kind of thing, but I can't. It wouldn't be right."

"No, it wouldn't be. But we can go somewhere it'll all be all right. Somewhere no one can find us."

"Where?" Owen laughed. "Where would it be? My god. *Where*?"

Jimmy recoiled as if he'd been slapped. "Out to sea. In the boat."

"For how long, Jimmy? How long before your dad cuts you off or before we move on? What if this is all lust? What if this isn't meant to happen? How long before you need to go off to your Ivy League school and then marry and meanwhile, I live in some kind of shame on this island. I'm not like you. I'm not like the kind of men who do this with other men. I'm just... Just."

"Just?"

"Just not sure what I feel right now. It's confusing. You're all I think about." Owen modulated his breath, his voice, changing the tone to a husky, low growl as he spoke slowly and carefully. "I just want you. Just you. Not her. That's all I know."

It was easy to lie once Owen knew what he would do with Jimmy. How he would destroy him. How it would go smoothly once everything was in place.

"Oh, baby," Jimmy moaned, leaning over, into him, pressing his scalp against Owen's neck. Owen felt wetness along his throat. "You don't know how long I've hoped you'd say it."

"We don't need Jenna, do we? Or girls like her," Owen whispered. "God, if I could, I'd kill her."

"Who? Kill? *Owen*?"

"I didn't mean that," Owen said, and kissed him on the top of his head.

Owen knew that he had him now. He had Jimmy right where he wanted him.

Where Dagon wanted him.

DAGON

"**O**wen?" his mother asked, holding something in her hand before he could tell what it was.

The statue.

It had always seemed enormous to him, but in her hand, it was only about a foot long. The base was cracked, a few of its teeth had fallen out, and all that remained was a grotesque statue someone had once carved and left behind.

"Where'd you get that?"

"Right where you left it," she said. She hefted it in her hand. "Where'd it come from?"

"I...I found it."

"You found it?"

"Yeah, I did. It's mine."

He held his hand out.

"Did you buy it?"

"That's none of your business."

"Why put it in the fishpond?"

"It's an ornament. It looked nice there. Give it back."

"It's terrible looking. Its eyes. Whoever made this thing was sick. I think some kind of animal was used. It smells, too."

"Mother."

"Don't 'mother' me. You may be a young man, but you have a thing or two to learn. I know you, Owen. I know how you think. I saw you that morning."

"What are you talking about?"

"I saw you. You cut your arm and let it bleed on this...this thing."

"That's crazy. Why would I do something crazy like that? Like—what—like cut myself? And what—did you say—bleed?"

"It's some kind of awful thing, isn't it? This thing. It's some awful thing for you. The way your mind works."

She looked at the small statue in her hand, and then back to his face. She squinted as if trying to see him more clearly.

"You've never been quite right. You know how you're different from other boys, don't you? Yes, you're crafty and you look good in a suit and you can make your muscles talk for you. But I know you better than you know yourself, Owen Crites. I know how cold you are. I know how you believe different things than most people do."

He felt her closing in like a bird of prey as she moved toward him.

"What exactly *is* this thing? A toy? Is this something you talk to? Is this...is this...some kind of devil god? Do you worship graven images now?" She said it in a half-joking manner and that was the worst of it. She wasn't taking Dagon seriously.

Owen felt as if his tongue had been cut out. He felt a heat rash along his neck. He looked from the statue to his mother and back again.

Then, he grinned.

"Don't be ridiculous," he said. "You have such a small mind. You're quick to judge when you're the one with the cold heart. You set a trap for Dad, and now you punish him for that same trap. You can't even love your only child. And your imagination—your *paranoid* imagination —finding some carved art in a koi pond, something that you claim you watched me bleed over...Did you ever for a single moment think that maybe I hated myself so much I wanted to slit my wrists? But something made me stop. Something kept me from hurting myself. But it wasn't the thought of you, was it? It wasn't the love of my mother that saved me, was it? It was the thought that maybe one day I'd have a moment just like this. A moment when Dad is out of the house. A moment when you're at your worst. Do you know what I am going to do with you?"

"What are you talking about? Owen?"

"Give me that," he said, snatching it from her hand. "It's mine. Not yours."

She stood before him, trembling.

Owen cradled Dagon in his arms. He closed his eyes, and whispered a brief prayer.

When he opened them, he said, "Here's something I hope you think about until the moment you die. I am going to be your dutiful son for a long time. But the moment that I get an inkling you're old and feeble, I'm going to show up at your bedside one night. I will press my hands over your nose and mouth and smother you to death. And in those last moments, you'll look at me and know that everything you were ever afraid of came true. Every single fear you have right now."

His mother pressed her hands to her lips, unable to speak.

It was the power of Dagon, of course. It was there, in the room. The god was there with him.

Dagon whispered within his blood: *You will die like the bitch that you are.*

Or had Owen himself said it aloud, in a whisper, to his mother?

THIS IS how it will happen, the voice came to him. *You will tell Jenna things. You will tell Jimmy some things. He harbors a madness. He is breakable. Then, she will kill him. You will save her. She will kill him and you will have her.*

He slept that night with Dagon next to him in bed.

He dreamed of the great realm beneath the sea. Owen no longer felt his age, but became a child again with Jenna beside him, the Queen of the Deepest Fathom.

"HELLO, SWEETIE," Mrs. M said.

She had just finished the Sunday crossword puzzle, and looked up from the paper. "You all ready for four more days of this...this tempest?"

The kitchen was like a brilliant day compared to the murky rain outdoors.

Owen had come in through the back, his towel in his arms.

"Up for a swim, Cathy?"

Mrs. M shook her head. "Feeling a bit downtrodden from the rain. Ask Frank, he'd probably love a race with you."

"Mr. M's around?"

"Back and forth. Here for now."

"That's great. I would've thought with the rain…"

Mrs. M crossed her legs, one over the other. Owen thought for a moment that it was the most luxurious movement he had ever in his life seen.

"You here for Jenna?"

"I doubt she wants to see me."

"Owen," Mrs. M said, setting the paper down on the kitchen table. She arched an eyebrow. "Something's changed about you. What is it? Turn around."

Dutifully, he turned about and then back to face her again.

"You're different now. What's that all about?"

"Maybe it's my hair? It's getting long."

"No, that's not it." She smiled. "Are you in love?"

"No," he said, too quickly. "Maybe it's all the swimming."

"Well Jenna's in her room. She sleeps later and later. Go call her if you want. She should get up. It's nearly ten. No one should sleep this late. Not at her age. Not in summer."

Then, Mrs. M leaned forward.

"Between you, me, and the wall, Owen, I think she's really depressed over something. But I'm the last person she'll confide in. I imagine it's about a boy," she whispered. "That McTeague character."

Then, she said, lightly, "I always thought there was something not right about him."

"Oh. It's you," Jenna said.

She was sitting up in her bed, the covers around her white cotton nightgown.

"Hi," he said from the doorway.

The room smelled of sandalwood and vanilla.

"It's the rain. It does this to me," she said, pushing her hair back from her face. "I hate storms. I wish we were back in the city."

"I'm glad you're not."

"I'm just bored. Where's the sun? It's like my summer got stolen. But you're my sun. You never fail to make me smile."

He stood there remembering the love he'd nearly forgotten. Why he care for Jenna so much. She was there for him, always. She had always been there for him.

"Okay if I come in? You know, like I used to?"

"Sure," she said, drawing her knees up. Then, "What is it between you two?"

He went into the bedroom, and sat down on the chair near her desk.

"Who two?"

"Don't be coy," she said. "Jimmy. Is it just sex?"

"Oh. That."

"Yes. That."

"I don't want to talk about it."

"I think you do."

"No, I really don't."

And then, something within him opened up.

It was like feeling a heat—a fire—in his chest, near his heart. It was Dagon. Dagon would inspire him. He felt that strength, suddenly, just when he thought he would falter.

Without even trying, tears poured from his eyes.

"Owen? Owen?" she asked, but he was nearly blind from the tears. She lifted the blanket, and patted a space next to her. "Come here. What's wrong? Owen?"

He bawled like a baby, and without knowing who—or what—had moved him, he found himself in her bed, her arms around him.

"Aw, Owen, what's wrong? What's wrong, my precious, precious, precious baby boy?"

She held him close, and Dagon was there. He felt it. He was not alone. Dagon was there. The voice that came from his throat didn't feel like his. It was some small boy's voice. Some crybaby who shivered and spilled emotion across the girl he loved.

"He...I didn't...I didn't want...I can't talk about...I didn't...he just kept...he just kept...he kept...he...I tried to...fight...fight...   fight...push...hit...but...he   just kept...he just kept...he just kept."

"Oh my god," Jenna said, her voice chilled and haunted. "No. He didn't. No. Did he? Owen? Did he *rape* you? Did he?"

"He just kept...oh god, Jenna, I can't face this...I

wanted to…I wanted to…I wanted to…kill…myself…I wanted to…"

And so it began.

She said all the things she was meant to say; and Owen told less than he needed to tell, because she made all the connections herself. He sat for hours in her arms.

Afterward, they made love.

HE WENT to the boat that night.

It was over now. It was all over.

He had won.

He wanted to take it to Jimmy. He wanted Jimmy to suffer from it.

If he could, he would've videotaped the afternoon, he would've tape-recorded Jenna's voice saying over and over again that she loved him, that it was all her fault, that Jimmy should never have come to the island, that he was bad, he was evil, and they should call the police, they should do something.

She even told him that if that bastard ever set foot on her property again, she would take that gun and shoot him right between the eyes.

The storm continued to rage across the gray expanse of sky. The Sound and the distant islands that could be seen were like watercolor images, fuzzy and melting.

Owen wore a bright yellow raincoat, a golden fire in the rain.

"Mooncalf, you look like a fisherman," Jimmy said. He wore cut-off jeans and a striped rugby shirt that was already soaked through, and his hair was like seaweed, hanging in his eyes. In his hand, a green bottle of beer. "Like, you know, a real New England Clam Chowder Fisherman!" He had to shout over a roll of thunder and a crack in the sky.

The world lit up for a moment and returned to gray.

Owen laughed, shaking his head. "You're drunk, boy."

"Want a beer?" Jimmy asked.

"Sure," Owen said. "How many you drink already?"

"Four. Maybe five. Who's counting?"

"Let's get out of the rain!"

"I like the jetty," Jimmy said, tossing him a small bottle just before he leapt to the dock.

He grabbed Owen's free hand. "No one's looking. We can hold hands, all right?"

"I don't know." Owen tugged away. He twisted the top off the bottle and took a swig. "God, I'm sick of rain!"

"Me, too!"

Jimmy tried to kiss him, but Owen stepped back to avoid it.

The rain lightened slightly; it was a warm rain; it washed across their bodies.

"She's sort of expecting us," Owen said.

"Who?"

"Jenna."

"Jenna?" Jimmy laughed, and then looked sidelong up the hill to the Montgomery place. "What for? I thought it was you and me tonight."

"She's...she's pissed. I guess that's what it is." Owen shrugged. "She's pissed and she wants us to talk to her. I told her."

"You...you *told* her?"

"After yesterday, in the truck, Christ, Jimmy, I can't not tell her. I've known her all my life. She's one of my closest friends. I told her about us. About how we're going to go away together. How you love me now. How everything's all right."

"You...you..." Jimmy stammered.

The bottle in his hand dropped to the rocky ledge, shattering.

"*You told her.*"

It was coming out now. The madness that they all had within them.

Owen wanted to smile, but knew that if he did, he would give himself away.

THE RAIN THINNED.

Minutes seemed to pass while Jimmy took in what had just been said. Owen could practically see the thoughts in his eyebrows as they squiggled around, flashing anger and confusion, and the way he chewed his lip, and how his eyes wouldn't stop blinking.

Owen reached over and touched his scalp.

"Sometimes I think I see a halo around your head. I do. I think you're some kind of angel," Owen said.

"You fucking told her?" Jimmy growled. "You goddamn fucking son of a bitch told her what we've been...what we've..."

"Do you think she didn't see?" Owen set his bottle down on the jetty, and put his hands on Jimmy's shoulders, pulling him into him. "Do you think she's stupid? We're her friends. She can see. She told me she watched us that first night. She saw us. There was enough light to see our shadows, puppy. She told me it upset her, but she understood. She wasn't sure if it wasn't just one of those drunk boy things...or something else. I told her it was." Then, he added hesitantly, "Something else."

"You fucking goddamn son of a bitch gardener's son living in your goddamn peasant fucking world, you don't even know what you've done!" Jimmy shouted. His face had contorted until it was a mask of pain and fury.

"You fucking think that," spit flew from his mouth, "that... that...you, you, with nothing to lose, can just throw what we have in front of her, in front of—you know what you're playing with? You're playing with things you can't even understand!" Jimmy began stomping around in a circle, alternating his shouts with lion roars.

When he finally quieted, Owen said, "What happened to yesterday? You looking up at God and telling me how this all felt, how you felt on the inside. How you felt you needed to let this out? What happened to that?"

"Don't you, you son of a bitch...don't use my words against me! I wasn't born to lose everything because I'm sleeping with some island townie whore, I wasn't born to have this get out, to have this ruin everything I've ever built."

"Listen to yourself. You talk like it's 1950. You won't lose everything just because..."

"You think so? You little *bitch*, you think I won't lose everything? You don't even understand what's going on here, do you? You think it's about me wanting you. Well, stakes are higher. I'll tell you something, boy: I want you, but I don't want you. You don't even understand why I have to be with Jenna, do you? Do you?"

Owen turned and began walking toward the strip of beach. Jimmy followed and kept right beside him.

"I don't want to hear about it," Owen said.

"Well, you need to. Maybe living in some little caretaker's house gives you zero perspective on this, but Jenna Montgomery means I will not be some poor shit like you."

Owen glanced back. "You're rich."

"Ha!" Jimmy cried. "You don't know the half of it."

"You're an heir to some fortune. Some sports store chain."

Jimmy shook his head. "It's not like it looks. My father has these stores. That's all he has. But the business is changing. It's changing, and he's had some setbacks. He's a terrible businessman, Mooncalf. All this stuff, this boat, the houses, all of it'll be gone in a few years. It's coming. He's going to be in jail someday, my father, and the IRS is going to eat him alive. And I don't intend to live like that. I do not intend…"

"Jesus," Owen gasped, and then began laughing. "You're just after her money."

Owen dropped to his knees on the wet sand.

"What's wrong with you?" Jimmy snarled, coming over to him. "You feeling bad now?"

"I actually thought you loved me," Owen said.

"It's not about whether I love you or not. It's not about that. But you've ruined even that now." He grabbed Owen under his armpits, lifting him up to a standing position. "You've destroyed something for me, Mooncalf. You really have."

Then, he looked up the hill to the house.

The lights were on in the pool area, and the upstairs light—Jenna's bedroom—was dim.

"I need to set this right," he said.

"No, don't, Jimmy, it's—"

"I need to," Jimmy said. "I'll tell her that it was weakness. I'll tell her I love her. I love her more than anything on the face of the earth. I'll tell her that I couldn't help myself with you, but that it was nothing. That you were nothing." He nearly laughed, but it had a cry within it. "You're just a little manipulative piece of trash. She'll understand. She's not like you. She'll understand."

Then, he took off in the rain, bounding up the wooden steps that crept like a vine along the side of the hill.

Owen waited two full minutes; an eternity. Then, he began taking the steps upward, but slowly. He waited along the top step, watching the house, seeing the light brighten in Jenna's room.

He heard the shots ring out before he reached the top step.

Soon dogs down in town were howling, and lights came up along the waterfront.

OWEN NOTICED the intense silence of the house as he stepped in through the doorway by the pool. He walked past the shimmering water to the kitchen.

He saw Mrs. M, lying in a pool of blood.

After that, Owen moved swiftly, his heart pounding.

Mrs. M resembled nothing of the mermaid or dragon or beauty she had once been. Death had robbed her of it. Blood took away the magic of her form.

Her eyes were open and fish-like.

Dagon, what is this? This isn't what was promised. This isn't what I prayed for.

He ran up the stairs to Jenna's room, and found *him* standing there, the gun in his hand—

On the bed, Jenna, bleeding, an enormous hole in her neck. Her hands moved as if she were trying to reach up to her neck.

She opened her mouth to cry out while blood pulsed from her throat.

He felt himself burning as he watched the last light flicker in her beautiful eyes.

Then, her eyes closed.

"MOONCALF, WHAT DID I DO?" Jimmy said, his skin red, his eyes narrow slits, his shirt torn and bloody. Tears and sweat shone like diamonds on his skin.

"What the hell did I do? I...I came up...I wanted to talk...and she...she had this..."

He held the pistol up.

"She...she threatened me...and then her mother came up...I grabbed it from her...I was going to leave...but they said things...her mother, too...they said things about

me...and her father...About something...some lie...
something you told her...something..."

"You killed them," Owen said as if even he didn't
believe it.

"I guess so. It's kind of a blur. Funny thing is," Jimmy
giggled in a way that seemed uncharacteristic, "the *funniest*
thing is it didn't really feel like me at all. It felt like something else. Like I got taken over. Maybe if she hadn't pointed
this gun. Maybe if I hadn't been drinking. I don't know. It
happened fast. I was about to leave, but her mother saw me
with the gun. She saw me and she was saying these things.
And then I just wanted to shut her up and this thing was
inside me. This feeling. Like something wanted me to point
the gun at her mother. Just to scare her. And then: *kabang*."

"Jimmy?"

"Her father starts shouting upstairs and I feel this...
this *wild thing* inside me. And I just go running back up
the stairs and down the hall and there's her dad, and I
think of my dad, and I think of all the things I'm never
going to have, and suddenly the gun is going off, and then
Jenna's screaming and she's picking up the phone in her
room because I hear that beep beep noise and I have to
stop her, I have to tell her not to call, that there'll be a way
to work this all out. And then, I feel it in me again. I'm
moving faster than I'm supposed to—the rest of the world
is moving slow—and I'm in her room and she has a look
on her face like she doesn't understand how I got there so
quickly and I'm feeling this—power or something—and
then I press the gun against her throat to shut her up."

Jimmy sighed, calming a bit. He pointed the gun

directly at Owen. "It's something you said to her. Isn't it? You said something terrible, didn't you?"

"Jimmy," Owen said. "Now, I know you're upset. I know this is difficult right now. But I want you to breathe. Take a few deep breaths. Come on. Just breathe."

Jimmy looked at him curiously for a moment, blinking, and then opened his mouth to inhale.

Then, *out.*

Then, *in.*

Slowly, carefully.

BELIEF

I can look at this past summer now and see that it was all Dagon.

I summoned a terrible god into our world.

There is no madness except the madness of the gods. There is no purity except the purity of love.

Here is where he took me:

Down to the sailboat.

Out to sea.

WE SAILED along beside the cliffs and caves of Outerbridge Island, beyond the Montgomery Palazzo; the flashing of green and white from the lighthouse; north and then east we sailed, beyond the Great Salt Pond; out into a diamond night where sea met sky while a new storm howled through my mind, a storm beyond any hurricane that nature could send.

I felt as if I could barely breathe.

Jimmy held me down, gun to my head, calling me Mooncalf over and over again, speaking with tenderness, gazing at me with a drowning affection, his warm hand against my cheek, forcing me to whisper an incantation to Dagon of the purity and madness of human love.

"*Mooncalf,*" he said. "*Mooncalf.*"

THE WORDS

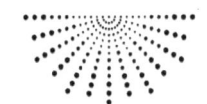

THE END IS LIKE THIS

After the last match goes out, he mouths the words to the Our Father, but it brings him no comfort.

He remembers the Veil.

He remembers the way things moved and how the sky looked under its influence.

He doubts now that a prayer could be answered. He doubts everything he has come to believe about the world.

The echo of the last scream. He can hear it, even though the room is silent. It seems to be in his head now: the final cry.

Hope it's final.

The scream is too seductive, he knows. He understands what's out there.

It's attracted to noise, because it doesn't see with its eyes anymore. It sees by smell and sound and vibration.

He has begun to think of it by its new name, only he doesn't want to ever say that name out loud. Again.

Your flesh won't forget.

Prickly feeling along the backs of his hands, along his calves. In his mind, he goes through the alphabet, trying to latch onto something he can work around. Something that will give him a jump into remembering the words.

He presses himself against the wall as if it will hide him.

Rough stone. No light. Need light. Damn.

He thinks he must be delirious because the goofiest things go through his mind: Michelle's phrase, *Unfriggin-likely, Spaceman Mark.*

Those aren't the words. Spaceman Mark. Hey, Space! What planet you on today? Planet Dark, that's what I'm on. Planet Midnight.

And out of matches.

The wind dies, momentarily, beyond the cracked window.

The damn ticking of the watch.

Someone's heartbeat.

The sensation of freezing and burning alternately — a fever.

The sticky feeling under his armpits.

The rough feeling of his tongue against the roof of his mouth.

The interminable waiting.

Seconds that become hours in his mind. In those seconds, he is running through sounds in his head — the words? What are they? Laiya-oauwraii…no. That's the beginning of the name. Don't say it again. It might call it right to you. You might make it stronger. For all you know. What the hell are the words?

He clutches the carved bone in his left hand. It's

smooth in his fist. Like ivory, a tusk from some fallen beast. Slight ridges where the words are carved. Like trying to read Braille.

If only I could read them. Need to get light. Some light.

Distracted by the smell.

That would be the first one it got.

Over in the corner, something moves. Darkness against darkness.

Someone he can't see in the dark is over there.

Eyesight is failure, Dash once told him. Perception is failure. All that there is, all that there ever will be, cannot be perceived in the light of day. At night, the only perceptions turn inward.

The words? The words. Maybe if you remember them, you can stop it. Maybe it reverses. Or maybe if you just say them…

Moves his lips, trying to form vowel sounds.

The dry taste. Humid and weather-scorned all around.

In his throat, a desert.

Every word he has ever heard in his life spins through his mind. But not the words he needs.

Not the ones he wants to remember tonight.

A beautiful night. Dark. No light whatsoever but the ambient light of the world itself.

Summer. Humid. Post-storm. One of those rich storms that sweeps the sky with crackling blue and white lightning, and the roars of lions. But the storm has passed — and that curious wet silence remains.

Taste of brine in the air from the water, a few miles away.

He remembers summer storms like this — their

majesty as they wash the June sky clean, bringing a gloom on their caped shoulders, but leaving behind not a trace of it. The smell of oak and beech and cedar and salt and the murky stink of the ponds and bogs. Their years together, all in those smells. All in the dark.

The night, summer, perhaps just a few hours before the sun might rise.

Might.

He wonders if he'll ever see another storm. Another summer.

Another dawn.

Those damn words.

"Your flesh will remember the name even if your mind forgets," Dash had told him, and he had still thought it was a game when Dash had said it. "The name gets in your bones and in your heart. Just by hearing it once. But the words are harder to remember. They don't want you to know the words because it binds them. So, listen very carefully. Listen. Each time I say them, repeat them exactly back to me."

He's shivering. Sweating. Nausea and dizziness both within him, the pit of his stomach. Something's scratchy around his balls — feels like a mosquito buzzing all along the inside of his legs. Twitching in his fingers. Tensing his entire body.

Afraid to take another breath.

A conversation replays in his head:

"It's not that hard. Watch."

"I can't. I just…"

"All you do is take the thing and bring it down like this. Think of it as a game."

"I can't do it."

"Don't think of it like that. Pretend it's a game. It doesn't mean what it looks like. You've been trained to think this is bad by church and school and your parents. And the world outside. But it is not real. It is just a game, only nobody else knows this. They're stupid. Nobody's going to get hurt. Least of all one of us. Least of all you or me. I would never let it happen. You're like my brother."

"I know. But I can't."

"All right. I'll do it. I'll just do it. Just remember what you're supposed to do. As soon as it happens. As soon as my eyes close. Promise? Okay?"

"Okay, okay."

"And the words. After. If it's too much. You know what to say. You remember?"

"Yes."

"You know how to pronounce them? You have to know. If this gets out of hand, you can stop it. The name for me, and the words to stop it. If it's too awful."

"I know, I know."

"Because it might get too awful. I don't know."

"Sure. Of course. I remember how to say them."

"And the name?"

He has no problem remembering the name. He'd like to blot it out of his mind. The name is on the tip of his tongue, and he can't seem to forget how to say it, how to pronounce it perfectly. The words have somehow vanished from his mind.

He tries to remember the words, now. How they sound. The language was foreign, but he couldn't read them off the bone. Especially with no light. But even if he had some light, he knew the letters looked like scribbles and symbols. They didn't look like sounds. All he can remember is the name, and he doesn't want to remember that.

A name like that shouldn't be said in a church.

A New England church. *Saint Something. Old Something Church. Older than old, perhaps.* Nearly a crypt. Made of slate and stone. Puritanical and lovely and a bit like a prison, now. Church of punishment. Rocky churchyard behind it.

He remembers the graves with the mud and the high grasses and the smell of wild onion and lavender, as if it were years ago rather than the past hour. Smell of summer, wet grass, and that fertile, splendid odor of new leaves, new blossoms.

The smell of life.

He is inside the church. In a room. The altar is at the opposite end.

Danny had the lighter, he thinks.

If I get it, maybe I can at least save her.

He wasn't sure if the shape in the doorway was Danny, or the thing that he didn't even want to name. Not Dash. Not anyone he had ever met or known.

An 'It'. A Thing. A Creature. Something without a Name.

But it has a name. He knows the name, but he does not intend to ever say it again. He knows the name too well, but it's the words he keeps trying to remember. The ones that are on the bone. The words that might stop it from continuing.

He tries to lick his lips, but it's no use. His mouth is dry.

Dry from too much screaming.

Nearby, there's a very slight noise. A sliver of a noise. He is sensitive to sound.

In the Nowhere.

Someone might've just died outside. He doesn't know for sure. Who? He just heard the last of someone's life in a slight moaning sound.

The open window. No breeze.

Just that sound.

A soft but unpleasant *ohhhhhh*.

The puppy whimpers. Somewhere nearby.

Other sounds, barely audible, seem huge.

Branches against the rooftop. Scraping lightly.

His heartbeat. A rapping hammer.

In the dark, the ticking of his watch is too loud. He slowly draws it from his wrist. Carefully, he presses it down into the left-hand pocket of his jeans. The watch clinks slightly against his keys. He holds his breath.

Needs to cough.

Fight it. Fight it. Swallow the cough. Don't let it out.

Closes his eyes, against the darkness. Closes his eyes to block it out. To make it go away.

Holds his breath for another count. The cough is gone.

Brief sound.

Someone's breathing. Over there. Across the room. Small room. More than closet, less than room.

Her? Thank god. Thank god. He licks his lips. Mouth, dry.

After a few minutes, he can just make out her shape.

He's staring at her, and she's staring at him, but they can't really see each other. Just forms in the dark. Michelle? Ambient light from beneath cracks in the walls creates a barely visible aura around her as he stares.

Dead of night. Dread of night.

The dread comes after the knowledge. He remembers the line from the book. That awful book that he thought was fiction.

But the words do not come to him. The sounds of them, just beyond his memory.

Breathing hard, but as quietly as he can.

Smells his own breath. The stink of his underarms. Glaze of sweat covering his body. Shirt plastered to him. Hair wet and greasy against his scalp.

The chill that hasn't left him, not since he came up out of the earth. Burning chill.

She's going to do it.

Or I am.

One of them is going to scream again. He knows it. He wasn't even sure if he had stopped screaming a half hour before.

Problem is, when the screaming starts, it happens.

And neither of them wants it to happen.

But the puppy is okay.

It doesn't want the puppy.

That's what someone said before. How many minutes ago? Did he say it? Had he said it and just not remembered it? "It doesn't want the puppy."

She whispers something. Or else he imagines she whispers.

Or it's the sound of the leaves on the trees, brushing the rooftop.

If it's her, it's wrong for her to whisper. Neither of them knows what decibel level it needs to find them, but she whispers anyway, "Please say it's a game. Please god, say it's a game."

He's not close enough, but he wants to hold her. Hold her tight. Rewind the night back to day, back a year or more, so he can undo it all. He wants everything to turn out okay, but he knows it won't.

Most of all, he wants her to shut her mouth up. He wants to hold her and press his lips or his hand against her mouth and keep in whatever she's trying to let out.

Silence. Come on, silence. Don't...

Even her whisper is too loud.

And it hears her.

And it wants to make her scream.

If she screams, it's all over.

Not just the game. The game will never be over.

If we can just hold out until daylight, he thinks.

But the noise begins. From her throat. He wants to shut her up, but he can't. He can't. She's over there in the dark, and he's on the other side of the room from her.

The scream is coming up from her lungs in a staccato gurgle.

She can't hold it in.

That's when he hears the sound.

Not her scream.

Dear Sweet Jesus, do not let that noise out of your mouth. Do not scream. It is inside here. With us.

He hears the sound it makes as it moves.

Wet, popping sounds, like bones springing free of joints, and then that stink of over ripeness.

Rotten. Steaming.

Then that awful thumping begins again.

And the steady hissing, as if dozens of snakes trail behind it.

He leans back against the wall, wanting to press himself into the wood as far as he can go. Wanting his molecules to change and move through the wood so he can just escape.

He's praying so hard he feels like his skull is going to crack open, only the prayers are all messed up and he's sure they don't work if you get them wrong. Dear God, Dear Jesus, please help this poor sinner, Hail Mary, full of grace, Hail Mary, full of grace and the fruit of thy womb, Jesus, Our Father who art in heaven, hallowed be thy name.

It whispers something in the darkness.

He begins shivering when he hears the words.

The girl in the corner finally begins to scream as if she already knows the game is up.

It sweeps toward her. *Sweeps.*

He can't stop it. He's too scared. He's so scared he's afraid he's going to pee his pants and start giggling because something inside his head is going a little haywire.

And then, he feels the wet fingers — he hopes they're fingers – along his ankles.

He tries to remain perfectly still.

Perfectly still.

Like I'm not alive.

Like I'm not even here.

Remember. Come on. Remember. Remember.

Damn it, the words.

BEFORE THE NIGHT

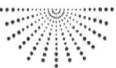

A ll that screaming and darkness happened one night when they were eighteen, but the truth was, it started long before, at least for Mark.

The longest day of the year; the shortest night of the year. But they didn't take off for the party until the dark had fallen. No one in his right mind went to a party early.

But that was the end of it.

The beginning was a game. A game within a game.

The game was about darkness.

THERE WAS a history of minor corruption between Mark and Dash that began when they were thirteen.

Dash was named, he told Mark early in their friendship, for Dashiell Hammett, a writer. Dash refused to read anything Hammett had written.

Mark was called the Spaceman because, he assumed, he must've seemed spacey at times. He didn't do any illegal drugs, but other kids were sure he did. Dash only called Mark "Marco."

"Names have power," Dash told him. "Only I can call you Marco."

Back when they were a bit younger, Mark was completely unnoticeable. He had few friends, and tended to mumble in school. Like the other students at the Gardner School, he had been pulled from public school for one mysterious reason or another.

He arrived, newly thirteen, at the Gardner School in Manosset Sound, at a spur in the Massachusetts coastline. It was nearly a forty minute drive from his home, which was in an outer suburb of Boston.

Some nights, he slept over at the boarding department, but most, he went home. Sometimes, his mother or father drove him to school; sometimes he carpooled with another older student who had a car.

The Gardner School was the only school that would take him after the little incident with the knife.

"I found it out on the blacktop," he'd told the guidance counselor at his previous school. "I did not bring it to school. I didn't threaten to kill anyone. And I didn't stab him. I held it up and I wanted him to get away from me. He was a bully. He tried to push me. He got cut because he pushed me on the blacktop and then he was about to hit me and I put the knife up between us."

Dash told Mark that he was at the Gardner School for something messed up, too.

"I have an IQ of 180, so I'm apparently really smart only I'm bored with school already. Why don't they get better teachers here? It costs a fortune to go here. You'd think they could hire a better group."

They'd bonded immediately.

They both turned up in French class, sitting next to each other in eighth grade. They found themselves with lockers side by side. Mark was an altar boy at St. Peter's. As he got into his robe one Sunday, *there* was Dash inside one of the confessionals, his head poking out from behind the narrow doorway.

"Wanna smoke?"

"How'd you get out here?" Mark asked. Dash lived closer to school than to Mark's neighborhood.

"Bus."

"I didn't know you were Catholic."

"I'm not," Dash said. "I don't believe in that stuff. I was just waiting for you to get off-duty. And have a smoke. I saw you smoke in the stalls at school. I like to hang out in graveyards, and there's a nice one behind this god place. I was having a smoke, and I saw you troop in with all the other god people."

Dash had a funny rhythm to his speaking voice, even then. As if he were preparing lectures, an old professor in the body of an adolescent.

"We're too young to smoke," Mark said. "And it's bad for you."

"Like I said, I saw you smoke at school. Or at least, I thought it was you. Do you have vices? Self-destructive ones?"

Mark only hesitated a moment. He had never smoked a cigarette before in his life.

"They might catch us in there."

"Nope. Confessional's all empty. Come on," Dash said.

He held up a pack of Marlboros. "This is the slowest way of killing yourself. One cigarette at a time, but if you start young enough, it'll help."

"Not everyone dies from that," Mark said.

"Everyone dies from something. That's the problem of life. You're just going to die," Dash said. "Me, I'll get hooked on any number of things if I can. It's always good to improve the odds if you want to succeed."

"That's like suicide. That's a sin."

"For you. You're Catholic. You have that whole resurrection of the body thing and the life everlasting, choirboy," Dash said. "Not that I don't find that appealing. I'd love to die and then come back. Conquering death should be the alternate goal if dying is the common one. I'd love to be a messiah. It would suit me. Now, come on, let's have a smoke."

IN SCHOOL, they went into the janitor's closet -- a deep broom closet that had stacks of *Playboy*s beneath a pile of cleaning supplies. The closet stank of *Comet* and bleach and oil.

"Just shut off the lights."

"Why?"

"Just shut 'em off."

"Okay."

Off went the lights.

"Listen," Dash said.

"To what?"

"Just listen. Hear my breathing? Now?"

Mark mumbled something about bad breath.

"See? This is the Nowhere," Dash said.

"This definitely is nowhere."

"*The* Nowhere. It's a different place than when the lights are on," Dash said. "Different rules apply. Hell, there are no rules. With the light on, it's all rules and regulations and laws and order. But with the dark, it's a different world. When you're dead, you're in the dark."

"When I'm dead, I'll be somewhere else."

"You think so?" Dash asked. "Now here's the thing. I know these people who believe they talk to the dead."

"Psychics?" Mark said.

"No, none of that crap. I mean people who actually believe they talk to the dead. They summon them from graves. They believe it. I don't know if I believe it yet."

"Are they in school?"

"Don't be ridiculous. I met them in a graveyard. Manosset has more than just the rocky beach. There's the Old Church. They were there. Doing a ceremony. They were sacrificing a turtle."

"Gross."

"It wasn't as gross as you'd think," Dash said. "They told me all about the Nowhere. How it changes the world. Darkness. Night. Absence of light. And in the dark, they think they talk to the dead. They have an old religion. Older than, well, yours. One of them told me that people still practice it, only no one ever talks about it. Bands of believers, basically. It's not so much different from yours.

Only, they believe in a messiah of darkness. A savior who comes by night."

"You making this up?"

"I wish I were. I don't really believe it. But they do. I find it a very attractive kind of belief system. It's this interesting idea. And you know how I like interesting ideas. And you've got this absolute connection between death and life. Bringing back the dead," Dash said this last part in full old professor mode. Then, he asked, "Do you believe in God?"

"Possibly."

"Well, then you might as well possibly believe in the Nowhere. I mean, virgins, miracles, and raising people from the dead. It's not that far from what they believe."

"You mean your made-up people who sacrifice turtles?"

"Not just turtles," Dash said. "Other stuff, too. Goats sometimes. Chickens. I'll introduce you to them one night. Did you know that a man named Crossing actually wrote several stories about their group? More than a hundred years ago. He was one of them. People thought he was writing fiction, but apparently, none of it was made up. I'll loan you one of his books sometime. He said that the darkness has a reality to it that lets illogic through. Isn't that a cool way of saying it? The darkness lets illogic through. He called it the Veil with capital V."

He paused.

Mark was about to laugh. Was this a joke? Was he *serious? I mean, with a capital V? Come on.*

Mark didn't say any of this out loud.

"It's not so different than anything else, really. It's

almost logical. There aren't any virgins in it. But there *are* some miracles. Take the streets: lights on. It's normal. Boring. At night? Lights out. No light. No moonlight even. It's a place where you make up the rules. You define the space. You create what's there and what's not," Dash said, his breath all warm. "You create what's there. And maybe *it* creates what's there."

"*It?*"

"The Nowhere."

"With a Capital N?"

Dash ignored this. "Believe what you want but there's something out there. In the dark. If you're in it long enough, it comes out. That's why they had to do the sacrifices. They told me it stops worse things from happening. You know about Eastern philosophy?"

Before Mark could answer, Dash kept going:

"Some of it is about how it's all an illusion. Everything we think we see. It's not what's really there. And if that's true, maybe what's really there is something else. Only we don't see it because we're too busy perceiving the crap we expect to see. We're taught from an early age to see things a certain way, and we name things so that they stay that way. But the darkness is fluid. It defies perception. You know how your eyeball works? How everything you see, you're really seeing upside-down, only your eye somehow adjusts it back again?"

Mark had never heard of this before. Sometimes, Dash's ideas went right over his head; or else they hit him square in the face and gave him massive headaches.

"Or a red rose. It's not really red. We see it because of the absence of some pigment and how all the other colors are there, and that somehow makes it red. But if you turn off the light, is the rose still red? Or is it no color? Is it even a rose? Does it become something else in the dark? And do you become something else in the dark?""

"Cool," Mark said. "But, I mean, I'm...me. I'm me even now. Even in the dark."

"Are you? Are you sure?"

Mark laughed a little.

"I'm not joking. Are you the same you in the dark as you were when the light was on?" Dash asked. "Would you do the same things in the light of day that you'd do if no one could see you? Do you ever wonder why people have sex in the dark?"

"Because they're embarrassed?" Mark said.

"Maybe it's 'because they can be something different in the dark. Or maybe they really are something different in the dark," Dash said. "Maybe right now, you're not even Mark. Maybe you're something else. Do you believe in life after death?"

"Well," Mark fumbled with his thoughts. "I'm sort of Catholic."

"Sort of?"

Mark shrugged. "I believe some things and not others."

"The only thing I believe about Christianity is the resurrection of the body," Dash said. "I mean, I think dead bodies still have somebody in them. Maybe we do them a disservice by burying them."

"What, you mean if you didn't bury a body it would just be fine?"

"Not saying that," Dash said. "If you can't think

deeper than that, Marco, I don't know about you. I just don't know. I mean, what are those caskets for? They're like little traps. What if we could all roll the stones away from our tombs after we die? Maybe there'd be more messiahs around. Who knows? Let me give you a rundown on deity.

"First, God's name is not God. Second, in the Old Testament, they called him Yahweh or Jehovah. In Greek, Deus. The Greek name for the top dog god was Zeus. Pretty close to Deus, don't you think? And Jehovah is pretty close sounding to the Roman god, Jove, alias Jupiter.

"I won't even go into what I learned about the goddess Ishtar and her relationship to your Queen of Heaven. You don't want to know what the word Easter comes from, trust me. It would blow you out of that little church world you're in. God, Yahweh, *what have you.* And none of these are the names of God, and even with God, there are other gods.

"That's why you have this commandment, 'Thou Shalt Have No Other Gods Before Me.' It's because there *are* other ones. And people can't say their names because no one really knows how to say the names. They used to. That's what priests in ancient times did. That was their power. They knew the real names of the gods. And naming them means bringing them. Invoking them.

"And that's what these people in the Nowhere have. For centuries, they've kept alive the name of a particular god. Maybe it's 'the' God. I don't know. But the name of the god is the power. And the god of the Nowhere is all about death and resurrection and darkness."

DASH HAD BEEN READING A LOT.

He claimed to have read the Bible three times till he knew it backward and forward, and a book called the *Aegyptian Book of Darkness*. He spoke of Kierkegaard and Kant and Buddha and Hesse and Yeats and Eliot and someone named Robert Graves and someone named Colin Wilson and about quantum something, and about transformations and chiaroscuro and shadows.

He loaned books to Mark, and asked him questions about what was in them.

Mark found it all irresistible, although the books were tough to get through.

Only the short stories by Wacey Crossing seemed to be any fun. In them, Crossing wrote about ancient practices that called up creatures of beauty and malevolence. He even mentioned Manosset Sound by name, as if these practices happened there in the 1800s. T.S. Eliot and Robert Graves were a little rougher going, although Mark loved a book called *Demien* by Herman Hesse.

Dash told Mark that, in the dark, everywhere was Nowhere. And it was better to be in the Nowhere than in the Somewhere.

Particularly if you were like one of them.

A bit outcast. A bit funky. A bit eccentric. A bit different.

"Nowhere guys," Dash said.

They loved to say to their parents – when asked, "Where are you going?"

"Nowhere. Honest. Just Nowhere."

And the Nowhere was always dark, and always somewhere else.

But Mark didn't ever get to meet these "people of
the Nowhere," as he began thinking of them.

Dash mentioned them now and again; he acted as if
he were getting close to them in some way that wasn't
expressed. He became secretive about some of the goings-
on when Mark wasn't with him.

"There's a ceremony they have called the Tempting.
Each of them cuts his left arm open and spills it over a
newly dug grave. They say some ancient words, and begin
chanting something I still can't make out. They have these
stones and they put the words on them, and dip them in
this syrupy mixture, and then put the stones under their
tongues, and the words are always inside them after that.
Their bodies memorize them or something. They don't
even use their minds. It's weird. And then, one of them
becomes possessed by the dead person."

Mark assumed it was made-up, stolen from Wacey
Crossing's stories, and as a year or so passed, he grew to
appreciate Dash's offbeat and dark sense of humor.

Once, together again in some dark place, hanging out,
Dash asked, "Do you love me?"

"Excuse you?"

"I don't mean that," Dash said. "I mean, *do you love
me*. Like a brother. Like we have a bond?"

Mark thought a minute, feeling uncomfortable with
the question.

"Sure. Like a brother."

"We've got to have that bond to make any of it worth-while. I mean, we'll get married someday and do all kinds of stuff, but if we love each other like that – like brothers – than we can move mountains."

"Sure," Mark said, but decided to turn on the light on the back porch at his parent's house.

He was surprised by what he saw.

Dash sat next to him, but he had a hypodermic needle in his arm, just withdrawing it.

"What the hell is that?"

Dash held the needle up. "It's not for you. Don't worry."

"You a junkie? Dash? What the hell is that?"

"It's not heroin. Jesus, it's the Veil," but Dash would not explain further. He took the needle, covered it, and pressed it into a plastic case that looked more suitable to a toothbrush. "See? I'm not tripping out or anything. Don't freak."

Dash reached up to shut the light off.

Dark again.

Mark sat there wondering if he shouldn't end the friendship or talk to someone at school about what seemed to be Dash's latest self-destructive habit.

But he didn't.

He did what others probably did when their best friends were on drugs – he somehow just put it out of his mind, because Dash never seemed high or wired.

And Mark didn't see much evidence of the hypo-dermic needle again. Nor did he look for it.

After a few months or so, Mark blocked that moment

from his mind. Everything seemed normal, in its own messed up way.

Dash was his only real friend at school, anyway.

ON A NIGHT-SMITTEN COUNTRY ROAD, Dash would flick the headlights off.

Suddenly, it was as if the world vanished. They were in a car with the world gone.

With just a sense of "road." A sense of "nowhere."

Dash started doing the headlight trick before he even had his license. This was back when he had managed to steal his brother's car and sneak out in the night.

He'd pick Mark up down the hill from where he lived. Always after midnight.

Mark would be out there waiting for him, waiting for the adventure.

"I been here forever," he'd say.

"Forever must last about fifteen minutes," Dash said, giving him a gentle punch to the shoulder.

They'd go to parties, or sneak off and grab a burger, or find out where some of the other guys were hanging out, smoking, drinking. Sometimes, they just watched people make out in their cars.

Neither one of them did much wild stuff. Mark even wrote down what he called the Nowhere Manifesto, but he tore it up one afternoon, worried that his mother might find it.

At the end of most evenings, they just called it a night and Dash dropped Mark off at his house.

But, on some nights, Dash took Mark to the graveyard behind the old church.

Mark never saw him draw the needle out again, but he knew that when Dash asked him to wait in the car a second, he might be going into the darkness to shoot up with whatever he used. *The Veil.*

Mark could ignore it. It didn't matter. They were friends.

Mark got out of the car this one time, and Dash, up near the church, whistled to him to come on up the path to the graves.

IT WAS NOT Mark's church, nor was it Dash's. It was older and more of a historic landmark than a functioning church. All Mark knew about it was that the founding fathers of the area had built it, or built the original building that no longer existed.

The graves behind it had those names like Goody Something and Sir Walter John Something, but most of the gravestones were rubbed smooth and coated with a slimy ooze of moss and yellow-green muck.

A bog, just the other side of a thin line of trees, had flooded the area, so they walked in mud and damp weeds.

"This is where I saw them," Dash said. "This is where they spoke to me. They showed me the Veil for the first time. Here."

Mark glanced around, but they were alone together.

"They asked me to tell them my heart's desire," Dash said. He went over and sat on a long flat stone. He patted the area beside him. Mark went over and joined him. "They told me that the Nowhere needed guys like me. Maybe like you, too."

"Are they some kind of witch cult?" Mark asked, chin in his hand. He stared across the expanse of field and wood beyond the old church. "Do they worship Satan?"

Dash grinned. "No. Not witches. Not Satan. That's all fairly new stuff. This is older than that. Long before. They're wise people, though. They know things. They believe that they talk to the dead. They believe the dead tell them things. They know the name of all the different gods. The *real* names. The names of power. I don't know how they do. They knew things about me that even my mother wouldn't know. Even you wouldn't know."

"Like what?"

"You don't want to know," Dash said. "There are some things I wouldn't want people to know. But *they* knew."

"Is it about why you had to leave the other school?"

Dash ignored the question. "Want to know something funny?"

Mark shrugged.

"They told me about you. This was before we met. They told me about that thing you did. When you were eleven."

"What thing?"

"You know," Dash said. "With the knife. Don't worry. It's kind of cool."

Dash put his hand on Mark's shoulder. Felt his breath against his ear.

"I did something terrible when I was twelve," Dash whispered. "Something you can't ever tell anyone else in the whole world, or I will hunt you down and kill you and tear out your heart and cut the eyes out of your face. Understood? We're fifteen, but when you're a kid – I mean a little kid – you do things without really knowing why. You're changing. Everything is changing. You have these impulses. You do things because something inside you tells you to do them.

"I once saw the most beautiful dead woman in the world, lying on the ground. She had killed herself, but it left no marks on her because she took pills. She was naked. I was caught doing something to her. But it wasn't what you think. Nothing perverted. She was so beautiful I didn't want to hurt her, even when she was dead and was beyond hurting. And they knew about what I did. They had spoken to her. The Nowhere people. After she died.

"They had gone to where she was buried, and they'd dug her up from the grave. She told them about me, about what I did, and they think I'm some kind of messiah because of it. Like it was a sign that I was the golden child or something."

On the phone, the next afternoon, a Saturday:
"I made it all up. None of it's true," Dash said, and then hung up.

Mark didn't see Dash for awhile, but eventually, Mark

saw Dash's car idling on the street beneath his bedroom window.

Mark was furious with his father for taking away his stereo because of a drop in grades, and he snuck out the back of the house and got in the car and told Dash, "It's about time you showed your sorry face."

ONCE, they narrowly missed being hit by a car that was following Dash's car too closely. They followed the car for miles just to annoy the driver.

They planned raids on some houses, too.

When a family was out of town, Mark and Dash would go out in the dark, late as they could stand and still feel awake.

They'd break in, way out in some suburban neighborhood. They wouldn't take anything from the home. They'd just get in through some window – it was easy to jimmy one of them open – and see what the house was like on the inside.

They wouldn't disturb anything. They kept the lights out, and wandered room to room.

Dash said he wanted to see how other people lived, what they owned, what they had.

Mark once said it seemed psycho to do it but Dash reassured him that they weren't doing any harm.

Sitting there, on someone else's sofa, Dash would sometimes speak in some language that wasn't English. They weren't any kind of language Mark had ever heard.

He would say a few of these words and, if Mark asked

about them, Dash would say that he hadn't said anything at all.

Sometimes, they'd move a book around on a book-shelf. Or they'd put a CD out of its case and put it on a windowsill. Just enough that it might seem curious to the family, returning from a weekend away.

But this was the worst of what they did together, and it really wasn't much. Some of the other guys at school regularly shoplifted. Others were smoking marijuana half the school day. Others were doing much worse.

Mark assured himself that what he and Dash did was fairly innocent. It really hurt no one. He tried not to think about that needle that Dash had. He didn't really see it, although sometimes he noticed the plastic toothbrush carrier inside Dash's green army jacket.

Although Mark and Dash loved girls and talked about them as much as any other guy in school, they really adored each other. They could've been brothers. Before they'd met – at thirteen – nobody would've thought they resembled each other. But by fifteen, they could've been twins.

Dash made Mark promise to be his Best Man at his wedding, whenever it happened; Mark asked Dash to be the godfather of his first kid, whenever it came into the world.

In the Nowhere, sometimes, Mark would say things to Dash that he never told anyone else. When Mark got dumped by Emmie, he told Dash first.

When Dash decided he was going to kill himself rather than grow up, he only told Mark.

"That's right," Dash said. "Why turn into some corporate robot and end up like our dads? I'd do it with a knife. I'll become one with the Nowhere. You?"

"Hanging. The front staircase."

"Do it at my folks' place. In the foyer. From the chandelier," Dash said. "In the dark."

They had a good laugh about it, and then shared a cigarette.

"What about those people?"

"What people?"

"The ones," Mark said, grabbing the cigarette from Dash's mouth, "that were in the graveyard. The ones you told me about."

Dash flicked on the light. Regarded Mark with a nearly mistrustful look. His eyes were bloodshot. "Listen, they're dangerous, sometimes. They showed me some things that were kind of nasty."

"Like what?"

Dash shivered slightly. Mark couldn't tell if he was just joking or not.

"Just some really bad shit," he said. "They have these ceremonies that you have to study. I've been studying them for a long time now, and I still don't completely understand them."

"Why haven't I met them?"

"They decide who meets them and who doesn't," Dash said.

"I thought you made them up," Mark laughed again, puffing on the cigarette. "To scare me. You told me you made it all up. Remember?"

"No," Dash said. "I got a little scared. I was worried they might come after you. The priests of the Nowhere are real. They're practically holy. They're really good people, but they do some nasty shit. I'm sort of into what they do."

"Sort of philosophically," Mark added.

"Maybe," Dash said. "Give me that cig back, or go buy a new pack."

DASH WOULD END the night out in the middle of godforsaken nowhere, spinning the car in the mud, or gliding down an icy patch of road, the back-end of the car fishtailing.

All around them, the dark, as if they drove inside their own minds, and the world existed only for them.

They could talk about their deepest thoughts, argue philosophy, their sense of the meaning of life and if there was one at all. They determined that there was no meaning to life, but to truly enjoy life, they each must act as if there were a meaning to it.

Their understanding of girls became legendary, as they discussed sexual availability versus the sacred virgin as it applied to the girls they knew; misunderstanding of other boys in school, which manifested in an open contempt for jocks and their football parties; they shared their love for Herman Hesse's novels and Joan Armatrading albums and this writer with the unusual name of Wacey Crossing who wrote *When Nowhere Comes* and other books in the 1800s.

Dash owned three Wacey Crossing books, all short stories, and their bindings were leathery and cracked like old Bibles, and inside the books, people had written messy illegible notes all in the margins and drawn what looked like dirty pictures of naked women with huge breasts in the front and back pages.

The Crossing stories were about a mystery cult that had survived centuries of persecution, misshapen creatures that lived beneath graves, and ancient ones that prowled the darkness.

Mark borrowed each of them, and read them thoroughly, enjoying the terribleness of the punishments meted out to those who treated the Nowhere people badly. There were six primary deities in the Crossing stories, all with nicknames: *the Devourer, She Who Befouls The Night, Hallingorianang-the-Eater-of-Souls, Oliara-the-Sword-of-Fire, The Swarmgod of the Thousand Stings, The Pope of Pestilence*, and *Julaiiar the Conqueror*.

Mark began calling Dash "the Devourer," and he in turn might call Mark "Swarmgod."

It definitely sealed their fates within weirdo-hood. Mark was perfectly happy with that.

They dreamed together, aloud, of what they'd do if they had the powers of Julaiiar the Conqueror who came in Shadow and cut the heads off friend and foe; or if She Who Befouls the Night decided to make it with Oliara-the-Sword-of-Fire, what kind of kid they'd produce.

It all happened when the lights went out.

HEADING DOWN SOME LONESOME ROAD, the headlights off. They'd light their cigarettes, and the world would change from its unsubtle self to some kind of dark wonderland.

Even though Mark might be in the backseat with a current girlfriend making out and doing everything two teens can do with each other while still keeping most of their clothes on, it was Dash who made him feel as if it were just their world: in the car, on a dark road, with nothing but the unexpected wonders of night around.

AND ONE NIGHT, Rachel Cowan had a big party out at the country place her folks had, a few weeks after graduation, and everybody they knew was going.

Michelle and Danny needed a lift, and even though Dash and Rachel went out once on a date and now didn't get along very well, Mark convinced him to go.

"This is a perfect night for this," Dash said.

"Yeah?" Mark asked, grabbing a cooler of beer. Checked his watch: 10:15. "I figure the party'll be hoppin' by eleven."

"It's a sacred night to the Nowhere. It's a night they call Lifting the Veil."

"Oh," Mark said, used to Dash's tales of the Nowhere and its priests.

Dash whispered to him, as Mark slid into the front seat next to him, "Let's have some fun with them. Okay?"

Mark couldn't reply, because Danny had already gotten in the back of the car, and Michelle rapped at Mark's window for him to unlock her door. In her arms, a plastic and wire cage.

She brought a stupid puppy from her sister's kennels as a surprise birthday gift for Rachel, who had just turned nineteen, and whose dog had recently passed away.

"Just a little fun," Dash said. "For a sacred night."

Then, he reached around to unlock the door for Michelle.

THE NIGHT BEGINS

Dash flicked the headlights off.

The night came up like veils of shadow against shadow – purple darkness, black darkness, and the curious ambient light of the earth itself – particles of illumination from unknown sources.

Reflections of slivered moonlight off distant ponds. It was beautiful, Mark thought.

The narrow, winding road was ripe with pot-holes and wounds, and the June-fat trees hung low over it – it was a beautiful world as far as Mark was concerned, and he felt comfortable there with Dash in the front seat, their world, their Nowhere surrounded them.

Mark glanced over at Dash, beside him. Dash in his green army jacket, with holes through out it. Beneath, he wore a black t-shirt. Even in the summer he wore the jacket, his emblem of weirdo-hood, of not abandoning his outcast nature.

Smoke from his mouth. The red glow of the cigarette lit Dash's features. His hair had gone from brown to dark blue with fiery tinges where it flopped around his eyes. His eyes seemed to have a light of their own.

Dash smiled, showing all his teeth.

It was not pitch black quite yet, for the moon half-lit the world. Its light, diffuse behind scalloped clouds, hinted the outline of a dilapidated farmhouse with its property cut in a ragged square from the encroaching forest, and a balding fringe of dead trees at the edge of the road before the property. A single light glowed in the house, and it somehow made Mark think about loneliness, despite being there with his friends.

He wondered what he would do – now that college loomed, and he and Dash would probably grow out of their friendship, as all friends seemed to after high school. He didn't want it to happen, but there was an inevitability to it – they would move on and stay friends, but lose that closeness, that brotherhood they felt. The farmhouse became a blur as Dash recklessly swung the steering wheel to negotiate a curve in the road.

Then, the woods appeared again, thick and dark, and another turn, another break in the woods cut by a stream and ditch to the left.

They passed what seemed at first an empty, desolate field, and there came the moon across it, a white sickle of moon. It was not empty, but was some kind of cemetery – Mark didn't recognize it at first, but then knew he had been there before – *of course, he thought, it was here, the Old Church is here. Saint Something.*

They had been mostly silent in the car – me and Dash in front, our world, our night world.

Mark grabbed another beer from the back, and nearly

stuck his hand down Michelle's shirt – she was sure I was making a grab for her, but Danny already had his hand halfway down her shirt, and suddenly something stank like a dead animal in the car, and I knew it was the puppy, in his crate. It was whimpering.

Michelle, after nearly slapping him, reached back and thrust a finger through the small Kari-Kennel opening and murmured, "That's okay, baby, that's okay," then, she reached up and flicked on the car's interior light. "Some light in here would be nice. What's this thing with darkness?"

"Darkness is cool," Mark said.

"Friggin' Goth," Michelle said; Mark was not a Goth. He was just a guy who felt better in the dark. With friends. In the car. It was his comfort zone.

"Are you sure Rachel wants a new dog?" Dash asked. "She can't exactly take it to college with her."

"I already talked to her mom about it. Her mom's going to keep it while Rachel's at Smith."

"She got into Smith?" Mark asked.

"Last minute," Michelle said.

"Where are you two going?" Danny asked, fairly innocently. With the question, came the unspoken: they were a couple to some extent. Mark and Dash were paired in the minds of their classmates.

"How could you not guess?" Michelle huffed. "They've practically been talking about it since sophomore year."

"Oh, yeah," Danny said. "I thought maybe Mark might go to Georgetown."

"I didn't want to go to Georgetown," Mark said. Then, he added, "Really. I didn't."

"U-Mass for us," Dash said.

Mark sniffed at the air. "Who farted?"

"That dog crapped," Dash said. "He needs to go outside. Not in the car."

Mark laughed, popped open the beer, and reached for the radio buttons. Dash rolled down a window, and the humidity poured in – a gentle steam. He switched the air conditioning up to a higher level.

Michelle began lecturing Dash on why the puppy was in the car in the first place, and how Rachel had wanted the puppy ever since her last dog was hit by a car out on the highway; and how, even though we were headed for "what no doubt is going to be some kind of brawl," the puppy would be fine, and when they got to Rachel's house, she'd let it out to do its business in the wild.

"Whoa!" Dash cried out, "that was close!" Another pair of headlights, in the opposite lane from them, fast approaching and crossing the invisible line in the road. Dash swung the car to the right a little too hard, and they all felt the car leaning into the ditch on that side.

Then, back to normal, driving in the dark.

"Do you really want to hurt me?" Mark began singing along with the radio, which he'd very wisely turned up slightly to drown out Michelle's whine. "Jesus, nothing but oldies."

He punched the radio buttons, but the best he could find was a heavy metal.

Briefly, he turned the sound up high; Dash reached over and switched the radio off. Then, he switched it back on, and a voice came up that was nearly monotone, "And the angel carried a crown and a burning sword, and sayeth unto…"

"'Jesus radio. I love it. Selling God on the airwaves without really knowing all about God," Dash said, switching to a soft rock station. "I like oldies better."

"Look," Danny said, rising from the back seat. "I think that's Carbo's truck over there. Hell, did Rachel even invite the dropouts?"

"That redneck," Michelle whispered, as if no one would hear her. "Carbo is such a hillbilly. I'm surprised he ever even got into Gardner." She drew the little yellow puppy from the crate into her arms. She let it lick her all over her face. Her shirt was still unbuttoned, and she wore no bra. Mark could make out the roundish mounds of her breasts, glancing back at her for a second too long. He found them unappealing. They weren't as big as they looked when covered up.

PERHAPS IT WAS because it was Michelle, whom Mark found generally unappealing.

She had a well-bred look, as if her parents had never been in love, but had know that between their check-books, their inheritances, and their basic health, they should mate and produce offspring with equally good checkbooks, inheritances, and health. Like some alien life form that must have progeny in order to conquer the earth.

Michelle was the natural product of this loveless but purposeful union.

He had seen her type throughout high school – she was not a prototype the way Dash was, or even Rachel, who was a true original. She was just one of the herd. Dash had a thing for her, but he said that his interest didn't go much past the flesh.

"She's a copy of a copy of a copy. But with an especially nice rack," he'd said at some point.

Michelle was mass-produced. She was one of many rich girls with not a lot going on other than her birth certificate and her trust fund. She had teeth – and a lot of them – and hair, and a strangely seductive little jaw of determination that waggled side to side when she was pissed off. She dressed like hot stuff, even in her khaki shorts, with visible panty line, and white top wrapped for maximum breastage.

Mark supposed there were boys with the low expectations of a Danny who found her completely irresistible.

But she was no Rachel.

She wasn't even an Emmie, Mark's girlfriend who had dumped him on Prom Night right after they'd made love on the golf course at the Country Club. Right after he'd lost his virginity. Just dumped him, and left him on the moist morning grass as the turgid sun rose somewhere – Mark, there, near the seventh hole, his tux jacket somewhere else in the world, cummerbund lost, shiny black shoes in a sand trap, and carnation shredded from passion.

Still, he had his cufflinks, and a hazy memory of his first time. Emmie had given him that, and she was more of a human being than Michelle could ever hope to be.

Unfortunately, Michelle and Emmie were best friends,

so Mark knew that Michelle knew about his getting dumped in that way.

She probably knew about how badly he'd fumbled with Emmie's shiny blue prom dress, how he probably was less-than-perfect at the whole sexual thing and how he may have said something stupid in the throes of *doing-it* that really made Emmie dislike him once and for all.

"You know, that dog has worms," Mark said to her, in the car, still looking at the sloping mounds of her breasts through her open shirt. "And you letting him lick your face could put wet puppy spit full of microscopic worm larvae on your skin, and from there, they could get inside you. And when they do…"

"Only someone like you could come up with something that disgusting," Michelle said.

"I want to hear," Dash said. He drove with one hand; he had a cigarette in the other.

"The puppy has roundworms, and maybe tapeworms," Mark said. "Almost all puppies have them. The puppy will get wormed soon, but right now, that poop inside that little crate probably has tiny strands of spaghetti – that wriggle."

"God!" Michelle shouted, kicking at the back of his seat. "Stop, now. Just stop."

"I want to hear it," Dash said. "So what do they do?"

Mark shrugged. "Well, to dogs and cats, they do a lot. But worming pills will take care of it, most likely. When those worms get into people, it's harder to get rid of them.

They make little canals under the skin. They like to go for the eyes."

"You're making that up," Danny said.

"No, for some reason, the roundworms can't mature into adults in people. So the larvae just make do, and they seem to really like getting the tissue around the eyes."

"If," Michelle said, slowly but with her usually dominating force, "you. Do. Not. Shut. Up. Right. Now."

"I won't even go into the tapeworm possibility."

"Jenny Patterson had tapeworm when she was twelve," Dash said. "Remember?"

"No," I said. "I didn't know her back then."

"She had it, and she lost twenty pounds practically overnight. She was sick for a long time. She said it was pretty nasty."

"They grow inside you," Mark said. "They grow as long as they can. They can fill your intestines, and just eat at you."

"I once saw a dead body that was opened up and full of worms," Dash said. "I almost threw up when I saw them in her mouth."

"Shut up!" Michelle shouted.

The puppy began whimpering.

Dash laughed and accidentally dropped his cigarette.

Michelle cried out something that Mark thought was "*What*," and that's when they hit something in the road.

4

THE DEER

The car didn't just hit something in the road.

It slammed into something like a brick wall.

Sounds of brakes squealing, metal crunching and glass breaking filled Mark's ears. He felt the world spin. His head knocked back into the head-rest of his seat. He slammed against the glove compartment, almost into the windshield. Something flicked against his scalp.

Michelle screamed. Danny made a noise like he'd had the air knocked out of him. Dash whooped as if he enjoyed the ride; Mark wondered if the puppy was going to be okay.

But it was over in a second.

MARK OPENED his eyes and saw something dark and liquid.

Covering his eyes.

He reached up.

"Shit." He was bleeding. Something had cut his forehead.

Someone touched him on the scalp.

"Not much, Marco." It was Dash. "Just a little blood. It just seems like a lot to you." Then, "Everybody okay back there?"

No answer.

Whatever they'd hit had darted out in front of the car from the edge of the bundle of trees at a bend in the narrow road.

Dash didn't turn the headlights back on. Perhaps they didn't even work. Mark wondered if something awful was going to happen now. If one of them was dead. Or if they'd killed an animal. Or if Dash's parents would ground him and take away all his privileges for the summer and beyond.

Mark wiped his face. It was a lot of blood for a little cut, but he felt the irregular slice at the top of his scalp, and it was, indeed, not much of a wound.

"Lots of bleeding at scalp level," Dash said. He grabbed a tissue and daubed it on Mark's forehead. "See? All better. You knocked it on the dashboard."

"I thought I was dead."

"Maybe you are," Dash said. "Maybe we all are. Maybe we're dead but doomed to stay right here in this wreck and never leave the dark road."

"Hmm," Mark said. "I think I saw that old *Twilight Zone* episode."

From the backseat, Danny gasped, "Oh my god, we hit a deer."

Michelle shouted out "Fuck!"

The word seemed to stretch into an eternity of several seconds.

Outside the car, the world was dark.

For seconds, they were all silent again.

Mark closed his eyes and wished it away. When he opened them again, he was still in the car, feeling bruised, a throbbing at the front of his scalp.

"Is everybody okay?" Dash asked a second time, breaking the quiet. He didn't bother turning around to check. He adjusted the rearview mirror, and glanced back.

"I guess I'm ok," Mark said, although the back of his neck hurt from the way he'd slammed back against the seat. His scalp stung.

"Just a little upside down back here," Danny said. "More beer, please."

"I'm fine. The puppy's fine. As if you care," Michelle said, coughing. "My arm hurts a little. And ow. My knee."

Dash began cussing up a storm. When it subsided, he looked at Mark, tapped him on the shoulder and gave a slight squeeze. "Damn, and I forgot to pay my insurance this month. I am so screwed."

It wasn't a deer.

At least as far as they could tell, although Danny insisted it had antlers, and since he was the drunkest of them, he was the least believed.

MARK GOT OUT LAST, generally pissed off that they wouldn't make it to Rachel's party at all.

They were somewhere between school, and the Sound, and it was a section of road he couldn't quite identify. There were no lights in the distance. There was no traffic noise from some nearby highway. Trees all around, thick with leaves. The moon existed somewhere, but not where Mark stood.

Dash had a flashlight and waved it around the front of the car.

"This car is fucked," Dash said. He spat out some more choice words, and Mark thought it was a bit like watching a three-year-old have a temper tantrum, the way Dash stomped around in a circle, muttering and shaking his head.

"It is, truly," Danny said. He hoisted a beer to his lips, and drank the entire bottle in one gulp. Then, he belched.

The damage to the car was extensive. The front end had completely smashed inward, practically wrapped around the engine; the front axle was bent; and Danny made a joke that it was a miracle none of them was hurt.

"Even the puppy," Danny said. "Man, that was a hell of a deer."

"I didn't see a deer," Michelle said. She had put the puppy on a short leash and walked around the front of the car. "I saw some people. A few of them."

IN THE FLASHLIGHT'S BEAM, she looked like a doll that had been through a windstorm. Pale white, her shirt half unbuttoned, her hair a mess. For a second, Mark thought her lip was cut, but it was just an odd shadow.

"If we hit somebody, they'd be lying here screaming right about now," Danny began, but Michelle gave him a harsh look that shut him up fast.

"I saw these people. I didn't see their faces or anything. I just saw a group of them. Maybe three. Maybe more." She began crying a little.

When the half moon came out from behind a cloud, beyond the trees, casting the slightest amount of light across the road, Mark noticed how her tears shone on her face.

"Somebody hold me," she said.

Danny obliged; his arms wrapped around her. "No, babe, it was a deer. I'm sure it was."

"We killed some people," Michelle said, but even as she said those words, it didn't sound like she really believed it, seconds after saying it. "They all had shaved heads. They might've been monks or something. I know. It sounds crazy. Maybe it wasn't people."

"We're not far from the old church," Danny said. "Maybe it was some monks."

"I didn't see any monks," Mark said.

"Monks, skinheads," Michelle said with a bit of venom in her voice. "I saw faces. And maybe one of them had antlers on." Then, she laughed. "Oh, my god, it sounds ridiculous. I've had two beers exactly and I sound ridiculous." She looked at Mark and Danny. "You would've seen it if it was people, wouldn't you?"

"Antlers?" Mark grinned.

"What?" Dash let out a huge laugh, like a balloon popping.

"Okay. Something on his head."

"It was dark," Mark said.

"Maybe," Michelle began. Then, seemed to change her thought. "All right. If I saw them, they'd still be around."

"Well," Dash clapped his hands together. "Mystery solved. You got bounced around back there. Maybe it jogged some memory or made you hallucinate."

"Well, I guess you three have talked me out of my mania," Michelle said.

"It was pretty dark, 'chelle, and it happened pretty fast," Dash said. He shook his head, chuckling. "Antler hats. Pretty good. Skinheads in antler hats."

Mark looked at Dash, but couldn't read anything in his face.

It was only later, when Dash went to take a leak with Mark, that Dash said, "It was them. The priests of the Nowhere. This is the night."

They stood at the edge of a mossy embankment that encircled what looked like a bog. Thin trees all around. Mark had the uncomfortable feeling that they weren't alone. He kept looking off in the woods as if he would see Danny or Michelle standing there.

Mark toggled his zipper and let loose a stream onto some twigs.

"This is fun, no?" Dash asked. "We're going to be part of a ceremony."

"What are you talking about?" Mark zipped up.

"I guess I didn't tell you. It's a sacred night. Remember in the Wacey Crossing story?"

Mark did. There was a Wacey Crossing story about midsummer's night, and how it was the weakest point of darkness in the world, so the Nowhere gods had their moment to come into the world of Man. It was a bit of a shivery tale, and Mark had a few nightmares after reading it.

"It was just a story," Mark said. "You nut."

"Everything Wacey Crossing wrote was true," Dash said.

Mark nearly looked at Dash straight on, but didn't. It looked like Dash was pulling that toothbrush case-that-didn't-hold-a-toothbrush out of his inside jacket pocket.

Mark didn't want to see the needle come out.

Or see Dash use.

Excerpt from "The Night of Changing" by Wacey Crossing, from the collection, In The Grave of the Devourer & Others published 1882, N.M. Quint & Sons Press, New York, NY. Used here with permission.

...The one called Rowan motioned to Petra, a flourishing movement of hands that reminded me of fish, swimming. Petra left my side, and I was loathe to let drop her hand, for fear, for the terror I had begun to feel in my heart. She was my beloved, and she was too innocent for this night of madness. Her mind would become twisted from their heathen perversions and dark callings. I looked upon her in the shaded and sickly moonlight, upon her luxurious dark hair, her figure so lovely and dress of gossamer. I was afraid of what this Unholy Man would do to her, what he might take from her, as he had taken my peace from me.

But it was too late. She had persuaded me to bring her, for she longed to speak again to her father. She begged me with tears and cries and silence until finally, weak man that I am, I allowed her to come with me to this ceremony.

Gudrun took her hand, and brought her into the sacred circle, drawing down her cloak, and painting strange figured upon her face and neck.

I did not know what to expect, for although I had been an initiate for nearly a year, I had not borne witness to this highest of their Holy Days, the shortest night of the year at Midsummer. From my studies, I knew that this was the thin sacred veil that flowed between the world of the Nowhere and the world we human beings occupied. The gods were at their most powerless to resist human intervention in their affairs. I was

well aware that invocations would be made, that the Names would be said, and the seven words of power would be intoned over the exhumed grave of one of the early Masters.

The bones of the Masters had been given, relic-like, to the handful of followers left in the world – one some distant European shore, hundreds of thousands of years ago. Each bone, whether a toe-bone or knuckle or entire skull, had been held in secret, and buried with one of the followers, and the circles of belief arose around the grave that held the relic.

I had known that this particular spot of worship held a rib from an early Master. On this rib, these bones, the runes of Boediccaeringon had been carved. These, the last words uttered in a time of famine and torture in the west of the British Isles in those ancient times. It was used, they said, to ward off the invasions of Romans and Norsemen. I had never seen this sacred rib, but now, Gudrun held it.

In the darkness, I saw only its knife-like appearance, curved slightly at the end.

Then, Rowan drew close to her. I saw their shadows nearly touch, and it filled me with both jealousy and dread.

And I knew what he was about. He had lied to me about what this ceremony was – yes, there was truth to his lie. But I knew in that instant that I would forever regret bringing Petra to this bloodthirsty tribe of worshippers.

He was telling her the Words, and the Words were sacred and known only to the few.

And the Words were the names of the Gods, the TRUE NAMES, THE NAMES OF TERRIBLE AND SWIFT POWER, NAMES THAT SHOULD NEVER HAVE BEEN REVEALED TO MANKIND!

To know the secret names of the gods, to be able to say them aloud, had been brought by one who had come back from the dead thousands of years ago. The legend of the Words was that the one who brought them could not get rid of them. They were accursed to the one who knew them, for he could not resist saying them. Could not resist intoning the names of the gods, and this brought terror and panic into the world, and with it, disease and ill-begotten monstrosities. So the first Masters had found a way to put a lock upon them, so that only part of the Names could be said by one, and the Masters knew the completion of the Names – but no Master knew the entire Name to himself alone. The priests that followed the Masters shared the Names as well, and for each gathering, two priests or priestesses would know the Names, and could perform the ceremony if times were needed to invoke the Wrath of Gods. The flesh of the one who heard the Words could not resist saying them, for the Words went wormlike not into the brain, but into the lips and the throat, and remained there until the point of Death.

Only in the last throes of Death would the Words emerge.

I knew then to what end they used my beloved Petra.

God have mercy on my soul that I had ever taken the woman I loved into their corrupt circle! Petra had been living within a world of despair since her dear father had died so horribly! Had I but known the lengths she would go to in order to reach him, in order to be with him again!

She herself took the sharpened bone and thrust it into her breast, and as she died, I heard her utter some insane language, a string of vowels and consonants that made no earthly sense. She fell; the others held me back, though I fought them dearly to get to her.

Rowan crouched down, a lion over its kill, and leaned into her ear to whisper something.

I struggled free and escaped my captors. I fled deep into miasmic bogs and woods, running from the terror and evil of it all. The visions of what I'd seen in the dark, of the dancing and singing of the priests and their minions, their shadows against the darker shadows of night, and within their circle, Petra, dying – and with her last breath, the demonic language!

At my apartment on Broad Street, I locked the door, and shuttered the window from the night. I lit candle after candle and lamp after lamp, to bring the brilliance of day into the late hours.

I heard a rapping at my door at nearly three in the morning.

She had found me. She had returned to me.

How could I resist her? She was my heart. She was my soul.

For her, I snuffed the candles, and turned down the lamps.

I left the Nowhere into my room. My soul.

Petra found me, before the morning had come.

She showed me the visage of a god whose true name should have been destroyed millennia ago. In the ancient tongue of the Chaldeans and Babylonians, a savage, devouring god whose hunger for children and the innocent is never-ending....

SHELTER

M ark and his friends found nothing in the ditch on the side of the road. Neither were there any people – or deer – moaning in the woods.

"Whatever it was, it was big and strong."

"Brilliant deduction," Michelle said.

"A bear, maybe," Dash said.

"We got bears out here?" Danny asked.

Michelle flipped out her cell phone. The green light came up, and she began punching in numbers. "You have triple A, Dash?"

"No."

"Who you callin'?" Mark asked.

Michelle turned her back to them.

Then, she said, "Rachel? It's 'chelle. Listen, Dash wrecked his car out – no, we're okay. Oh my god, I know," she said, her voice dropping to a whisper as she said stuff that Mark was sure had to do with what geeks they were and how she'd been stuck riding with them because Danny was too drunk to drive. Then, her voice returned to normal. "No, no idea. We're not far from some farmhouse. And a graveyard. Yep. We have a special gift for you. I am not telling. Can you send your brother out to Route -- Rachel? Rachel? You're breaking up. Damn it," Michelle said, slapping her phone shut. She spun around. "You guys have a cell phone?"

"I'm technologically challenged at the moment," Dash shrugged, and went to grab a beer from the back of the car. When he got there, scrambling around the backseat, he shouted, "Jesus, Danny, did you drink two six packs?"

"I don't think so," Danny said, looking at both Michelle and Mark with the look of an innocent puppy. "Did I?"

"Found one. Wait, found three. No, five. Who wants a beer?"

"I do!" Mark shouted.

"Yeah," Danny said.

Michelle opened her cell phone again, and tried dialing. "We're in one of those dead areas."

"Dead?" Danny grinned.

"Can't get through," Michelle said, practically under her breath. She went over and stood beside Mark, and touched him lightly on the shoulder. "I guess we can't just walk to the party? Jesus, Danny, you always have that damn cell phone."

"We can find another phone," Dash said. "There's that church."

"Or the farmhouse."

"Church is closer. There's either going to be a payphone or an office phone in there."

The sky began dripping with rain. The soft distant rumble of thunder.

"It's coming back," Danny said. "One-one-thousand, two-one-thousand."

A few seconds later a flash of lightning hit that was so bright it seemed to illuminate the forest, and for a moment, Mark thought he saw people standing there, behind some trees.

Danny began counting again, and a louder rumble of thunder sounded.

The rain began coming down fast, and Dash called out, "Come on, this way," and Michelle put the puppy in the little carrier; Danny took it in his left hand and held her hand with his right, and they ran together. Mark jogged behind them all, down the now-slick road.

Within minutes, Dash ran to the right, up the grass-covered path that led to the Old Church. Mud sloshed all around. The rain came down in sheets, and Danny was laughing and running, and the puppy in the carrier was barking; Mark held the flashlight up so they could see their way up the path, and couldn't wait to get inside the church and be dry again.

As they got closer to it, Mark noticed that there was a flickering light from within the church.

"God, we should've just stayed in the car," Michelle said.

She was soaked, her hair, dripping, her shirt pasted to her breasts. "This feels a little déjà vu in the junior high department. I can't wait to get out of this place and get to

Northampton. May this be my last rainy night in Manossett."

"Yeah," Danny said. Then, he added, "God, I feel wasted."

"I'm amazed you're on your feet," Michelle said, nearly cheerfully.

"I can always go down the road to that farmhouse, too," Mark said, not breaking eye contact with Michelle.

"No need, Marco," Dash said.

They huddled inside the arched doorway of the church, Mark pressed against the thick wooden door.

"This is more of a chapel than an actual church," Dash said. "It's one of the oldest in this area."

"It's locked," Danny said.

THE WINDOWS WERE all shuttered and locked from the inside, as well – Mark had checked when they'd first arrived.

Lightning lit the night again, and Mark saw the rocky graveyard lit up. Again, he thought he saw people – a group of them there – but they seemed blurred to him, and he wasn't sure if perhaps he should quit drinking beer.

"This kind of place," Dash said, "has to have a key. This isn't the kind of hangout people worry about getting broken into. Not way the hell out here."

He felt around in the recesses of the arch as it peaked and then dipped, and cried out, "Gotcha!"

He held up a thin round key. "Ask and it shall be given to you."

"Thank god," Michelle said. "I just want to be somewhere dry."

Mark kept looking out through the heavy rain at the darkness of the graveyard. He heard the door open behind him. The puppy whimpered in its carrier, and Danny made baby noises to it as he lifted it and took it inside.

One-one-thousand, two-one-thousand.

The sky lit up with whiteness.

There, in the graveyard, shadows of people.

And what looked like an open grave.

Then, darkness. Rain. The grumble and crack of thunder.

"The world's smallest chapel," Dash said. "You probably know its history."

The chapel was one oblong room, with angles cut into it to create recesses with shrines along its gray stone walls.

Mark noticed the windows first – barely slits to let in light, with stained glass in them. The shutters outside were deceptive – they were large, and made Mark think the place had large windows as well. When he and Dash had been in the graveyard before, they'd never thought to venture in the church itself. It was a plain, nearly bare church, with flat, long benches for pews. The altar looked very much like a wide flat stone of four or five feet in length, and two feet wide.

There were fat long candles in brass holders up and down the aisles, all lit.

"Well, there's no phone here," Michelle said. "At least it's dry."

"Yeah. And it's better than being out there."

"How's the puppy?" she asked.

Danny crouched beside the carrier and looked in. "Doing fine. Chewing on his rawhide."

"Damn," Dash said. "My ciggies are ruined." He held his pack of Marlboros up.

"I have some," Mark said. He reached into his pocket, and drew out two cigarettes. "Got a lighter?"

"I do," Danny said, feeling in his pockets.

"I got matches," Dash said, withdrawing some from within his jacket. "And shockingly, they're dry. Five left." He struck one against the matchbook, and Mark passed him a cigarette.

"You keep these," he passed the matches to Mark once he'd begun puffing on the cigarette. Mark thrust the matches into the back pocket of his jeans. "You got four more cigarettes and four more matches. Perfect, Marco."

"I hope Rachel appreciates the effort we go to for her birthday," Michelle said. She reached into her handbag and withdrew a comb. She ran it through her hair, her head tilting sideway. She wandered over to one of the pews near the front of the chapel. "So now what?" She patted the bench where she sat, and Danny sat down beside her. Soon his arm was around her waist, and she leaned against his shoulder, looking up at the candles at the altar. "This is one ugly chapel. Those puritans really – holy crap, look at that!" she pointed toward the curved wall behind the altar.

Mark immediately looked up. Behind the flickering candle, there was a painting that reminded him of something from his sophomore European History book. It was nearly medieval looking – a faded painting of what seemed to be several monks, their heads shaved in tonsure.

"Those look like the guys I saw," Michelle gasped, and then giggled. "How bizarre."

"Oh yeah, the monks we hit," Dash said, his voice brimming with contempt. "The ones wearing antlers."

"Gives me the creeps, a little," Michelle said. "Now I really wish we'd stayed in the car."

"And risk getting hit from behind by another car? No thank you," Dash said. "What good would that do? Your cell phone won't work. I know this place. I'm sure there's a phone in it."

Mark said something about how seeing a painting of monks in a chapel was not the strangest thing in the world, but the whole time he felt like he was lying. Wasn't sure why, but there was something funny about the painting.

He walked up the aisle to get a closer look. Stepped up the worn, uneven stone steps to the altar.

The monks had faces that were like softened inverted triangles, and large wise eyes. There were four of them. In one of their hands, there was what looked like a thin white flute that bore markings – *Hebrew? Latin?* Mark had no idea. As he gazed at it in the shimmering candlelight, he thought it might be the thin tusk of some wild animal rather than a flute. One of the monks held a round stone in his hand, or perhaps it was a large wafer of some kind. Again, this had strange marking upon it. The third monk held both his hands out. The third monk's hands were merely presented as having nothing in them.

But the fourth monk in the group held a small human skull in his hands.

The skull had small bumps along its scalp – two just above the forehead. And its front row of teeth seemed unusually sharp, nearly wolf-like.

"It's funny," Mark said.

Behind him, Michelle. She had gotten up and looked around the altar, too. "What?"

"I was sure I'd been in here once. A long time ago. Some time. But I guess I never have. I've been outside before. But never in here. I've never even seen anyone go in here before."

"Look at this," Michelle said. He turned, and she was reading something off the top of the slab.

He went to look. The stone tablet was covered with a stubble of mold or some kind of dusty lichen. Michelle brushed some of it off. "Look at that, Mark," she said, pointing to something carved into the stone.

Mark thought the drawing was a squiggle of circles and lines intersecting – some abstract Christian imagery. He noticed that it had eyes.

"It's some kind of bird," she said.

"Or bug. Look at its wings. There are four of them," Mark said. In his mind, the words *Swarmgod of the Thousand Stingers* seemed to surface. Words beneath the carved figure. "Is this Aramaic or something?"

"It's Latin," Dash said from the back of the room. "Or Greek."

"I took Latin in ninth grade," Michelle said. "It doesn't look like anything I remember."

"Then it's Greek," Dash said. "I've been in here before. I got a guided tour. This is one of the oldest churches in New England."

"How old?" Michelle asked, idly, her eyes never leaving the altar top.

"I would guess the 1600s."

"No, wait, I know what language this is. This is just French," Michelle said. "It's just carved in the stone with such a strange script, I didn't notice it. Let's see, this means, no, maybe it's not French. It's something I recognize." She leaned against the stone tablet. "Why would the pilgrims write in Greek? Or French?"

"I'm sure more than just pilgrims have been using this in the past five hundred or so years," Mark volunteered.

"That's right," Dash said.

"This is Latin, this part of it." Michelle's fingers traced the engraving. "VE. DEU. VI. Well, it's all broken up. It could mean anything. And what the hell is that? It looks like a round mouth full of sharp teeth."

"Deu is probably Deus," Mark said. The words seemed to be in his head: *The Devourer. She Who Befouls The Night. The Pope of Pestilence.*

"Maybe," Michelle nodded. "These drawings are fascinating. They almost look like caveman paintings. This word – AMOR. That's easy. Unless it's part of a longer word – too bad it got rubbed away here. I just wish I could figure out the letters in between."

"I didn't know you studied Latin," Mark said.

"Two years, but I switched to French junior year. I

stopped enjoying it," Michelle said. Then she arched an eyebrow. "What, you think I'm just some dumb rich girl skating through life?"

"No, no, really, I don't," Mark said.

"Well, there's always more to people than you think. Even you and your buddy," Michelle offered a sweet smile. "I'll probably major in comparative lit at Smith, if I can take German and handle it at the same time. Someday, maybe I'll translate great works of literature. Or be a foreign correspondent."

"Or a spy," Dash said.

Mark almost wanted to tell Dash to shut up. He had his own interest in language, and had been studying Spanish in school, but had wanted to learn French, too. He looked at Michelle carefully, as if seeing her for the first time. She noticed, and laughed.

"I guess it takes a car wreck and a storm for us to get along," she said. He felt warmth from her, just standing beside her. Connecting in some way that he never thought he could with a girl like Michelle.

"Well, obviously, there's no phone here," Dash said. "Maybe we better take a hike."

"Yeah," Mark said, feeling a bit more like a man.

"I'll be fine here. I'm going to try and decipher this stuff," Michelle said. "Danny, you want to go with them?"

Danny, the puppy in his lap, made a motion that seemed to indicate that the puppy needed him.

"Me and Mark will go to that farmhouse," Dash said. "You two stay here. What, it's maybe a mile down the road?"

Mark nodded. "Yeah."

"We can run."

"Sure," Mark said, but dreaded the rain.

"You two just continue the party here, dry off, and we'll be back," Dash said. "Feel free to chug the last beer, Danny."

THE RAIN HAD SLOWED to a steady but light sprinkling. The lightning was off in a distant sky, barely lighting the path from the old church.

"Okay, now, here's what we do," Dash said.

"What's all this?" Mark said.

"Huh?"

"'Huh?' You planned this," Mark said. "I know you did. What *is* all this? The church. The crash. Huh?"

"Come on, Marco, I told you, we'll have a little fun."

"It's not fun. It's the opposite of fun. Fun would be the party. Fun would be anywhere but here."

They walked out among the graves. Mark kept the flashlight on the ground to avoid any rocks and stones.

"She's a bitch, you know that? Don't let her fool you with all that Latin shit. She spent half of high school thinking that guys like you and me are less than toads, so don't suddenly get all sugary just because she shows you her rack."

"Maybe we *are* less than toads, Dash. Maybe all this Nowhere crap makes us warts on toads."

"Blasphemy." Dash reached over and slapped him hard on the face.

It stung. Mark reached up and touched his cheek.

"Tonight is the night." Dash said grabbed him by the elbow, and pulled him close to him. The flashlight fell from Mark's hand. Dash's breath was all beer. "Look, you've known since you were thirteen that you were going to be part of this. You knew. And tonight is the night. Just like in the book. It's the Night of Lifting the Veil. It is nearly midnight. It is midsummer's night. The shortest night of the year. The night when the Veil between our world and the world of the Nowhere is thinnest."

Mark laughed. "Come on, Dash. Come *on*."

He pulled away from Dash, walking ahead on a narrow, scraggly path between gravestones. "Get real."

Then, Mark thought he saw something before him – some shape that was all shadow, and he saw that at the edge of the graveyard, like a gate, there were people standing there, in long coats or cloaks, he wasn't sure, but he could see them.

He heard Dash groan behind him.

Sound of sudden movement.

Mark was about to turn around to see what was wrong, when something hit him hard on the side of the head, and he was out.

MARK AWOKE A FEW SECONDS LATER, feeling dizzy. His vision blurred. All shadows and scant moonlight around him.

The rain kept coming down.

He lay in mud.

He thought he saw others there, those people, those

monks, whoever and whatever they were, and it seemed nearly natural to see them. He almost expected them. Had it all been true? Had everything Dash had been telling him about the Nowhere – all those stories – been true?

He lay there, blinking, in the rain.

Of course, a cult could survive. There were all kinds of cults and religions in the world. But right here? In Manosset, in the 21st century? And could they be so backward and ignorant as to truly believe that there were gods with such ridiculous names as She Who Befouls the Night?

But those were just nicknames. He knew that from the Wacey Crossing stories. All names for the gods were not their true names. Their true names were only known by those who held the power.

The back of his head throbbed.

He looked up into Dash's face, shadowed with night.

Were they alone? He felt alone.

"Here's the thing. You've got to listen very carefully, Marco. Very carefully. There are words, and they're on this," Dash pressed something into Mark's hand. His fingers curled around it instinctively. "Sometimes, the god that enters gets out of hand. And has to be stopped. The words will stop the god. The words are the only thing that stops the god. Listen. Just lie there and listen or I will hit you again so hard so help me god Marco you might never wake up. Listen! This is so important," Dash said.

Was he weeping? Was it rain? Mark couldn't tell.

"I have to fulfill something here. It is my destiny. I am chosen for something, and tonight is the night. When this happens – and it has only happened nine times since the dawn of recorded history, Marco, nine times, I will be the tenth. I will be the tenth, and this hasn't been arrived at lightly. They are very smart people. They have waited more than a thousand years in their religion to allow this to happen again. They feel it's time. And I am the one. But you have got to remember the words when you hear them, Marco. I can only say them once. You are the only one who can stop this with the words. Only the one I...I," Dash's voice broke.

Then, strength returned.

"Only the one I have given my heart to can stop this once it starts. And the words have got to be remembered. These others," Dash nodded to darkness, although Mark saw no one, "they have had their tongues cut out lest they utter the words. The one who told me, taught me, drilled me in this -- he's dead. I can say the words to you, but you must remember them. And with the words, I will tell you the names of the gods. This is an enormous responsibility. The world is corrupt. The time of human life is nearly over. The gods want to return and end the stupidity of this race of men. The names of the gods," he leaned into Mark's face, and pressed his mouth to Mark's ear, he began whispering something that Mark tried to remember as soon as he heard it.

"There's really a Nowhere?" Mark asked, pleading in his voice.

"Oh," Dash sighed. "Marco, wait til to you see it. I mean really see it. There's something you need to drink. Here, sit up."

Mark felt Dash's hand slip behind his neck. "It's easier to see like this."

Mark moaned a little – the pain at the back of his scalp intensified. "You hit me too hard."

"Sorry." Dash withdrew the hypodermic needle from the plastic case.

"What – what are you – what – don't," Mark whispered.

"It'll take the pain away. And you'll understand. You'll see. You will really see," Dash said, and he held Mark's arm down, tore his shirtsleeve up to his bicep. Dash squeezed his bicep, and then Mark felt the needle go in, twisting into his flesh.

"This isn't junk. This is ambrosia. Believe me," Dash whispered. "You'll have a taste of the Nowhere. What it really can be like."

THE SENSATION OF FLOATING, *but not floating*.

Hands moved in bird-like blurs before his eyes.

It was already morning. The rain had stopped. The sun was out.

But the sun was white, not a warm yellowish gold, it was white – all the light was pure white in the sky.

Mark sat up against the gravestone. The throbbing in his head was gone. The trees were funny, the woods seemed weird. Something moved along the bark of the trees. Snakes and worms wriggled along them.

The strange thing was: some things were missing. The trees themselves didn't move in a light wind; and there was no rain, although there had been second before.

Dash was there, only he was Dash with a difference: he seemed better looking. Color in his face. A rosy glow. His eyes were like a little boy's – all happy and expectant. Mark's eyes went in and out of focus. He heard a strange humming in his head. He looked at his hands, and he saw them as liquid, contained within some invisible boundary that defined "hand." When he waved his hand, some molecules of flesh dispersed – just a few -- and seemed to form into an insect of some type in the air – a ladybug, flying off.

"Ain't it cool?" Dash asked. "It's like the world only different. If you stay still, you disappear. Watch."

Dash closed his eyes and mouth, and clasped his hands together. Within seconds, he seemed to evaporate like steam.

Then, he laughed, and suddenly was there again. "The world we're used to has to move a lot or make noise for things in the Veil to see it. Otherwise you become invisible, even to the gods. It's a strange place, no?"

Dash kept laughing, but it all seemed to move slowly, and Dash drew back his black t-shirt, tearing it, only it didn't tear like fabric. It formed droplets of black goo that absorbed against his green jacket.

Then, Dash pressed his hand against his pale, hairless chest and drew back the skin – not as if it were cut or scraped, but in that liquid medium, as if Dash himself were a soap bubble – malleable and shifting, but within a boundary that kept the liquid in place.

Dash's fingers went deeper into his flesh. He drew out what appeared to be a pulsing mass of purple and poppy red.

Smiling, Dash brought it closer to Mark's face.

"My heart," he said. "My heart and your heart."

Dash reached into Mark's chest, and it tickled. Mark laughed, and felt Dash's fingers inside his flesh, moving along the organs within his ribcage.

A feather-like tickle of his heart.

All the while, the liquid between their bodies, the floating droplets, merged and mixed, splashing together.

Dash held both hearts for Mark to see.

"We're brothers," Dash said.

"The Veil," Mark murmured, feeling particularly good, as if he had never know what it meant in life to feel good.

Dash nodded. "Yep. The Veil. From a garden that existed thousands and thousands of years ago. A garden destroyed by mankind when it learned the secret names of the gods. But the wise ones who knew its value rescued this flower and its seed. And they've planted it and cared for it in secret all these years, Marco. And it shows you the real world. The Nowhere. If I told you this was Eden itself, wouldn't you believe me? Look, we flow. Look at the sky. This is night, Marco. Not daylight. This is true night. The blackness is an illusion. See? Look –" Dash pointed to the sky. An eel wriggled in the white air as if it were moving through rippling milk. "This is the realm of the gods. This is what we're blinded to. This is what the Nowhere people know. And always have. We can't be here long. We can't take the Veil too much. It's addictive, but it can be horrible as well as beautiful. Do you see now? Marco? How beautiful? Marco, I've seen magnificent cities on the surface of the sea – I've seen creatures that have only been drawn in ancient texts – sea monsters, mermaids, all here, all within the Veil. And the gods, too. They cause what happen in our world, but we are blinded and cannot see – we see through darkness. The Nowhere is the true light."

"I feel a little sick," Mark said, reaching to his stomach. "Sick."

"It's your first time. But you'll get used to it. You'll enjoy it more. Right now, you can only tolerate a few minutes. But later, you'll be able to have more of it. I'll show you amazing things, brother. Amazing. One more beautiful than the next," Dash said, and then he held something in the air. It looked like a white horn -- *or an animal bone?* Writhing around it, tiny red insects. "You'll come out of this in a minute or two, Marco. When you do, you must say the names as soon as I've said the first part. And if it gets too much out of hand, you can stop it. There's always a way to stop it. Just remember the Words. They're here, on this bone. See?" He said them quietly and made Mark repeat them. "The Words are hard to remember. But once you hear the names you can't forget, even if you try. You hear them and your molecules take them in and hold them. The flesh remembers. You have to say the names as soon as you see me die."

"Die?" Mark looked at him, uncomprehending. "You're going to die?"

"Not really. Not die like you think. You ready?" Dash held the bone in front of his chest.

He began saying the first halves of the names of the gods of the Nowhere.

ALONE, with Dash, in the rain.

Out of the Veil. In the real world. The ordinary, awful world again.

Mark sat up.

Sky, black. The earth, sucking mud.

Taking the smooth thin bone, Dash pressed the sharpened end of it into his chest.

Mark reached for the bone, pulling it out. "No, Dash, please, no!"

As he let out a final breath, Dash whispered the names of the gods.

WHEN DASH'S eyes were closed, Mark said the last half of the names. He didn't know how he could remember them – they were a long string of sounds and clicks and howls. They hurt his ears to say, like a strangely out of tune sound of pipes being played from his throat.

He almost wanted to say the Words, as well, out of fear.

The Words that could stop this.

But he hesitated. He tried to think of the Words, but none of them came to him. He tried to remember Dash's voice speaking them, but it was like a wall of silence.

Dash opened his eyes again.

They glowed like the ends of cigarettes in the dark.

THE CHURCH

Mark began shivering in the darkness as he watched what had been Dash rise to its feet. It no longer seemed to be Dash, not in the sense that he had felt Dash had been. It had glowing eyes, and its teeth were sharp at the ends, small nails of teeth, and even in the moonlight, Mark could see the way spurs had burst from his joints -- elbows and knees -- and writhing worms, long night-crawlers, moved along his fingers.

"Nowhere is here," Dash grinned, and for a second, Mark thought it was a trick.

The drug, perhaps. Still lingering in his system.

Of course. The drug. The Veil.

The needle that had gone in his arm.

"Jesus," Dash said. "I'm *hungry.*"

DASH TURNED, glancing toward the church. Then, back

to Mark. "You're not going to understand this, Mark. If you could see what I see, you would."

The red eyes burned and then seemed to fade into Dash's normal eyes.

Mark heaved a sigh – it must've been the drug. He was still hallucinating. He still felt weak and dizzy, and he had to sit down again. His head was spinning.

It was the drug. That's all it was. None of it had happened.

"Look, give me a minute," Dash said. "You need to rest. You're going through a lot. Shit, I've been through a lot."

Mark turned, and threw up onto a gravestone. He wiped his mouth; a sickly sweet taste lingered in his throat. *The Veil.*

When he turned around, Dash was gone; by the time Mark rose up on his feet, he thought he saw some enormous winged bird – almost a pterodactyl, given its wingspan – landing at the door to the old church; but it was a man – no, it was Dash.

Mark walked toward the church, lurching with each step, stopping every few feet to cough.

God, what if I die? What if that drug kills me? He slid in the mud and had to pick himself up. His heart beat rapidly. It was poison. I'm going to die.

By the time he reached the door to the old church, he heard Danny's shout.

THE CANDLES along the altar were lit. It was warm and

humid within the church, as if the summer storm had turned it into a steam room.

"What the fuck?" Danny laughed. "Holy shit, what the hell have you been drinkin', Dashy? Or maybe it's me, maybe it's just me!" He was beer-soaked at this point; the last couple of bottles of beer lay beside him on the stone altar. Michelle glanced up – they were making out, which is what they seemed to do whenever they had five minutes to themselves.

"Dash, don't, just – just – get away," Mark shouted from the doorway. He stepped into the back of the church. "Just come outside!"

"Oh Danny boy, the pipes, the pipes are callin'," Dash began to sing, and practically skipped into the church. Danny had his pants off, briefs intact, button-down shirt still on with a few buttons missing; Michelle's shirt was open; she made an annoyed sound in the back of her throat.

"Sorry to interrupt, lovebirds," Dash said.

"Get the hell outta here," Danny said, but he began laughing – it must have struck him as funny to be caught nearly doing it with his girl on the altar of this rat-hole church.

Michelle pushed Danny away and began closing her shirt up.

"Enough," she said.

"Just a little fun," Dash said.

Mark stood at the entrance to the church, watching Dash, unsure of what he was really seeing. Dash seemed to move with a grace he'd never had before, like a dancer or gymnast, and he went right up to the altar and pressed his hands down on two of the candles to snuff them out.

Only one left.

"Dash!" Mark called out. "Come on, let's go. This won't be fun."

Dash turned back to him, and in the final candle's glow, laughed a little – laughed the way he would when they'd first met, back in eighth grade, a *let's-have-fun* laugh, and said, "Oh, wait and see."

Then, he snuffed the last candle out. The room was plunged into darkness.

"Hey, who turned off the lights?" Danny shouted.

Mark saw shadows against shadows. Michelle started cussing, and saying she just wanted to get the puppy and get to the party, and why didn't her cell phone work? Danny began laughing and telling her that it was going to be better in the dark, but Mark heard a strange groaning sound.

The door behind him slammed shut, as if by a great wind.

But there had been no wind.

And then, the screaming began.

MARK'S first instinct was to run away; but he moved forward in the darkness, hitting against one of the long benches. He dug into his jeans for the matches, and drew them out.

Only four left in the matchbook.

He lit one, and for a fizzing few seconds, the light lit

up the room – there was Michelle, screaming, and some-thing with enormous leathery wings, and crab-like appendages studding its body – it was Dash but it was no longer Dash –it had hold of Danny by the throat and was shaking him hard, side to side.

The match went out.

ANOTHER MATCH; he struck it, and it flared up for a moment.

Michelle was running toward him, halfway there– her eyes were wide and seemed to have lost all intelligence –

A creature that seemed both insect and dragon – it was only an impression, like the flash of a dream – chewing on Danny's scalp --

Mark dropped the match. Darkness blinded him.

GURGLING SOUNDS FOLLOWED, and then the wet shred-ding noise and cracking of bones.

He heard footsteps near him -- *Michelle?* Brushing past.

Dash's voice:

"Ye*sssss*," snakelike and hollow. "Marco, the Nowhere is here, you helped bring it, it's all true," and then the sounds of a dreadful slobbering and gobbling, as of a wild dog swiftly devouring prey.

MARK DREW OUT A THIRD MATCH, and struck it in the matchbook.

Dash stood so close to him that they were practically touching.

Shocked by the closeness, Mark dropped the match, and it went out.

IN THAT SECOND, he had seen the white and pink worms encircling Dash's throat and hands, growing in pulsating movements from his flesh, and soft fuzzy tendrils gently fluttering from his bare waist and ribcage.

His mouth painted a dark red.

In his arms, he cradled what was left of Danny's body. Torn and ragged, more meat that human.

"Any shape I desire," Dash said, and tossed Danny's remains to Mark when the darkness again engulfed him.

MARK FELT nausea sweep through him. He dropped the body and turned to run, but fell to his knees instead.

"Pray to your little god," Dash said. "Pray like a good altar boy. But you're in the wrong place, Marco. This is the altar of the Nowhere. The Church of the Veil. Now, where do you think Michelle's run off to? Not outside. I made sure the door was shut tight and locked. She must be here. Hiding. Oh, yeah! This makes it more of a game, doesn't it? But I can see with more than eyes now. You know that,

Marco. You've been through the Veil. You know that it's a world of liquid white now."

Mark wanted to cry out, or scream, but his voice had abandoned him – or else he had screamed so much in the past few moments – without realizing it -- that he had none left. He felt cold and hot at the same time.

The Words. Remember the Words.

You can stop him with them. They're the words of ending. The god will return to the Veil. The Words. He imagined the bone with all the scratching on it. Dash's voice saying the Words and making him repeat them back.

Some kind of trick.

"I can hear her breathing," Dash said. "She's gonna love what I do to her. I hope you're there to see it, Marco. I hope you'll partake."

Mark thought he heard Michelle cry out from behind him.

"Run! Get out! Michelle! Just get out!"

The sound of her sobs echoed.

"It's locked!" she cried out, banging on the door, "Somebody! Somebody help me! Help!"

"Michelle! Shut up! Just shut up!" Mark yells. "Stay still and shut up!"

It needs movement and noise. Maybe it will leave now that it had Danny. Dear Jesus help us. Help her.

The Words.

Remember them.

IN DARKNESS, THE ENDING

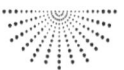

*A*nd so, in the room in the church, the thing in the dark
feels his ankles.

He presses himself against the wall, halfway between
scared shitless and ready to do something – *anything* – to
keep it from going after Michelle.

Slick and sticky and wormy, it seems to lick his calves
with its feelers.

Michelle by the door, moaning out little noises.

The thing that Dash has become slithers and feels its
way over to her.

In Dash's mind, he must be seeing the whiteness of the
darkness. He must be seeing the liquid move and the
unseen things that wriggle in the air and along the walls.

Dash must see Michelle, too, not as a terrified young
woman of eighteen, but as some collection of molecules to
be devoured, to be fed upon, to increase its happiness and
its mission as it moves through the world, but sees and
feels all through the Veil that Dash has now destroyed
within himself.

The last of the tendrils that Dash-thing drags with him slides away from Mark's foot.

Leaving him. Letting him go.

Moving toward *her*.

She is groaning as if she can't contain her fear.

And then, she lets out a bloodcurdling scream – and another, and another in quick succession.

He hears the throaty laugh.

"Come on, it's only me, Michelle, come on," Dash says, and for a fleeting instant Mark thinks that it might be a game. It might just be all fake. *The drug. Yeah, it's the drug. It was some kind of illusion. Some trick of light and dark. A bad acid flashback.*

This is some kind of trip. This isn't the real world.

Michelle's sobbing, with diminishing screams in her voice, jagged shards of sound.

Get to Danny. Something on him. His jacket. Jeans.

A lighter.

It's afraid of light. The Nowhere can't exist where there's any light.

Any genuine light.

If darkness is light to it, *then surely light is its own kind of darkness.*

"You always wanted me, Michelle, you always did," the thing that Dash has become says. "Rachel told me how you thought I was quirky and cool. When she did, when she whispered those things to me, it got me so revved up, baby. I knew that someday you and I would have this moment."

Mark hears the whirring sound again – a soft, rapid fluttering.

If I just get to Danny's jacket, Mark thinks. *The lighter.*

"Please," Michelle whimpers. "Dash, please. Don't hurt me. Please. Oh god. Please."

Her "please" becomes bleating like a sheep. In a horrible way it's funny, it sounds like a joke, but Mark knows it's not.

Why doesn't she try to run? Is it blocking her way?

Mark estimates that he can get to the doorway.

To where Danny's body rests.

Just grab the jacket and thrust his hand into the pockets.

He can get the lighter, flick it up, and scare the monster away.

"Oh, Michelle, baby," it says. "I want to love you so badly. I want you to be my girl, don't you know that?"

"Please," she says in such an awful tone that tears came to Mark's eyes even as he takes a step toward the opposite corner of the room.

"Take my hand, Michelle, don't be afraid," it says. "I want to love all of you in every way."

The sound changes – it feels like an alarm has gone off somewhere. A sound like hissing and spitting and the crack of a whip.

"No!" Michelle screams, "Oh my god, oh my god, god, god, god, god." Her screams turn into giggles and jets of laughter.

Mark races to Danny's body, pushing through the

wetness, tearing the shorts from what remains of the lower half of him, sifting quickly through the pockets until he finds something cylindrical and hard.

The lighter.

Hang on, Michelle.

The sounds are wet and bubbling.

Mark turns, flicking the lighter.

Doesn't light up.

Flick!

Again no light.

Then, a spark.

A SMALL FLAME erupts from the lighter.

He cups it in his hand, a yellow and rosy glow around his palm.

He calls out to Dash, but the splattering noise and that whirring has begun again.

Mark brings the flame up to see:

Shadows cast against the old bare wall of the room.

He sees what looks like the spread wings of a gigantic shiny beetle. Long white and pink worms –slender tentacles – move between Dash's body, which floats barely a foot in the air – holding Michelle – caressing her – she struggles against it -- the worms inside her mouth, her nose, tearing her shirt off, scraping at her skin until it's nothing but torn flaps hanging down. The wormy tendrils shooting and pulsing from Dash's mouth and eyes and ears.

His ribcage opens like two doors creaking apart. Long feathery whips emerge from his torso and stroke her skin.

Mark feels frozen in terror – the worms are wriggling, from Dash's ribcage – boring out from them, feathery, barnacle-like fans – moving swiftly, tickling her breasts and along her ribs. Her eyes are wild and the worm-appendages of the thing reach into her ears – and they are –

Mark shouts, "I have light! You have no power in the light!"

He waves the flame around, his arm outstretches, his body taut. "I'll set you on fire!"

Shivering, he walks towards what Dash has become:

A creature with huge beetle-like wings, four of them, spread wide, another layer of nearly-transparent wings in between.

Mark stands, bone in one hand, lighter in the other, the flame shooting up high.

Mark tries to read the bone, but he can't – *not while Michelle is still…*

But he tries. The symbols on the bone seem different than they did before. They seem to have smudged or moved around and he can't quite see them for the flickering light.

With the light, he can see the sores and pustules along Dash's spine.

Dash turns for a moment, his face covered with many small black eyes, and he says, his words rapid-fire and ripe with excitement, "the light doesn't matter now, Mark. Not once the incarnation has happened. All the world is white light. Once in the flesh, I'm indestructible. Unless you remember the Words. But you don't, do you? You will never read the bone, will you? How can you? Only the priests who have studied for decades can remember them, can speak them," and then the creature turns about to Michelle's beatific and glowing form, blood shining along her body, and begins devouring her like a spider feeding upon a wriggly fly caught in its web.

"Oh, so delicious, such a de*lee*cious treat," Dash says, his mouth foaming with white and red.

Then, his opening body, like a mouth, covering her, a Venus flytrap, a devourer.

Mark moves toward him and thrusts the flame against his neck, but the worms shoot out from beneath wings and tear the lighter from his fingers.

The creature turns, its face bubbling with sores, its eyes blinking in unison.

It regards Mark with some interest.

The wings close, and it floats inches downward until it touches the floor.

Then, it shoots slender tentacles around Mark's waist and chest. He presses against them, but he can't pull free.

It lifts him up, and he feels the invasive, parasitic wormy fingers moving against the holes in his ears, pressing down onto his lips, forcing them open.

Lower, his navel is stretching as the worms push inward.

Wave after wave of nausea hits him.

The slick, wet tendrils pry the sacred bone from his fingers.

What feel like bundles of worms thrust down the back of his throat.

He feels the sharp jab against his stomach –
the bone –
going into him.

DASH'S VOICE, nearly sweet, whispering along with the dreadful humming of the wings as they move rapidly. "I won't let you hurt for long, Marco. I want you and me to be together. We can do anything now. Anything, and we'll bring the Nowhere into daylight. We'll tear the Veil."

DYING? Mark wonders as pain seeps through him. Blood is pouring from his stomach and legs.

Dash, in the dark, seeming human, seeming not to have a thousand wormy tentacles and barnacle feathers, lifts Mark up.

Lifts him with two arms.

Broken bones shift. Freezing pain.

No screams left in him. Mark is sure now that he screamed the whole time that the creature slaughtered Michelle.

Through the narrow hall they go, Dash seeming human but not human, carries him like a soldier holding a beloved friend on the battlefield.

Smell of fresh air.

Outside again.

Sky, clear.

Moonlight, very little, but enough.

DASH STRIPS Mark's shirt off. With his fingernails, he scratches markings on his chest and stomach.

"You can be like this, too. Just like we said. We never have to be apart. We can be in the Nowhere. And still here, too. Still alive. There's a way."

"No," Mark tries to lift his head, but can't. "Please, I need help, Dash."

Dash lets out what can only be a sigh of contentment.

"None of this has to change who we are. This is just the god thing. It's what gods have to do. Look, Mark, I know things now. I gained knowledge. Yeah, it hurts some, and part of me feels bad, but when it takes me over, man, you have got to experience this. It's like…like *life*. Like there's no darkness at all. There's a whole other world you can see when you're like this. You can see things without your eyes. You have feelers. You have these parts of you that can stretch out and find things without even opening your eyes.

"And them? Michelle and Danny? Shit, they're in another place. Death isn't bad for them. They're the food of the gods, that's all, They're chow. Gods eat life. That's how it goes. The god of grass eats grass and the god of the flesh eats flesh. You can't have life without this. It's some-thing we've all gotten away from, but the worshippers, the priests of the Nowhere, they know. They kept the ritual. They put themselves at one with the gods to do this.

"*We* are anointed ones, we're gods in flesh. You can't be afraid. You can't look at this with the same eyes you had before, not once it happens. It's stupid and human of you to do it. When you die, you're not going over there. You're going to come back here. Do you know what the gods are? Do you? *Do you?*"

A hiss comes from Mark's lips as he looks up at the dark figure.

"The gods are creatures, just like us, but they don't have boundaries. They reshape themselves at will. They let their hunger loose. Their lusts. Their wants. We think things happen because we do them or there are natural laws, but Marco, there aren't natural laws – the gods make things happen, they make it all go. But their names are power. I have the power. It's within me," Dash says, passion swelling in his voice. "I can be anything, Marco. *Anything.*"

MARK, in the muddy grass, at the edge of the grave.

He looks up at what once had been Dash.

What is still Dash.

The moonlight is soft around his scalp, almost like a halo.

Dash has a beautiful face. Dash has an ugly face.

Michelle. Danny. Gone. In less than an hour.

It still looks enough like Dash, with his hair, stringy from rain, matted with mud. His longish jaw and his eyes that shine even in the absence of light.

Just two eyes. Two human eyes. No thousand eyes of some monster. Darkness around his lips. Blood?

"You're dying," Dash says. "Don't be afraid of it. Just say the names. Just say them, Marco."

"Mmm," Mark said.

"We never have to live anywhere but in the Nowhere again. Not ever," Dash says.

"You're dead," Mark whispers, but isn't sure if Dash can even hear him. Mark feels so weak, his life draining.

"The names," Dash says. "Remember? You say then as you die. The first part. I say the other half of the names after you breathe your last. I know all their names now, Marco. I know each of the gods, and their wonderful hungers and the way they look – I can see them all around us. We are their children. I have them incarnate within me, too. I can be a thousand different things. I can be a hornet or dragon, Marco. I can bring up a wind or burn with fire. I can see clearly, more clearly than I could in daylight, see with more than just these useless eyes. I can smell my sight, I can feel sight. You will, too! We can go to Rachel's party. We don't have to miss it. We can bring her the puppy. I'm not going to hurt the puppy. It's not like that. What's inside me now, it has meaning. It doesn't want puppies and turtles and goats and chickens. It wants more than that. Everyone will be there. Everyone from our class. And we'll show them that we're not just there for their pecking order and social put-downs. We'll be there to show them the faces of the gods. We could even bring some more of them back, if we're careful with their bodies. We could make all of us live forever, if you really want. I mean, yeah, it's too late for Michelle and Danny, but I let it out too much. I hadn't learned how to pull back on the reins yet. But I think I understand now.

"And the Nowhere is with us. They think I'm a messiah. They'll know you as my lieutenant. We'll change everything. Everything in one night if we have to. We'll pull back the Veil. You and me, both. After you say the name. And then you'll be here again. We can fly, now. We can swim under water for hours. We can turn to liquid, or move within the bark of a tree. We can become the darkness. Or light.

"It'll be you and me. Brothers. Everything we are to each other will matter. In the Nowhere. We'll be gods *here*, Marco. We'll do things we couldn't have imagined before. Before it was just a game. Now, it's real. *We're* real. And the others? The people in the world, your mother and father and mine and the teachers at the Gardner School, they're the unreal ones. We can go on to Rachel's next. Just the names. Let me whisper them to you."

Mark closes his eyes.

Soft rain falling. Just drips of it. On his face.

Cooling rain.

The feeling of Dash's wet slippery hand touching his face.

"The names," Dash says, as gentle as the rain. "Just say one of them for me. I love you so much. Just say it."

Dash may have tears in his eyes or perhaps it is the raindrops falling gently on Mark's face.

OPENS HIS EYES.

The shadow of Dash's face is all he sees. The smell of his breath – the same stink of the dead body, its flesh torn open.

Mark mutters something.

"Marco?" Dash leans closer.

Mark says it as loud as he can. It comes out a whisper. "You. Not my brother. I don't love you. I don't want to be with you after I die…far away from you."

All his energy in those words. He feels smug. Numb and smug. A worm of pain somewhere in his gut, but otherwise, he's ready to go. Into the arms of Death.

Mark wants to close himself up.

To die without remembering the names.

DASH IS HOLDING HIM NOW, cradling him, practically kissing his ear as he begins to whisper something that Mark can't quite make out.

Dying. Please take me, God. Take me now. Break me out of life. Crush my spirit and body and slam me into another place. Or just cut off whatever it is that life is within me. Keep me from the Nowhere.

But even as he dies, without wanting to, without desiring this, Mark parts his lips.

No! something within him fights against it. *Don't say it. Don't say the names!*

But his flesh is at war with his heart, and he realizes that Dash's remark had been true: *the flesh remembers.*

Mark utters the unspeakable names of the gods of the Nowhere, of the Veil. Like the worst profanity coming from his tongue.

Permission to be called back.

He cannot remember the Words that would stop this.

Only the names to begin it.

HIS LIFE SLIPS AWAY, just as if it were dropping into a pool. A rock in water, hitting the surface and slipping down into the murky depths.

He's angry as he goes down to a place where the lights dim and flash and dim.

The lights are nearly out.

He can't even sense that he is breathing or whether is holding him or not.

Dash sings some painful song in an unknown tongue as if he'd been singing it his whole life.

Mark has a sense of the others that are there – the priests and believers of the Nowhere.

Standing in a circle around them both.

The part of Mark that still has a speck of thought and life feels terror and calm all at once, knowing that after he goes, that thing that Dash has become will hold him in his arms and intone the other part of the names, the response – the litany – until Mark's eyes, once again, open.

THE PARTY

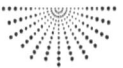

An hour or so later and several miles away, a girl of nineteen – her arms around a boy of roughly the same age – says, "Oh my god."

The lights in the house go out.

The boy kisses her again, his breath all beer. "Rachel, you know what? I hope we spend every night together this summer. Our last summer together."

"Damn, I'm not even sure where the fuse box is," the girl says, pushing her boyfriend away.

"It's a brown-out," another girl says. "They'll come back on."

"Where the hell's my beer?" a boy whines just before he begins cursing.

"Lights!" someone shouts, laughing. "Somebody hit the lights so Jack can find his beer."

"What happened to the music?"

"Party must be over. Nice hint, Rachel."

"Yeah, you want us to leave you can just ask us."

"It must be the storm," somebody says, drunken slur to his voice.

"Looks like somebody forgot to pay the bill."

"It must've been the storm."

"Yeah, or a burglar."

"I love it in the dark. There's more to kiss."

"Perv!"

"Got a flashlight?"

"Yeah. We all do."

A cell phone light comes up. Then, another.

"Jesus, it's nearly two. I better get home."

A half-dozen more lights comes up as phones are drawn from pockets.

"We've got a bunch of candles under the sink," Rachel says.

"Get your hands off me, Josh. And go get me some more beer."

"Somebody's knocking at the door."

"No, something hit the window. That a seagull? What the hell *was* that?"

"A bird. A bird hit the window."

"No, it's the front door."

"Come in!" a boy shouts.

"Where are those candles?"

"The kitchen," Rachel says. "Under the sink. Should be maybe six of them."

"You get the candles, I can light 'em up," some boy says.

He flicks on a lighter.

For a second, the small blue-yellow flame lights his face. The light-dappled shadows of others surround him.

The phones cast eerie patches of light across wall photographs and furniture and faces, flattening all of it.

In the wide mirror on the back wall the reflection of the light reveals more: the enormous living room is packed.

"We need more light," someone says.

"Knock knock," a boy, a junior from the Gardner School, reaches the front door.

He draws the door inward.

A gust of steam. Humidity has risen after the rain.

Two figures in the dark, on the front porch.

"You're late," the boy says, sleepily, not quite recognizing them in the dark but thinking one of them is a geeky kid he saw once with his older sister even though he can't quite see the two guys on the porch all that well.

Can't quite remember that kid's name. Mark something. Or Matt? Marty?

"Party's almost over," the boy says.

For a split second, the boy who opened the door has an instinct but ignores it.

He thinks he should shut the door and lock it.

He hears a strange fluttering like the beating of wings of some large bird flying just above his head.

The boy takes a few steps backward as two dark figures cross the threshold and move toward him.

AND THEN, it begins.

THE ATTRACTION

CHAPTER ONE

W atch the desert. It is out there. This abomination. Keep an eye along the ridge, over at that mesa, after sundown.

You can hear it, sometimes, when it's completely dark. So dark, even the stars have died out.

In the Southwest. In Arizona.

Not among the cities and towns. Out where the scrub brush and ocotillo cactus take over the landscape.

In those places where the tumbleweed blows through like a whisper of the past. The coyotes at twilight on the ridge of a mesa, their *ki-yi*s sing of something sinister, something unnatural.

And something, at sunset, scuttles along the dark lip of a cave—a crack in the wall of a cliff—some creature.

STRANGE THINGS LIVE in the desert.

Strange people, too.

I heard from an old man over in town that some dogs got torn up bad out on the mesa, right near where the new housing development's going in.

Maybe it was just coyotes, or maybe even a mountain lion from up in the hills, driven down from its home by hunger and thirst, but it didn't sound like it.

Someone said they found a deep hole in the ground where someone started to dig up an area for a new house and a swimming pool.

Fools. They break up the earth, tear into it, and change it.

They don't think there's anything in that desert, do they?

They're idiots to expand this town out there, out where nobody in his or her right mind should live.

I'VE SEEN a lot of strange things out there, in the desert. I've seen a man who seemed to be turning into a dog. I've seen rains come out of nowhere, and from their pools, in the crater depressions of the mesa, strange fish generate from fossilized eggs. I've heard of a snake so large it feeds on wild burros, and of a mountain lion who hunts only children.

But the one thing that was undoubtedly the strangest in my existence was something that was called Scratch, and lay within a glass case inside a gas station's roadside attraction.

It happened a long time ago.

Let me tell you.

1977. No cell phones. An old-fashioned, pre-tech world, if you will. An innocent world that seemed guilty. A year of death, pardon, disco, and, as the year wore on, gas lines. The death penalty was reinstated with the execution of Gary Gilmore, the first man to be executed in the US of A since 1967. Gerald Ford, then president, pardoned Tokyo Rose. Jimmy Carter arrived in the White House just about the time when the economy began taking a downturn. Soon enough, gas lines lengthened.

It was a strange year of unrest and discontent, and nobody knew why. Maybe it was because disco had become the dominant force in pop music. Who knows? If you were in college at the time, and it was a little private middle-of-nowhere college in Virginia, in the mountains, you probably wanted to get the hell out of there except your folks were divorced, nobody really wanted you home for the spring break, half your friends were heading to Virginia Beach, half to Florida, but the girl you wanted badly was going to make a fast trip to California and get back to campus within two weeks.

And you owned a car and wanted to drive her out there and back. Four days out, four days back, four days in LA.

Not bad.

It was a crazy thing to do.

But you were nineteen, hated your life, and crazy was something you needed.

She was someone you needed.

"Attraction can really fuck you up." So said Josh.

He stretched out on the lawn because he drank too much that night and felt too awful and wished he were somewhere else and could be someone other than Josh, youngest son of a farmer, first to go to college—on a scholarship, no less—and further from his dreams than from the stars above him.

CHAPTER TWO

The stars were out in full force—thousands covered the night sky.

Josh tried to identify the constellations—the Pleiades, Orion, Scorpio—but he'd nearly flunked astronomy. To him, they just looked like jumbly pinpricks in the fabric of the world. The darkness, with the holes in it that hinted at another side, a bright paradise somewhere far away.

He got drunk on the cheapest beer from a warm keg out back in the driveway, and he stumbled to the front lawn, where girls stepped over him on the way into the party.

The party roared—its music and screams spreading out into the night—but he heard it like the ocean in a shell.

"Attraction can really fuck you up," he repeated to no one. "It can fuck you up good. You gotta choose the right person. If you don't, and you choose the wrong one, or you let nature take over so you always pick the wrong ones, it sends you to Hell. Hell in a handbasket."

He thought of Bronwyn.

BRONWYN SHAPIRO: brown hair, straight, long. Five foot three, wore black too much, smoked too much, no breasts to speak of, but somehow looked more skeletally advanced than other sophomores, wore glasses but looked intellectual instead of geeky, never put up with shit from the guys at the frat, wrote poetry that she considered puerile.

Josh first saw her: freshman year, *Expository and Creative Writing 101*, Michael Framington—the short story writer—teaching.

Bronwyn read a poem about setting fire to her roommate's hair.

Framington called it the worst case of overwrought emotional baggage with the sensibility of a disturbed eighteen-year-old that he'd heard in years.

Josh wanted to hear that poem again. He remembered the line: "The kiln of her skull explodes; a hundred broken memories burn."

After class, he dogged her steps, followed her to a bench shaded by an oak tree and asked what she was reading.

She glanced up at him.

"It's called a book," she said.

"Now that's a suitably bitchy thing to say," he said.

She took a drag on her cigarette, narrowing her eyes as she looked beyond him. "You know, when I've noticed you in class, I assumed you were a loser. Now you've just confirmed it for me. Please leave."

And that was the moment he felt that he had to have this woman in his life no matter what.

A year later, lying on the grass, looking up at the stars, Josh wished she were with him.

BRONWYN SAT ON STAIRS, nursing a beer, wishing she were anywhere else but in a frat house the night after second semester finals.

"See him?" she nudged her friend Alli. Her target was Mitchell Sloane, from Poughkeepsie, New York, wearing his cardigan and khakis, vodka gimlet in one hand, cigar in the other. "He's a classic closet case. His friends think he's male bonding or something, but look at how he's sizing up Joe Welsh. He wants to plant a big wet one on Joe's puss."

"Half this frat are closet cases," Alli said.

"How'd you do on the accounting final?"

"Okay, I think."

"I bit the dust," Bronwyn said. "I thought that last question about debits and credits was a trick question. I wrote a note to Jones that he was trying to trick us on the final and that the answer was that it was impossible. I think I just flunked. Look at him." She pointed with the bottle toward Dave Olshaker. "He's pathetic. He's looking for Tammy Detweiler."

"The hose queen," Alli said.

"Exactly. He thinks because he gets a boner when he looks at her that she must love him."

"Detweiler's incapable of love."

"So's Olshaker. Maybe they're made for each other. Besides, Olshaker's a psycho, and him—" Bronwyn's bottle tipped over to a guy with filthy long hair and dirty jeans and a stained T-shirt.

"He looks like a scrappy dog," Alli said.

"Ziggy. He's just looking for weed. He dropped acid seventeen times before he was eighteen. You can be declared legally insane for that. He's legally insane too many times over. But hell, he's got a lighter and I definitely need a light."

"WHERE'S GRIFF?" Bronwyn asked, leaning over Kathy Emmons to light her cigarette from Ziggy's magical torch.

Ziggy gave a blank look. "No idea."

"God, this cigarette tastes like shit." Bronwyn took another drag off the cigarette, and then stubbed it out against the wall of the frat house. "He's with *her*, isn't he?"

Kathy nodded. "Of course."

"Damn it," Bronwyn said, and then let out a vile string of profanity, but her curses couldn't be heard above the thud of the music coming from the basement dance floor below. She lit another cigarette.

"Let's get high," Ziggy said.

"You're already high." Bronwyn sucked at the cigarette. A cloud of smoke surrounded her face for just a moment. "Give up the drugs, Ziggy. I'm telling you. You are going to mess up your entire life and maybe even your chromosomes so your future wife might have turtle babies someday. You're going to end up in rehab. Just stop now. 'High' is not the natural state for human beings. Low is. Get low. Low is good."

"I'm going to get *so* high," Ziggy said, as if he hadn't heard a word. He glanced around before wandering off while mumbling about how he'd left a bong somewhere in the kitchen.

"Why are you obsessed with Griff?" Kathy asked. "He dumped you."

"Not true," Bronwyn said. "I dumped him."

"Okay. Either way, a dumping was had by all. Many moons ago."

"I don't give a damn about him," Bronwyn said. "I just don't get what he sees in Tammy. Jesus, she has him *and* Olshaker wants her back. What is it about her? She's the poster girl for the living dead. Is it just boobies? Is that all boys are about? Boobies?"

Kathy cocked her head to the side. "I think so."

"Yeah, sadly, sometimes I think so, too," Bronwyn said, her cigarette nearly gone to ash. "You know, I am just about done with giving a damn."

A ROOM UPSTAIRS in the frat house. Smell of beer and sex in the room. Tammy Winthrop on top of Griff Montgomery. His pants around his ankles, which dangle over the edge of the slender bed. His starched white button-down shirt open at the chest.

Tammy's jeans on the floor, her tank top half-pulled up around her neck, the small gold cross that hung from her neck bouncing up and down as Tammy's thighs wrapped around, obscured and engulfed Griff's self-described dong in the kind of banging that led college boys to believe that sex would always be like this—wild and free and stinking of marijuana and tequila and ripe breasts like plums, no, like great melons bobbling, and pleasure that was urgent and wonderful and eternal and kind of skanky. He loved the stink of sex in his bed after the fact. He loved the way she looked when he was inside her.

"God, do you feel my dong?" he asked, too loud.

"Uh?"

"My wang. My big boy. Do you feel it? I feel like…like I'm God or something. It feels so big."

"Uh," Tammy muttered, "uh, *sure.*"

"Don't you like it? Tell me how much you like it."

"Oh yeah, I like it. I love it."

"Say it."

"No. You know I don't want to."

"Aw, please. Baby. It does so much for me."

"Okay. Okay. Your…*wang*? Your wang is so good." She began giggling a little, but he didn't notice.

"Oh yeah. Oh yeah!" he groaned against her ear as she leaned into him.

"It's the biggest one I ever had. It's the biggest. I don't know if I can take it all. Oh," she whispered. "Oh."

In her head, Tammy was thinking about how she was working too hard and how he needed to move around some more.

In his head, Griff was thinking about two other girls at school, and pretending that it was both of them, kissing him, taking him into themselves, flicking their tongues all over him, and whispering obscenities like they were good-luck charms.

Outside of both their heads, they thrashed, and finally, they fell over on the floor, on the heap of dirty laundry that Griff left there.

She didn't kiss him afterward, but got up, pulled on her underwear, and looked in the long mirror on the back of the door to his room and said, "I think I'm getting fat."

Griff, lying on the pile of clothes, some of which bunched up uncomfortably under his lower back, considered whether or not he should shower.

Without saying another word, he bounded out of bed, grabbing a towel from the second heap of laundry-to-be in the corner by the dresser.

Gave her a wink, and a too-brief hug, and went out into the hall.

IN THE SHOWER, one floor down from his room, Griff took the Ivory Soap and scrubbed away because there was this smell Tammy had that he couldn't stand and when it got on him, it reminded him too much of his mother's closet where he used to hide, and he hated that smell.

Then, he thought of someone else, someone other than Tammy, and he got aroused again.

"YOU WHORE," Dave Olshaker said.

He stood in the doorway of Griff's room. He'd been

waiting on the stairs, and when he saw Griff run out to the showers, he knew he had his chance.

Slammed the door shut behind him.

Reached back, and twisted the bolt.

He was a big guy, maybe 240, six-five, overalls and a white T-shirt, a townie with a scholarship for football, and he looked—to Tammy Detweiler—as pissed as anyone could be.

He turned his back to her for a second, double checking the lock on the door.

"Dave? What the hell are you doing in here?"

"You slept with that asshole," Olshaker said, turning around to face her. "You told me you loved me."

"That was last year. Dave? Get the hell out of here. I'll scream."

"You won't. You can't do this to me. You whore. You know I gave you my heart. And now you're just stomping all over it. Look, look, I forgive you. Okay? I forgive you for your bad nature, baby. I do. I love you that much."

"You aren't gonna forgive me for anything. Now get the hell out of here, right now."

Tammy leapt out of bed, trying to find the gun that Griff kept. She was pretty sure he kept it in the top drawer of his dresser. He wasn't supposed to have it, but then, in college, you weren't supposed to have a lot of things you ended up having.

Olshaker rushed her, grabbing her by the wrists. "Just come back to me. Just tell me."

She was shocked to see tears in his eyes.

"Let go of me, damn it!"

His face turned bright red. He was angry. She knew

the look—it was half the reason they'd broken up before midterms. He had slapped her a little too hard, and she had seen that red face.

Her wrists hurt where he gripped her.

"Let me go. Please," she said more calmly, looking down at his hands. "Please. You're hurting me, David."

"I just want you," he said. His breath was all sour beer. Right then and there, he began blubbering like a baby. He released her wrists.

"Enough!" She shoved him backward, and he fell backwards on Griff's bed.

"You don't know what it's like. To love someone so much. To love them, to want them, you just don't know. Honey, honey, I love you. I love you like no man is ever gonna love you." His tears came in hiccups and heaves.

She began to feel bad for him, despite everything.

Once completely dressed, she went over to the bed, and sat beside him. She put her arm around his back.

"Look. You're a good man," she said, but felt as if she were telling the biggest lie on the planet. "You'll find a girl who loves you because you're wonderful. I'm no good. I really am not right for you. Maybe I'm not right for anyone. But you, you have a lot going for you."

"I know," he said, weeping bitterly. "I know. But I can save you from your sinful life, Tammy. I can make you a good woman."

"Poor baby," Tammy said, hugging him to her. "Poor, poor baby."

"I love you," he said.

He looked up at her with his tearstained face.

To her, he looked like a puppy dog that had just been

hit by a car and lived to whimper about it. He leaned in to kiss her, and she felt badly enough for him that she let him.

And that was when he grabbed her tight and thrust his tongue into her mouth.

She pushed him away, but his grip was now around her arms and waist like a straitjacket. He maneuvered to the side and brought her down on the bed, turning her around so that her face pressed into the blanket.

"You know I love you," he said, slobbering. "You know you're my woman."

She tried to cry out, but the blanket acted as a gag on her mouth.

She felt him grind against her.

IN WHAT WAS CALLED the Persian Room, in the basement of the frat house, off beneath the stairs, away from the loud music and dancing, a small room full of a haze of blue smoke, Ziggy pressed a bong to his face while clouds of sweet smoke billowed around him and somebody said, "You look like a fire-breathing dragon, Zigster."

Ziggy laughed and felt his face go all red. He wondered if he'd ever been this high before. He looked at his hands to make sure they weren't sprouting leaves.

For a second, he thought he was turning into a tree.

"What's up with that?" he asked his partner-in-high, Joe Metheny.

"With what?"

"My hands? It's like they're ripping out of my arms."

"Holy shit."

Both of them laughed at once. Then stopped. Then laughed again.

There were others in the haze of smoke, but Ziggy only noticed Joe, who had the most hilarious look on his face—a red smile and sparkling dust around his eyes.

"You know what I like about you?"

"What's that?"

"You're always happy," Ziggy said.

He took another hit from the Monster Bong.

"WHERE THE HELL IS JOSH?"

Bronywn picked her way through the rabble of the party—students passed out on the floor, others leaning into their girlfriends' faces in the corners of rooms, still others managing to keep dancing to music that stopped ten minutes before, all the while the stench of beer and vomit, up and down the stairs—and just as she got to the top of the stairs, coming out of the bathroom, naked, in full swing, Griff.

She felt as if she'd been shot with a raygun and couldn't move.

She tried not to look at him. He was a golden Apollo. His hair, slicked back on his scalp, and it emphasized his high cheekbones and his pool-blue eyes and the way his nose was the slightest of ski slopes and she couldn't help herself—she looked down at his chest, developed from football and wrestling, and then along his abs, the striation of muscle prominent, his pale skin slick with water, and down to the blond tufts of pubic hair, and the artistically arranged penis itself.

Then, the millisecond passed. He didn't notice her watching, and passed by the stairs, heading back to his room.

Bronwyn caught her breath and sat down on the stairs. Another cigarette, this time for several long, drawn-out puffs.

The doorway at the top of the stairs went to one of the upperclassmen's rooms. It was open, and she got up and walked through it to the balcony. She went out to the edge of the balcony and looked up at the stars that were just fading as morning came up along the horizon in a new day that was still too distant from the night.

When she glanced down at the murky front lawn, she saw a guy she was pretty sure was Josh.

"YOU'RE DRUNK," she said. She crouched down in the dew-wet grass beside his prone body.

"I'm not," he said. "I'm stargazing."

"You didn't touch *any* booze?" She kicked at the empty bottle of Jack Daniels at his side.

"Okay. Busted. Just a little."

"Damn it. We go in three hours."

"I'm ready."

"Jesus. We're never getting to LA."

"We'll get there. I drove from Chicago to Atlanta in one night once. We can get to LA in three days. At the most, four. I promise. How many people are coming?"

"Total, five. I think. You, me, Griff, Tammy, and maybe Ziggy if he doesn't get too messed up tonight. Everybody chips in, so it's a free trip for you."

"That'll be cozy," he said, laughing.

"You need to sleep this off before we go. Damn it," she said.

"You want to see Orion?" he asked. He pointed to a group of white specks in the dark sky. "Come on. Lie down. Here, use my jacket. There. Now, look."

"That's not Orion."

"Okay, it's something else. It's the unnamed stars. Let's connect the dots and make them into somebody."

"Like who?"

"There's Ziggy," Josh said, drawing an invisible line with his finger, swooping it in the air, from a cluster of stars to a single bright one. "See, he's got his bong."

"I see it," she said. "And there's Tammy. See the boobs?"

JOSH MADE a wish on the last star, just before it extinguished.

Bronywn drifted to sleep beside him, her last cigarette falling on the wet grass as morning arrived.

They both woke up at the same time, hours later, late in the afternoon on Saturday with Josh's arm slipped beneath Bronwyn's neck. He opened his eyes to what seemed like midday, and knew, instinctively, that she had also just woken up. She sat up, drawing away from him.

Glanced at her watch. "We're already late. Please tell me the Pimpmobile is running okay."

ZIGGY HAD AN ACID-FLASHBACK DREAM. In it, something small and nasty with eyes like green stones on fire and claws like shiny black hooks leapt for him like it was a jaguar from Hell.

He awoke and drank an entire pot of coffee before going off in search of the others about to leave on the road trip that would get him away from the drugs for a while.

He hoped.

THE PIMPMOBILE WAS MORE than its name could ever suggest. Not just a car. *The* car: a boat on wheels.

A big fat honkin' Lincoln Town Car sedan.

Given to Josh when he went to college by his grandmother, who was a doctor's wife and changed cars every two years. She drove her cars hard and put them up cracked and dried out, and often was in accidents, so something always went wrong—a headlight that blinked, a strange push on the brakes, something about the shotgun seat that didn't feel entirely comfortable. Small problems that could be worked around. His grandmother was named Alfreda, and she used to spray perfume in the car so much that Josh was sure it still had her overall smell. She died soon after giving him the car—her smoking and drinking got the better of her—and he missed her and kept the car despite the fact it was held together by duct tape and got about ten miles to the gallon. Even with its negative issues—a little low in the trunk, a backseat covered with tape, smelled permanently of cigarette ash, and there was this noise it made every few miles that sounded like the squeal of a cat getting hit —Josh took care of the Pimpmobile as if it were solid gold.

He had spent all of Thursday, not studying for his *Survey Course of the Early American History* final, but washing and waxing and tuning up the boat for the big trip.

HERE'S how the trip evolved:

Back in February, Bronwyn's dad and his new wife moved to LA from Chicago. Bronwyn hated the new wife, but loved her dad, and even though her dad didn't want to see her, she told him she was coming for spring break come hell or high water.

Josh's Pimpmobile was the only ride she could get.

"I can pay all gas," she told him. "And two nights in a motel."

"You don't have to do that," Josh said.

She looked at him strangely. "Yeah—I *do*. It'll take four nights at the most. But I know we can make it in under three if we take turns driving. Plus, I've got a radar detector. We can go a hundred on some of the desert roads. They're straight lines with no traffic at four in the morning and I love drinking a pot of coffee and driving through them before the sun comes up. Plus, we can get other people to pitch in on gas."

Because Griff and Tammy were going to go, too, plus Ziggy, the car would be packed tight.

Bronwyn claimed the shotgun seat three weeks before the trip.

CHAPTER THREE

The day of the journey's start—which turned into Saturday evening —the only person who hadn't shown up at the designated spot was Ziggy. They had to drive around for forty minutes before they found him in the college library, asleep on one of the leather couches.

He opened his eyes to see all four of them standing over him.

"What the hell?" he asked.

"I don't love druggies," Bronwyn said as she took a long, last drag off a dying cigarette. "I just don't like the idea."

She pointed down at him. "No weed goes on this trip. Understood? Beer's fine. No drugs. We get pulled over, we all go to jail. And that's not happening on my watch."

"Beer's a drug," Ziggy moaned, scratching himself under the arms like a dog after fleas. "Nicotine's a drug. Coffee's a drug."

Bronwyn squinted and pursed her lips. "I think you know what I mean."

THE ROAD TRIP began about an hour later.

By nine they were on the main highway toward Tennessee. It took too long to get through the South, let alone reach the Southwest.

Josh drove first shift, then Bronwyn, then Griff.

After Griff's six hours were up, he got in the backseat and—without anyone being aware of it—put Tammy's hands on the bulge in his pants and whispered in her ear that she should just keep stroking it. Tammy pretended she was getting the little bottle of Vaseline moisturizer from her handbag because her hands were drying out. Ziggy pretended to be asleep, but he told Josh later how— when Josh was driving and Bronwyn was talking a mile a minute about why Ayn Rand was the most brilliant human being who had ever lived but really should've understood why people without money genuinely had no money given the capitalist system's inherent flaws— Tammy had unzipped Griff and gave him a slow, easy hand job that had driven Ziggy nearly crazy as he watched from half-closed eyes.

"He's got a big boy," Ziggy said when they got out to pump gas. "And Tammy was licking his ear the whole time she did it. Man, he is one lucky dude."

"Ew," Josh said. "In the back of the Pimpmobile. Nasty, nasty, nasty. I really wish you hadn't told me."

"He's like the Alpha."

"What?"

"The Alpha. Like in wolf packs. One male gets the hot

chicks. All the other males—that's you and me—never get laid."

"I get laid."

"Yeah, sure."

"No, I do."

"That's why you're all alone on this trip. Like me," Ziggy said.

Then, Ziggy sniffed his fingers. "God, even my fingers smell like sex. I can't believe you and Bron didn't notice. It was freaky."

"Sleazy's more like it. And go wash your hands. This whole thing's disturbing."

"You're just jealous," Zig said, and then went over to the restroom at the back of the gas station.

Josh glanced at Tammy, just going into the ladies' room. Griff stood outside its door, grinning, hands in his pockets.

Then, thinking nobody was watching, he tapped on the door to the ladies' room. The door opened. Griff went inside.

Bronwyn remained in the car, smoking. Josh went over to her rolled-down window.

"You hear what Zig said?"

Bronwyn took the earphones to her Sony Walkman tape player off. "You need money for gas?"

"No, not that. Did you know that Griff and Tammy… had sex in the backseat today?"

Bronwyn's eyes seemed to squint into tiny cuts, then opened wider. "Men get trapped by sex. That's all it is."

"Yeah, they do," Josh said.

"Like you're any different."

"I am."

Bronwyn smiled, blew out a puff of smoke and touched the edge of his wrist. "No, you are. You're so different I thought you might be gay when I first met you."

"I'm not gay."

"Don't get all defensive. It was the poetry you wrote. For creative writing. It was sensitive. That's all. Not like the other guys stuff that's all about them and their exploits. You wrote about something different."

Oh Christ, he thought. Oh Christ. *She sees me as a dickless wonder.*

"I think they're going at it in there," he said, nodding toward the restroom.

"Gross." Bronwyn sucked back some smoke, and then heaved it out in a long sigh. She leaned forward into the dashboard, stubbing her cigarette out in the ashtray. "Let me tell you something, Josh. Something about some girls. There are these girls like Tammy who boys really like because of this whole sex issue. But girls know about who she really is. She's a sad pathetic idiot who thinks her whole life should revolve around giving the worst kind of men what they want."

"I thought you were still hot for Griff."

"Once. Maybe. Not anymore. I don't think I could ever want someone who slept with some of the girls he's slept with. Back when I dated him, you know, he'd only slept with a few girls. At this point, the numbers are reaching the population size of small villages. Tammy's just one of many, I'm sure."

"You don't fool me," he said. "Not one bit. You like bad boys. Nice girl like you, rich family. It's true, isn't it?"

"Bite me, preppie boy," she said, and then put her earphones back on."

"I'm not a preppie," he said, but she couldn't hear him anymore.

NOBODY THOUGHT Tammy should drive because she had too many beers during the day and Ziggy somehow managed to get stoned even though no one could specifically say when. It was assumed he'd somehow managed to smuggle some weed (despite Bronwyn's initial search among luggage and pockets) and would smoke a quick joint in the bathrooms of various truck stops and diners.

They stopped six times the first day because Tammy had to pee so much. Or else, as Josh and Ziggy assumed, she and Griff had to sexually christen every sleazoid gas station bathroom in the Bible Belt. They drove through Memphis with Griff telling a story about how he got lost in downtown Memphis once and went to some big party there and passed out and woke up the next day in New Orleans. He thought it was a funny story, but no one laughed.

In Little Rock, Bronwyn called her father collect. He told her that she was an idiot to plan a trip like this with people she didn't know and that he'd send a plane ticket if she wanted to come out. She hung up on him and chain-smoked the rest of the day and evening, which got them to Oklahoma City, where they all crashed in one room at a Howard Johnson's. They slept for eleven hours, when the maids finally banged on the door the next afternoon, trying to get them up and out.

They went from Oklahoma down through the Texas Panhandle, and Ziggy wanted to stop at El Paso for something, and that's where things started to go seriously wrong. Griff and Tammy wanted to spend a day in Juarez, barhopping, and Bronwyn's period had started (she didn't need to announce it, everyone knew when she went into snapping turtle mode), and Josh had to go rescue Griff from a fight at a badly lit bar, even though Griff had been the creep who was coming on to other men's wives in the bar.

"What the hell are you doing?" Josh asked, yanking Griff by his wrinkled button-down shirt, out from the darkness of the bar, into the searing white light of midday. Griff crumbled to the ground, shielding his face as if expecting to get hit one more time.

"I'm havin' a little fun. You know about fun?" Griff giggled, and wiped a smidgeon of blood from the edge of his lips.

"That guy could've done some serious damage to you. You asshole."

Griff raised his eyebrows in a "who cares?" attitude, and reached his hand up to Josh. "Come on, help me up."

Josh gave him a lift up, and smacked him lightly on the back of the head. "Get back to the car. Jesus, now I've got to go back in there and get Tammy. Could you just stay out of trouble for once in your life?"

"This isn't trouble," Griff replied, stumbling off in

search of the others in the car, parked out on the main road. "The lacrosse trophies. Now that was trouble."

Who could forget? Josh thought. Who could forget someone having stolen all the lacrosse trophies at Jackson College that had been won over the past ten years, the prize sport of Jackson, the Gods of Jackson had played lacrosse. Griff and his frat brothers had stolen all of them and then pissed in them and left them in front of Dean Egan's house at the edge of campus. Griff was a moron and a thief, and he'd been doing shit like this as long as Josh had known him, which was only two years now.

IN LAS CRUCES, New Mexico, they got pulled over by the cops. Griff told Bronwyn to show the cop her boobs and they wouldn't get the ticket. "My sister did that once. She had these big boobies. And I was riding shotgun, and this cop pulled her over for going eighty-five in a fifty-five zone, and she just unbuttoned her blouse three inches down and acted all baby-like and he didn't give her a ticket. It works. Honest."

They saw the first billboard before they reached the eastern edge of Arizona. None of them really noticed it at first. Only Ziggy. But he had been smoking a joint for lunch, and started laughing after they'd passed it.

"What'd it say?" Tammy asked.

"Something about the Unspeakable."

"Unspeakable? What the hell is 'unspeakable' supposed to mean? You can't speak it or something?"

"Exactly," Bronwyn said, only nobody detected the bitchiness in her tone.

"Something unspeakable and unknown. An ancient wonder of the world. Coming up somewhere. Off some exit," Ziggy added.

Ziggy kept complaining that he couldn't sleep because of all the bumps they hit in the road, so Bronwyn had them stop the car. She went to the trunk, opened it, and drew out a couple of blankets. She rolled one up for Ziggy's pillow and threw the other one over him for comfort, although it was a warm day. Ziggy closed his eyes soon after, and they all snickered a little as he snored.

Then, he let out a bloodcurdling scream, to the point where Griff nearly pulled the car off the road.

Ziggy glanced around to the others who all were staring at him.

"I had a nightmare," he said.

THE SECOND SIGN stood about fifty miles further up the highway among a mass of billboards about trading posts and outlet malls in Tucson.

This time, Josh read it aloud as it went by:

"Come see the mystery! The great ancient wonder! The Unspeakable, Unknowable Attraction! The Secret of the Ancient Aztecs!"

Then, the last bit, about mileage and turnoffs to get to the site. "Hey, we're apparently only two hundred miles from the great mystery of the asshole of the universe."

"I love those kinds of places," Bronwyn said. "When I

used to travel with my dad, we'd stop at all the roadside attractions. Sometimes they were just rattlesnakes in cages. Sometimes they had what looked like babies in jars."

"I saw John Dillinger's dong once," Griff said.

"Bullshit."

"I did. It was in this museum in DC. It was so big they kept it in this long jar. Just floating in this formaldehyde shit."

"Nasty," Ziggy said. "That's nasty. You die and then they cut off your dick and stick it in a museum."

"Don't worry, Zig. Yours is safe." Griff laughed. "There's no itty-bitty museum."

"I want to go see the unspeakable and unknowable attraction," Bronwyn said, flicking her cigarette out the window. She stretched out, and pressed her bare feet up against the dashboard. Josh looked at her feet, and noticed that they were small and perfect, with toes that didn't intrude on each other, as his did.

"What route was it on?"

"No idea," Josh said, watching the road, watching her feet.

That night, in Tucson, they stayed at the cheapest motel they could find (The Roadrunner Inn) and then got out on the road after a big breakfast at Denny's.

Nerves were shot by the time they got back on the highway, only this time Griff insisted on driving, and nobody had gotten a good night's sleep in the motel because Ziggy had the shits and the toilet wouldn't flush and the smell alone kept them awake, to say nothing of the broken-down air-conditioning and the way the heat had shot up sometime after crossing Texas to New Mexico, and then, at its worst, into Arizona.

Bronwyn spotted another billboard for the Unknowable Mystery, and this time it was more explicit.

YOU'RE NEAR THE MYSTERY! THE UNKNOWABLE, UNSPEAKABLE TERROR OF THE ANCIENT WORLD IS JUST DOWN ROUTE 19 AT THE BRAKEDOWN PALACE AND SUNDRIES. NAVAJO BLANKETS!   TURQUOISE!   ARROWHEADS! FIREWORKS!

"I INTEND to be the unspeakable, unknowable mystery of the modern world," Bronwyn said.

Josh watched as she closed her eyes gently. He thought she was the prettiest girl he had ever seen.

He knew he shouldn't shut his eyes and lean against Bronwyn to fall asleep. But he couldn't help it.

HE DREAMED that he and Bronwyn were in a deep green forest. The trees towered over them, a cathedral of nature.

Wispy fern beneath their feet formed a bed. Bronwyn began to undress, stepping out of her panties, finally, and he began to feel her all over. She gyrated against his touch, and soon his clothes had fallen away, and Bronwyn went on her hands and knees. She glanced up at him, smiling. He took her there, on the fern, on a soft mossy floor. He felt the intense pleasure of warm wet heat when he went inside her, and she began whispering something about how he needed to wake up now. Only he didn't want to wake up.

Then, something shifted in the woods, and the trees began to vanish, one by one. He didn't care, because he felt so good inside Bronwyn, but soon, they were in an open space, and it was not Bronwyn beneath him at all, but Griff who said, "This isn't trouble, Josh. Don't worry. This is good times!"

That's when he woke up.

"Holy shit," someone said.

Reality banged against him.

Light of day. Heat in the car.

Leaning against Ziggy now instead of Bronwyn.

The car had come to a stop, in what seemed to be a ditch.

"WHAT THE HELL WERE YOU THINKING?" Bronwyn shouted from the backseat. She lit up a cigarette.

Josh glanced from her to Griff, at the steering wheel. It was almost as if cartoon steam came out of his ears. Griff wouldn't turn around and face the backseat.

Tammy, however, would. "You bitch, just shut your hole. All of us were sleeping. We're all too goddamn tired. And somebody stinks. Who stinks?"

Josh glanced at Ziggy, who shrugged. "Don't look at me, dude."

Griff pressed his face down, almost to the steering wheel.

"What happened?"

"Mr. I-Can-Drive-Now fell asleep at the wheel," Bronwyn said. She lit another cigarette and sucked back the first smoke and then spat a ghost trail of it out into the already smoky car.

Josh—still half-asleep, his back soaked with sweat, feeling cranky, sore from his cramped position between Bronwyn and Ziggy—realized something.

"Jesus. We're sideways."

"No shit, Sherlock."

"Didn't anybody notice?"

"I was snoozing," Ziggy said.

"I think we all were," Tammy said in that little girl voice of hers that didn't quite go with the big boobs.

"Exactly," Bronwyn said. "Griff included."

"Shut your hole!" Tammy shouted. She got on her knees, swiveling around in her seat. Her face looked less like blonde hose queen and more like pit bull with wig as she began listing all the ways Bronwyn sucked. "You're like the bitch queen of the universe with your 'I'm so sophisticated and together and I know everything and I look down on everybody' bullshit. And second, you are after Griff. Just say it. Just because he didn't care for you anymore, just because he dumped you—"

"Correction," Bronwyn said. "I dumped him."

"Bullshit, Miss Perfect Bitch, he dumped you, because you were too clingy and annoying and too much into proving everybody around you wrong, why is that? Why is everybody else always wrong? And don't sit there with that smug Jewish look."

"Excuse me?"

"You know what I mean, that 'Jewish Princess from Intellectual Hell' look."

"That's a bit better than my 'smug, Jewish look,'" Bronwyn repeated, slowly. "As opposed to your shiksa moronic face?"

"You're jealous. You're jealous because I have him. Because he wants me. Just admit it. Just admit it and get over it."

"First, admit that you're a raging anti-Semite whose boobs are bigger than her IQ."

"Suck my dick," Tammy said, and then pushed the car door open and gingerly got out by the edge of the ditch. More obscenities flowed from her lips as she stomped off a ways down the road.

Bronwyn, to her credit, took it all, enveloping her face in a cloud of smoke, a mask through which she could make sour faces back at Tammy without being noticed.

Josh briefly remembered his dream: taking Bronwyn like a whore, on her hands and knees, in the woods. Conveniently, he had already begun to forget the part where Bronwyn suddenly had become Griff.

"I didn't know Tammy was anti-Semitic," Josh said to no one.

"Also anti-semantic," Bronwyn said. "She probably doesn't even know what it means. We gotta get the car back on the road."

More calmly, she added, "I hate you all," and Josh laughed because it sounded so funny.

"WHERE THE HELL ARE WE?" Josh asked.

He stood outside the Lincoln and glanced from the torn and twisted map of the US to the sunlit lunar landscape surrounding them.

"Don't get mad at me!" Griff said. "It's not my fault! I took one turn."

"You took a turn?"

"I got tired of the highway."

"You *what?*"

"I thought Route 66 was here somewhere. I thought that's what the sign said."

"Did you go south or north?"

Griff shrugged. "Maybe north?"

"How long you think you were driving like that?"

Griff closed his eyes as if it helped him remember. Then, he opened one eye. "Not sure. Maybe an hour? Maybe…maybe a half hour?"

"All we have to do is turn around," Bronwyn said calmly. "If we're north. We just go that way."

She pointed to what she assumed was south, then, glancing at the sun, adjusted her aim slightly.

Josh thrust his hand out. "Give me those."

"Give you what? My smokes?"

Josh grabbed the pack from her hand, shaking it until a cigarette popped out. He thrust it between his lips, wrested the Bic lighter free from her grip, and spun the wheel until a small flame came up.

He lit the cigarette.

Bronwyn glared at him.

"Thief," she said. "Although they are appropriate for this kind of occasion. Even if they kill you."

"Everybody dies from something." He took a long draw of smoke into his lungs, coughing most of it back up. "All right. We need to figure out how to get the car back on the road. There are five of us. There's no reason in hell why we can't all get down on the other side of that ditch and push. We can bounce it back up."

"I'd say it would be a smarter use of daylight to go back to the highway. It can't be more than twenty or thirty miles back, over that ridge." Bronwyn pointed with her cigarette. "Three of us stay here, two walk it. I don't mind a walk. I can walk ten miles. It's not that hot. We go back and we flag someone for help. There's gas stations and rest stops all over the place on the 10."

"I'm boiling," Tammy said.

"I'm not walking twelve miles," Josh said. "Damn it."

"Me, neither," Griff said.

"I can do it. Ziggy?"

Ziggy shook his head. "I got bunions." Then, he added, "I inherited them from my grampa. Third-generation bunions."

Bronwyn looked at the others. "I'm not going alone." Her eyes narrowed to slits as she stared at Griff.

"If we all work together," Josh said, "we can get the car out of the ditch."

Bronwyn looked at him with squinty eyes, her head cocked slightly to the side.

Quietly, she said, "So, you really think we can get it back on the road?"

He glanced at the others, then back at Bronwyn. "Yes."

"It looks like we'd need a tow truck. Or some other kind of way to lift it."

Josh glanced back at the Lincoln and then at Bronwyn. He felt his heart racing, and he wasn't sure why since
he wasn't panicked or all that worried. He felt something
he hadn't generally experienced in life. Something that no
one had ever demanded of him. He felt as if he knew how
to handle this.

"We can seesaw it up," he said.

"You study engineering?"

"I didn't have to," he said, grinning. "When I was four,
I spent a lot of time on seesaws. I got the gist. Look, it'll
take hours to walk back to the highway. If we all just pitch
in, we can get out of this ditch and be on the road in less
than an hour. I'm sure of it. And if it doesn't work, I will
walk with you. No, I'll do better than that. You can wait
here and I will walk to the highway and get help."

Her face brightened, and she nodded, slowly. "Okay.
But will you do me one favor?"

"What's that?"

"Don't pretend." She reached over and plucked the lit
cigarette from his mouth and dropped it to the gravel.

JOSH HAD BEEN WRONG.

It took the better part of two hours, and Tammy
whined, Ziggy was no real help at all, but Griff and
Bronwyn both put some muscle into pushing, and when
they finally got back on the road—with the sun going
down a bit to the far western hills—the car made some
funny rattling noises that Josh guessed originated somewhere in the rear axle.

Josh turned the Lincoln around, and headed back toward what they hoped was the highway. Instead, he found a confluence of ribbon roads, a narrow crossroads with what looked like pyramid-shaped hills in the distance and that strange cast of sulfurous light and purple shadow in the sagebrush, which meant night would seep across the desert roads within a few hours.

Without asking the others for their suggestions on which way to go, he took the road that seemed to be headed west, and soon it went from a narrow two lanes to a wide two lanes, and he felt pretty good about his choice of roads until he heard the back left tire blow out.

But he didn't even know about Dave Olshaker.

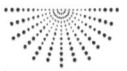

CHAPTER FOUR

Now, let's back up a few days.

Back to the Saturday night when the rest of them all took off in the Pimpmobile for the West Coast. Picture a big strapping guy of twenty, in the back of a pickup truck, with eyes that just popped open like he'd come back from the dead. He'd had a dream, and it involved a couple of things he didn't like to think about, one of them being his friend Billy Dunne, and it freaked him out to think about it. Dave Olshaker snarfled awake, farting as he woke, and he was royally pissed. He'd been up till at least six or seven a.m., and after leaving Tammy in the frat house, he'd gotten in the pickup with his buddy Billy Dunne and gone to do 360s in the mud of the cow pasture out by McCrory's lake. Sometime, in a haze of beer and piss, he passed out. Woke up, looking at the back of Billy's head, too. What a shocker that had been.

It was like the dream! Just like the dream!

He didn't like to think about what happened the night before. Even if he could remember, which he wasn't so sure about, given the Mother of Hangovers that held him in its grip. He had a taste of what he had come to think of as sour ass in his mouth, and a hammering in the head that so distracted him he barely realized he'd woken up in the backseat of his Ford pickup truck.

He got on the road once he found out from one of Bronwyn Shapiro's friends exactly what route they were taking. He told her Bronwyn's dad had called, and he needed to call him back to let him know. "For safety."

That was when a girl named Kathy Emmons stepped forward and told him how to track them down.

HIS HEAD HURT SO MUCH, Olshaker ended up having to pull over at a place he liked to call Motel 69. Billy got the room, and Olshaker barely got his sorry ass to the bed before passing out again. Before he turned off the bedside light, he told Billy he had to sleep on the far side of the bed.

"Why?" Billy's eyes were all bloodshot and his face was pockmarked from too many Milky Way bars and Mr. Pibbs and Pabst Blue Ribbons in between to wash it all down. He looked like an old man with a mop of bright yellow hair thrown on his scalp.

"'Cause you stink," Olshaker said, but it wasn't completely true. He was a little afraid that he'd start dreaming about Tammy and in the dream wrap his legs around her, only when he woke up it might be Billy's thighs rubbing against him.

Out of this general fear, Olshaker kept his clothes on that night.

They'd lost a day, but they got back on the road and ended up pretty much following the route that the Pimpmobile had taken.

And he was there, in Arizona, when the Pimpmobile took the wrong turn off the main highway.

He drove his truck up to a plateau, and got out binoculars to watch what Tammy was up to with her friends.

And when they got the flat tire, he turned to Billy Dunne and said, "Holy shit. We got 'em, buddy. We got 'em."

"What do we do now?"

Dave Olshaker thought a moment, cocking his head back to look up at the blank white sky.

Then he reached down under his seat and drew out a warm can of Pabst, popped the top and took a chug down. "Kee-rist, I don't know. But that jockstrapped asshole has my baby. And I mean to get her back any way I can. She belongs to me."

CHAPTER FIVE

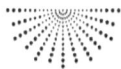

"Son of a bitch!" Griff said. He had kicked the tire six or seven times as if he could bring it back to life.

"You really don't have a spare?" Bronwyn whispered to Josh, pressing her lips so close that he could feel her heat on top of the heat of the day.

Josh looked out over the highway. Nothing but scrub, dust and a long barbed-wire fence. Sweat trickled down his back. He felt a mushiness of sweat around his balls. He wished he had a nice motel room with a long cool shower.

Ziggy was already toking out on a big rock above the highway. "Hey, I see somebody coming!"

"Yeah?" Tammy shouted back.

"A trucker! We're gonna get a lift. I know we are!" Then, he shot his arm out, pointing to the west. "There's something way over there, man! It looks like a gas station. All we have to do is get the trucker to give us a ride and we're set."

"Thank god," Bronwyn said, lifting a cigarette in the air like she was flipping the bird. "This is my last smoke."

THE TRUCK WAS an enormous Kenmore and the guy slowed down, pulling on his horn.

Tammy stood in the middle of the highway, jumping up and down. It was her looks that did it—that's what everyone felt without having to say a word about it.

"Someday, someone's going to build a memorial to her beauty," Griff said.

"Men never cease to live down to my expectations," Bronwyn said, shaking her head, and dropping the last of her cigarette in the dust. She stubbed it out with the toe of her shoe before shivering a little.

"You okay?" Josh asked.

"Just that sense. You know, the one where they say a goose walked over your grave. Like something's wrong." Then she laughed. "Maybe I just need another cigarette."

BRONWYN HAD to scrunch up next to the trucker but she didn't mind.

He was a rugged, road-weary kind of guy with a face that must've been pretty at one time, but had turned into baked granite from the sun, cracked lines along his smile and around his eyes.

"Best I can do is dump you up ahead. About two miles up, there's this place."

"That'd be great," Josh said.

"It was nice of you to stop." Bronwyn leaned very slightly against the trucker's shoulder. He smelled like axle grease, but there was something comforting about it for her.

"I drive this highway eight times a week, back and forth. There ain't much here." He introduced himself: Ely. He told them about his life, which was mainly travels on the road and a little shack out in a town called Naga. It wasn't too far away. You knew you had reached his place because a paved road ended where a dirt road shot off to the west. From there, you could see a silvery glimmer from all the hubcaps hanging on the front fence, and you could hear the music he blasted from his workshop out back.

"Mainly ZZ Top," he said. "Mainly. Sometimes I get into the mood for Boston. But mainly ZZ."

"That's quite a life," Josh said.

"Ha," Ely spat back. "I bet you kids are rich and are on spring break and just tooling around because you got nothin' else to do."

"I think that pretty much sums it up, except we really don't have money." Bronwyn glanced sidelong at Josh. "Don't you think?"

"If I had money I'd be in LA right now," Josh said.

"Ha," Ely said. "Well, you get out here, and life smacks you like you're the bug and it's the windshield. Ass first, and you got about two seconds to dodge."

"So what's this town like?" Josh asked. "*Nada?*"

"Naga. It's a little town. You'd hate it. Jesus H, why even talk to you about it. You'll never go there. Look," Ely said, pointing toward a rise to the left toward a long flat corrugated metal roof beyond the old gas pumps.

Further back, they could make out a long rectangular building with a curved metal roof, and three giant signs with various versions of: "SEE THE ATTRACTION! DON'T GO HOME WITHOUT SEEING THE ATTRACTION! THE UNSPEAKABLE UNKNOW-ABLE MYSTERY! IT'S THE EIGHTH WONDER OF THE WORLD AND THE SECOND WONDER OF THE NEW WORLD! 75 CENTS ADMISSION! BUY INDIAN BLANKETS! GET COFFEE! GAS IS CHEAP! COFFEE'S CHEAPER!"

"Wow. It's where I wanted to go," Bronwyn said. "It's the Unspeakable Mystery place. How lucky are we?"

"They sound a little desperate," Josh said.

"I usually never stop here," Ely said.

"Why's that?" Josh asked.

"That thing they got. That attraction. Gives me the creeps."

Then, Ely slowed the truck, which groaned and rattled a bit. He turned the wheel to the left, crossing the empty highway, and then spun the wheel to the right, taking the truck onto the gravel service road.

WHEN HE DROPPED them off near the pumps, Ely said, "Now, if you ever get lost out here, find your way over to Naga,. Look for the end of the only paved road you're going to find. Go down there until you see silvery lights from hubcaps in the sun and maybe ZZ Top blasting from the back. You're welcome to stop by and check out Naga. It's a cool town, but probably not as sophisticated as you two. And listen, you kids be careful on the road. Lots of good people maybe, but a few crazies out there, too. Some of them, scary as hell."

The Brakedown Palace Gas and Sundries was the biggest man-made thing for miles—mainly because there was nothing else around it. Bronwyn went in to buy more cigarettes and Josh walked around by the garage bays to find the boss.

A big man, the size of a bear and with a growl not far from one, rose up out of a grease pit in the back. He had sunbaked copper skin that had begun to go from tan to alligator hide. "Whatja want?"

"Our car's got a flat. Just back a little ways. Down the road."

The man's eyes were almost like fish-eyes, nearly perfectly round. A nose like a hammer, and big lips that held an unlit cigarette between them. He wore a black bandanna tied around his head, and an enormous white T-shirt that clung tight to his barrel chest and potbelly. His hips were wide, and he wore stained jeans that looked like they were homemade. On his feet, boots with steel tips at the toes. He was exactly what Bronwyn would call "a real character."

"Hell, kid, I'm busy. You need a tow? It'll be twenty minutes at best."

"Okay," Josh said.

"Fifty bucks."

"Fifty? It's just a couple miles away. Fifty bucks?"

"Take it or leave it."

"I don't know. I just don't know. Fifty? Doesn't that seem a little absurd?"

The man shrugged, then wiped some grease-sweat off his brow. "There's another gas station, twenty-five miles up. You want to go there, I ain't stoppin' you."

AFTER A DISCUSSION WITH BRONWYN, the fee was paid, the tow truck went out, and soon enough, Tammy, Griff, and Ziggy showed up, looking as if they had been drained of all energy, with the car hooked like a mackerel to the back of the truck.

The big guy was named Charlie Goodrow, and after introducing himself around, he told them they could each have a Coke on him.

"Fifty bucks' worth of Coke," Josh said.

The sun was moving westward too fast, and someone finally asked Goodrow how long it might take for the tire change, and Charlie Goodrow laughed and said, "Go wander the shop. I'll have it down in twenty minutes. Or less. I'll check your brakes, too. Free of charge."

"Fifty bucks' worth of checking brakes," Josh said, only barely under his breath.

"I want to go see the Great Unspeakable Mystery," Bronwyn said. "It's less than a buck and you enter in the back of the store."

ALL OF THEM went into the Sundries Shop for the free

Cokes, and Tammy wanted to look at the cheap jewelry they had near the Indian blankets. Bronwyn grabbed Griff by the elbow, and tugged him toward the back of the shop. There was a narrow door there, and it had a sign that read, "For the CHEAP ADMISSION PRICE of just 75 CENTS! See the Eighth Wonder of the World! The Mystery of the Southwest! The Aztec Demon Known as Xipe Totec! Found many miles south of here, smuggled up by an outlaw who believed it contained treasures! SEE THE UNSPEAKABLE SAVAGE MYSTERY OF THE ANCIENT PRE-COLUMBIAN WORLD!"

"Come on," Bronwyn said, pulling on his arm. Griff pulled away.

"I'm waiting for Tammy."

"Josh?" Bronwyn let go of Griff and stomped over to Josh, who stood near the glass refrigerator sipping his Coke.

"Okay, but we're not paying," Josh said. "We've already blown tonight's motel room budget on the car. I don't intend to make Charlie Goodrow a little richer."

CHAPTER SIX

Griff and Tammy followed them, and Ziggy showed up soon after, slurping his Coke through a straw. There was just a little box for the quarters, but none of them put any in, and since it was honor system, they snuck through the entry feeling like delinquents. Josh didn't, though. He felt damn good when he went in there and said, "Fifty bucks' worth of the Unspeakable Mystery of the Universe."

The corridor was dark, but with fine spears of light that came through at the roof's edge. They'd left the rectangular building of the Brakedown Palace, and had entered on a concrete floor, down a walkway with corrugated metal walls and what seemed to be a curved roof.

"It's a Quonset hut," Josh said. "They had them on the sub base when I was a kid."

"Navy brat," Tammy said, in a way that was so sexy it nearly turned Josh on to hear her voice. She purred like a kitten sometimes.

Then, the spears of light became brighter. Bulbs had

been strung along the roof, hanging down like clunky Christmas ornaments. The wiring above their heads was exposed as the lights brightened.

"Holy shit," Ziggy said. "This is like some freak show."

He pointed to the metal walls. Small dried animals hung by strings—lizards, rats, rabbits, quail.

"That's sick."

"It's just shit you find on the desert," Griff said. "Dried-up crap and dead animals."

Then, as they ventured forward, they entered into a well-lit space that contained poorly made wood and stone sculpture.

"The ancient Aztecs were a fierce, bloodthirsty people," Bronwyn read from the sign above the sculpture. "Jesus, some moron wrote this up. Ignorant desert scum."

She glanced at the diorama.

"Oh my god, look at that," she said. "They're Aztecs sacrificing someone. How adorable. And repulsive. The level of historical accuracy seems pretty low here."

Josh crouched down and peered over the divider that kept diorama and sculpture protected. "That's funky."

He guessed he was looking at a replica of a pyramid, about knee-high. At the flat top, a little stone-carved man held a blade against the chest of another little stone-carved man.

On the wall, beyond this, a cheap plastic replica of a Mayan calendar.

"Someone's obsessed with human sacrifice here."

"It's like a dollhouse of death," Tammy said, a sweet edge to her voice.

"You're *my* doll," Griff said, pulling her tightly into

him, and somehow managing to unbutton the top two buttons of her blouse at the same time.

They moved on, down the long corridor that went, alternately, dark and then light again as various kinds of bulbs and lamps lit sections, highlighting pictures that had obviously been torn from a book on the Aztecs. There was a scene of blood running from a warrior's chest, a look of horror on his face, as several priests stood around him, with one raising his still-beating heart high. Other large pictures included a poorly done painting of what appeared to be a tomb with stone jaguars and scorpions and what Josh guessed was the Aztec god, Quetzalcoatl. A crystal skull hung suspended above their heads. They all giggled and snorted or just laughed out loud as they passed through a spotlighted area with a tall carved-wood sculpture of a naked woman. The sign behind the sculpture read, "This work of art was found behind the arroyo and is believed to have been carved by the Ancients."

Finally, a new doorway, and over it, the sign, "It's not too late to turn back! You don't want to see the Unspeakable Mystery! The Ancient Savage Flayer of Men! The Flesh-Scraper of the Pyramids of Teotihuacan!"

Josh was the first one through the door, and what he saw there made him cry out.

DAVE OLSHAKER HAD BEEN on the road too long, and was sleepy as hell. He and Billy Dunne had to slap each other a few times just to keep their eyes open, and then the heat of the day just fried them out, that and the piss-warm beer. Dave had to take a dump twice back in the sagebrush because something he'd eaten the night before hadn't set well.

But they had watched it all.

Billy had wanted to go help with the tire change. "It's our chance. We can help 'em, and then beat the shit out of Griff. And you can get Tammy."

But Dave, not feeling so great, held back. He'd just driven around and around the narrow, dusty side road off the highway, trying to keep out of sight of the gang with the Pimpmobile.

Once the tow truck had come out, he decided to follow it up to the Brakedown Palace, but he still stayed a ways back until he saw all of them go inside the shop.

When he drove up to the Palace, he gassed up the car, and then, he went inside.

"Fuel," Billy said, grabbing snacks from the shelves, stuffing them down his pants as if the bulge wouldn't be noticeable.

"That a Twinkie in your jeans or are you just happy to see me?" Dave chuckled.

"Where'd they go anyway?" Billy asked.

Charlie Goodrow had come back inside the shop, and pointed to the doorway in the back. "They went over there. And you're paying for every damn Twinkie you got in your pants, kid."

INSIDE THE INNER SANCTUM, Josh was shocked by the

smell—it was of some kind of church incense. The room was smoky with it.

The others came up behind him, Tammy coughing, Ziggy saying something about getting high off "sacred fumes," and Bronwyn pointing out the lack of ventilation, despite adding to the interior pollution with a cigarette hanging from between her lips.

But Josh had already gone over to the display case.

The Mystery. The Great and Powerful It.

With spotlights on signs and images behind it—signs that warned of ancient curses and Aztec savagery, and images of the pyramids of the Sun and Moon as well as of some man-creature covered with blood, holding what looked like a human head in his hands—a glass case stood at the center of the room, lit from beneath and behind with a cool blue and white light, and within the glass display, some kind of curved rock.

It sat in what looked like a large stone bowl, as if a geode the size of a desk had been cracked open to cradle it.

"Holy shit, that's a dead kid," Griff said.

"You're way off. Look at the hands."

"And feet," Josh added. "Christ."

"It's disgusting," Tammy said.

"I don't know," Bronwyn said. "Makes me feel a little creepy. But it has its good points."

"Like?"

Bronwyn shrugged. "It looks like the kind of baby someone I know will have someday."

"Like a baby freak," Griff said.

The only one not talking much was Ziggy. Josh noticed

how he just stood off to the side and wouldn't do more than peer at the Great Unspeakable Mystery from the corner of his eye, as if it reminded him of something not so wonderful.

The thing itself was a light dusty gray color all over with a sort of brackish, almost seaweed undertone to it—faint, but noticeable. Its skull seemed enlarged, as it if were too big for the rest of its skeleton. Wrapped around its head and along its collarbone were gauze-like strips that crisscrossed all the way to its shriveled belly. Its skin was somehow glued to the gauze, and Josh just blurted out, "It's a mummy. A creepy little crappy mummy. These people are whack jobs to sell tickets to it."

Its hands were elongated, with fingers like fins that curled into talons at the tips. At the end of its fingertips, what looked like long, sharp, curved, shiny, smooth black glass that ended in hooks. Its feet and toenails were similar.

In its eye sockets, two rounded turquoise stones.

Bronwyn read aloud from one of the signs. "'It is a creature of the night, although it never sleeps. But the Sun God is its enemy, and so it prefers darkness'. Who writes this kind of crap?"

Its hands were crossed over each other, a twisted, knotted rope held them in place.

"It looks like a big baby, sleeping," Tammy cooed.

"Baby from Hell."

"Big ugly bondage baby," Griff chuckled.

"Maybe it's a small adult. I can't tell," Bronwyn said.

"I like the turquoise," Tammy added. "I kept hoping we'd find someplace to buy some decent jewelry out here. So far, this is the closest I've come to it."

"Maybe I should pop his little eyes out," Griff said. "Put them in a necklace for you."

"Ew," Tammy said.

"How could they do this?" Josh asked. "They had to dig up a grave and then do something to the body? It's sick."

Bronwyn lit up a new cigarette. "Maybe. But you know, out here on the desert, people die, bodies are found years later. The desert mummifies them. Maybe it's fake. I mean, it could be plastic."

"I bet it is," Griff said.

"Nope, it's real," Josh said.

"No way. Look at those hands. Nobody can have hands like that. Look at them. It's so fake it's funny."

Josh leaned over the glass cover of the display. "I can't tell. Maybe it's all fake. Who knows?"

"Just lift the lid up," Griff said. He pushed Josh back a little and went to feel under the glass lid. "Here's the hinge." He lifted the lid up and held it back. "Nice security system. I'm amazed nobody's stolen this yet. Hell of a Halloween decoration. Touch it."

"No thanks."

"You chicken shit."

Griff reached in and touched the forehead of the skull.

For just a second, Josh felt as if something happened.

Not anything awful, just as if something changed. Then, he began coughing. It was dust—the dust of the display case had come up in a brief smoky cloud and then dissipated.

"Hell," Griff said.

"What is it?"

"It's warm. This thing is warm."

"No shit," Bronwyn said. "It probably bakes in here every day."

"No, I mean, it's...it's...*alive*!" Griff shouted and then cackled gleefully. Then, stupidly, he let go of the glass display top.

It fell backward, shattering on the floor.

Each of them looked at the others.

"I wonder how much that'll cost to replace," Bronwyn said.

After several seconds, Josh said, "They didn't hear it in the shop. We're too far out here."

"Well, we can't leave it like that," Bronwyn said.

"Oh yeah we can," Griff said.

That's when Josh noticed the sign.

He read it aloud. "'Please Do Not Touch Glass. We at the Brakedown Palace have nicknamed this special ancient mummy Scratch, and he has been good luck for us all these years. We must warn any who view it of the legend that once Scratch gets fresh human skin under its fingernails and the taste of blood, he'll come back from oblivion to reap the human harvest. Do Not Touch. Do Not Feed'."

"*Scratch*. Now that's original," Bronwyn said. "That's nothing but some little kid mummified and they stuck fake longer fingernails on him. But they call him 'Scratch.' Lovely Mr. Goodrow."

"There's something wrong with this," Tammy said. For the first time since he'd known her, Josh felt he heard something adult in her voice, as if she'd been hiding behind a little-girl persona. "I don't feel good about it."

"I know. It's not right," Ziggy said, startling the others because he'd been so quiet they forgot he was there.

Josh turned—Ziggy had pressed himself up against the metal wall. It looked as if he'd finally hit the legendary limit of too much weed and too much speed.

"What's up. Zig?"

"I had a dream about this. A vision. Like a shaman."

Griff snorted. "Doin' 'shrooms, was ya?"

"It was real. I saw this thing coming for me, only it was all bloody and torn up, but it had eyes just like this."

"It was a dream. That's all," Josh said.

"I don't know. Shit. I am never ever taking anything again," Ziggy said. "Crap. My brain is fried. I *know* it is."

Bronwyn went over to him and touched the edge of his elbow. "It's okay. It's okay. Look, let's go back down to the shop. I'm sure the car's nearly ready. We can get some Cokes. Want a Coke? My treat."

"Some freak put this together," Ziggy whispered. "Some freak. Some sick nutjob. That's a kid. Or a dwarf. Or a very little person. Jesus Holy Mother of Mary."

"It's okay," Bronwyn said, softly. She tugged at his arm, and Ziggy, head down, began walking with her down the long corridor, past the paintings and the stonework of the Quonset hut, back to the shop at the Brakedown Palace.

"I never wanna get that burnt out on drugs," Tammy said. "I like weed too much."

"Remember that acid?"

"Only three times," Tammy said.

"Let's get out of here," Josh said.

"Eh, we just broke some cheap piece of glass. It's no

biggie," Griff said. "Hey, let's find out if this thing is real. Let's feed it."

"Hardy-har-har."

"I mean it. Come on. We can just give it a little skin. Just a little."

"You're getting creepy on me, baby," Tammy said.

"Creepy can be good." Griff reached for her left breast and gave it a squeeze. Tammy slapped him hard on the cheek—the smack echoed as much as the breaking glass had.

Josh stood there, wishing he could disappear.

"You slut," Griff spat, and swung a fist out at Tammy, who dodge it but barely. Off-balance, she fell to the ground.

"Hey!" Josh moved forward, grabbing Griff's arm, pulling it back.

Griff tugged hard, pulling Josh off balance.

"Leave me the hell alone!" Griff shouted. Josh wasn't sure what he yelled back, and he was only dimly aware that Tammy was screaming and weeping in a heap in the corner, but the next thing he knew, he was thrown backward into the glass display case.

He felt a sliver of glass slice into his side and heard a crunching sound.

At first, he thought he'd broken his back, but then realized it was just the Unspeakable Mystery Attraction beneath him.

"Shit," Josh moaned, finally. "You probably killed me."

Griff's face was deep red and sweaty—but the smash-up of the display had got his attention and stopped the fight.

"*Did* I kill you?" Griff said.

Griff gingerly pulled him up by the waist from the broken display.

Josh felt a pain in his back and side, but after a minute, lifting his torn shirt up, Griff only found two small bits of glass, and they had just scraped his skin a bit.

"Oh man," Griff said.

"You are one big dumb fool," Tammy said, as if it were the worst insult she could toss his way.

"Okay. Just leave me alone," Josh said, pulling away from Griff.

"I want to make sure you're okay."

"I'm fine. Don't touch me. And do not hit her ever again."

"She hit me first," Griff said. "And I didn't hit her."

"You tried to. *What,* are you two years old? She slapped you because you copped a feel. And you slug her. Get a grip. See a psychiatrist. But don't ever hit her again."

"Quit saying that. I didn't hit her."

Ignoring him, Josh turned to Tammy.

"You okay?"

She accepted his outstretched hand as a lift up. "I'm fine."

"Oh baby, I'm sorry," Griff said. "I'm so so sorry, baby."

"I know you are." Tammy let go of Josh's hand as she moved closer to Griff.

I do not believe this, Josh thought. *They're going to kiss and make up.*

And that's when he happened to glance down at the body of Scratch.

"Fucking corpse," Griff said, squatting in front of it.

"Holy shit," Josh said. "We broke it."

"Goddamn it," came a gruff voice from down the corridor.

Josh spun around.

It was none other than Charlie Goodrow with a big shotgun at his side.

"HOLY MOTHER OF FUCK!" one of them shouted.

Josh wasn't sure who'd yelled; might've even been him.

They all went running—at least that's what it seemed like—Josh pushing Bronwyn forward through the final door that expelled them into blinding sunlight. They ran as fast as they could to the car, which was parked just outside the garage bay at the side of the *Brakedown Palace Gas & Sundries* building. Josh noticed that the gas cap was off, but that didn't matter. They had to get the hell out of there.

"Where's Griff?" Tammy cried out, alternately laughing hysterically and whimpering.

"Just get in!" Josh said, shoving her into the back of the car.

Ziggy had already managed to squeeze into the backseat, ahead of them.

"Hurry up! He's crazy!" Bronwyn shouted from the front seat.

Then, there was the sound of a shotgun blast.

"Griff!" Bronwyn shouted. "Hurry the fuck up!"

But Griff came running around the corner with what looked like a kid in his arms.

"Go! Go!" he shouted and then leapt into the front passenger seat of the car, squeezing Bronwyn up against Josh in the driver's seat.

Josh got the car in reverse and his foot went down hard on the accelerator.

The car screeched and he put it in drive, but it went to neutral instead.

The thought flashed through his mind that the engine would stall, but he knocked the lever into drive and at that moment, here's what he saw, frozen in some strange tableau, as if he'd set off a flash camera to stop the action of life:

Not Charlie Goodrow running from the back of the Palace, but someone who looked big and slovenly and had a little blond sidekick with him.

He registered who it was:

Dave Olshaker? What the—

Then life sped up again, and Dave limped and half-jogged toward them.

"I been shot!" Dave shouted, clutching his ass. "I been shot!"

"Sons of bitches!" his sidekick shouted at them.

"Tammy! I love you, baby! Come back to me!" Dave howled as he fell to the pavement, his hands still massaging his backside.

But the Pimpmobile was already heading out onto the service road, kicking dust and gravel in its wake.

CHAPTER SEVEN

"This is just too much to process," Bronwyn said when Josh finally slowed the car down, having driven off the road a little, out behind a hill, at least twenty miles away from the Brakedown Palace.

"What the hell was Olshaker doing there? What the hell?" Josh asked, glancing in the rearview mirror at Tammy, who glared back at him.

"Don't look at me," she said. "I dumped him a long time ago. I guess some people just never give up."

"He's a prick," Griff said. "But looks like he got shot up in the hiney."

And it was sometime between spinning out of the gas station, and getting out onto the dusty road, that Josh realized what Griff had brought with him.

The Unspeakable Scratch.

"Little bastard," as Ziggy started to call it.

"You stole that thing?"

"Come on. It's not just a thing. It's the Unspeakable Mystery of the Ancient Aztecs," Griff said, holding his prize up on his lap, like a ventriloquist's dummy. "Hello, my name is Scratch."

"I gotta pee," Tammy said. "Come on. I gotta pee. When I get nervous, I gotta pee."

"Okay, okay," Bronwyn said. "Get out and go take a leak."

"Come with me. I'm scared."

Bronwyn made a noise of moderate disgust from the back of her throat, but flicked her cigarette out into the dirt and pushed Griff and his stolen Mystery out of the car.

"What, are you two years old?" she asked Tammy.

"There might be snakes. And scorpions."

"One can only hope," Bronwyn said.

"WHAT HAPPENED BACK THERE?"

"It was funny as hell," Griff said. "That old man came at us with the gun, but he didn't know that Olshaker and his buddy were right behind him. God knows what the hell Olshaker's doing out here. He's obsessed with my girl, and I guess he's been trailing us. Well, the old guy spun around, Olshaker squealed like a little kid and tried to grab the shotgun. I was surprised to see the little shit myself, but after you guys took off, you missed the best part—Olshaker and his buddy fighting with the old guy for the shotgun, and I just saw this little fella and decided he'd be great back at The House."

Griff always referred to his frat house as The House. Scratch would not be the first thing he'd ever stolen for

The House. He had a stag's head from one of the dean's homes, up in the balcony room on the second floor and a trophy from a rival football team hidden in the attic.

"Imagine this little guy up on the mantel during a party. Cowabunga!" He laughed, pulling the little mummy's arms up in the air, pretending to talk with a babyish voice. "I'm the Monster of the House! Wheee!"

"Why'd you steal it?"

He shrugged. "Chill out. He's all broke up around the ribs. We'd have had to pay for it anyway." Then, he held up one of Scratch's fingernails. "See? Broke right off."

He passed it over to Josh, who nearly pricked his finger on the sharp tip.

"It's obsidian. Like a knife. Sharp as hell."

"I think it's a cool souvenir from this crappy trip," Griff said.

Ziggy in the backseat had already lit up a joint, and he and Griff passed it back and forth, waiting for the girls to come back to the car.

They were all quiet for a minute or two, and then Ziggy said, "Just don't feed that little bastard."

"Huh?"

"It said don't feed it."

"I wonder what it eats," Griff said. "I mean, if it eats skin or blood, then I hate to say it, but our buddy Josh already gave it it's first meal. Look." Griff pressed his finger to Scratch's clenched jaws. He drew his finger back and held it up. A tiny spot of blood. "When you fell on it, buddy. It got a little taste o' Joshua."

"We're so very, very screwed," Ziggy said.

"Don't be ridiculous." Josh laughed. "Oh my god,

Ziggy, give up the weed. It's messing with your head. I mean it. Give it up."

"No, we're cursed. I know we are. That little bastard was in my vision dream. Shamans used mushrooms and herbs and weed to see things. I saw it. I had a shaman trip. I saw the little bastard in it. We're up shit's creek like nobody's ever been up shit's creek."

"Further up the creek than you'd guess, Plow-boy," Griff said. He pointed to the gas gage.

It was just beneath empty.

"Great. Just great," Josh said, hitting the horn with his fist.

The sound of the horn echoed across the dusty road.

AFTER A MINUTE, Ziggy said, "Throw the little bastard out. It's bad luck."

THE TRUNK of the Pimpmobile popped up.

"This is the ugliest, nastiest thing I've ever seen," Josh said. "When we get going again, we're going to return it. We are."

"No way," Griff said, heaving Scratch into the back of the trunk, among the girls' suitcases and the guys' backpacks and clothes.

They both stared at it.

"What were you thinking? What was going on in that mind of yours? You thought, 'I'll add robbery to my college career. Not just robbery, but stealing a nasty stupid sick little gas station mummy that's probably covered with some diseases or lice or something.'"

"Look. Live slow, die slow if you want. I watched my grandpa live like that and he ended up spending ten years in a damn nursing home. You live like that, you get a long boring life. Go ahead, have that life. Someday when you're in that nursing home sucking back pea puree and shittin' your diapers, you're going to remember this moment," Griff said, chuckling. "You'll remember its face. Look at it. With its little grin. It's kinda cute."

"That's not a grin. That's dried-up flesh around clenched teeth in some old corpse with an enlarged skull. That is the ugliest thing I've ever seen."

"Don't say that about my newborn baby. It's grinning," Griff said, and then slammed the trunk closed. He slapped his hand around Josh's shoulder. "It does not get cooler than this."

"You just put a corpse in with my clothes," Josh said.

"Don't think of it as a corpse. Think of it," Griff said, "as a memento."

TAMMY DROPPED her jeans and pushed down her underwear to squat and take a leak.

"You okay?" Bronwyn asked, facing the opposite direction.

"Fine."

"Olshaker must really love you," Bronwyn said.

"Like a bounty hunter," Tammy said. Then, when she

was done, she got back into her jeans, zipping up. "He's a guy I'd like to put in jail."

"He steal something of yours?"

"Maybe," Tammy said. "You got a smoke on you?"

"Sure," Bron said. "Here ya go."

She passed her one of the few remaining cigarettes. Then, she slid one out of the pack for herself and lit it up. Sucked in that first taste of smoke.

"I know I'm going to have to quit someday. Everybody either quits or gets cancer."

"Or both," Tammy said, lighting hers from Bronwyn's.

"When I'm having a bad day, a smoke just takes the edge off things."

"I started when I was fourteen. I saw an ad with these beautiful women smoking and I wanted to be one of them. Stupid, huh? But I was fourteen and I didn't look like much then and had no idea how life worked. I just wanted to be grown-up more than anything in the world." Tammy blew a perfect smoke ring into the air.

"I started smoking when my folks split. I was a little younger than fourteen. I thought I was intellectual to do it. I thought all these French intellectuals smoked, why not me?" Bronwyn laughed, coughing out a brief white cloud. "I think that's pretty stupid, too. I snuck cigarettes from my mother's purse. She didn't smoke much, so she always had a full pack."

"We have a lot in common." Tammy grinned. "I snuck smokes from my older brother's sock drawer. They always smelled a little like dirty feet because he rarely washed his gym socks, and he just balled them up and threw them in there on top of his packs of Marlboros."

"I had a boyfriend once who never washed anything. He smelled like a locker room half the time."

They both puffed on their cigarettes.

Tammy said, softly, "You still love Griff."

Bronwyn took a breath. "Yeah, I guess I do. I guess I do." She glanced over at Tammy and chuckled slightly. "It's stupid, I know. I'm practically the top of our class, I'm planning to get a master's and then maybe even a Ph.D., and he probably wants the kind of woman who..." Realizing what she'd begun saying, she added, "I don't mean... what it sounds like...I mean...I mean...what I mean..."

Tammy cut her off. "I know how you think of me. I know what the other people think, too. But what you don't know about me could fill a book. But I do know *exactly* what you mean."

"I'm a jerk," Bronwyn said.

"Maybe everybody is. I like Griff," Tammy said. "But he's not the kind of guy you're really supposed to fall in love with. He's like a ride at the county fair. You pay for it, but it's not going to last very long anyway."

Bronwyn's eyes started filling with tears, which she quickly wiped away.

Tammy slung an arm over Bronwyn's shoulder. "You should find someone new to think of in that way. He's not the best guy. He's a fun guy, maybe, sometimes. He's an asshole most of the time. But he's not right for you. Or for me. We're gonna break up."

"What? You have all this...sex all the time."

"Sure," Tammy said, puffing on the cig. "I like sex with him. He likes sex with me. But there's not much else."

"Oh."

"Yeah, I know what that 'oh' means. 'Oh, you're happy being a slut.' Just because I like to party and have a little fun, doesn't mean I'm just some mindless bimbo. Look, we're in college. Someday I'm going to be like my mother. I know it. I can feel it. All uptight and full of rules and making sure the silver's polished for Thanksgiving, even if I have some half-assed career. I know I'm headed that way. And I want to put that off as long as possible. I don't want a ring on my finger, not yet. Not for years. And Griff is… Griff is a pretty boy. He's a jock. He's a guy who's young and has fun and gets along with nearly everybody when he's not acting like a four-year-old. He's not long-term for me. Or for you."

"Says you."

"That's right," Tammy said. "Says me."

"You don't think you might be hurting yourself?" Bronwyn asked.

Tammy drew back a little and began walking to the car. After a few steps forward, she turned around to glance at Bronwyn. "You could just ask yourself that same question."

ONCE EVERYBODY WAS in the Pimpmobile, Josh drove another few miles along the road, but finally the car came to a sputtering halt.

"End of the line," Ziggy said. "Nowheresville, USA."

Josh felt a pain in his stomach—a knot of tension.

"You know, you'd think I'd be smart enough to fill up with gas at a gas station."

"I didn't think it was near empty," Griff said. "I'm almost positive we had half a tank left."

"Almost," Tammy said, somewhat archly.

Bronwyn said, "It's nearly six. I wonder what time it'll get dark."

"We've got food in the back," Griff said. "We still have the cooler full of beer, too."

"And a mummified body stolen from a gas station," Josh said. "Or did you forget that? Will the beer taste better with a little corpse on it?" Then, he slapped his forehead. "Christ Almighty! My dad told me to get a CB radio in case I ever got stuck somewhere. He told me. He said, 'Josh, you never know when the car's going to break down.' He doesn't give a flyer about me most of the time, but this was one of those few times when he did," Josh said slowly, softly. "I'm so stupid. Stupid. Stupid."

"I wonder if the guy at the Brakedown Palace is calling the cops," Ziggy said. "We stole his big attraction."

"That piece of crap?" Griff snorted. "He'll dig up another corpse in some old Indian graveyard around here. And then he'll have a whole new pile of bullshit to sell."

SOMEWHERE NEARBY, in some dark, airless place, a breath was exhaled and motes of dust and bits of bone coughed from a jaw that had not opened in a long, long time.

CHAPTER EIGHT

They made a fire in the dirt.

Bronwyn's lighter had come in handy. Josh and Griff gathered some slender sticks of wood for kindling, and then a larger piece of some dried-up gray wood that burned really well. They spread a couple of thin cotton blankets out on the ground, and spent some time making sure there weren't any creepy-crawlies nearby.

They distributed the contents of a bag of junk food that Bronwyn had bought at the Brakedown Palace. The passed around gas station sandwiches, snack cakes and a couple of warm Cokes like it was Holy Communion.

Afterward, they shared some beers as the sun went down in a blaze of pink and gold glory.

Josh felt pretty good.

"This is an adventure," he said, leaning back against Bronwyn's knees.

"Some adventure," she said.

"Nope, he's right," Griff said. "My uncle told me to have a lot of adventures in college. This could be cool."

"When we're completely dried up and burning up in the sun, we won't call this an adventure," Bronwyn said. "We'll call it the last day of our life. And I'm never making it to LA. I can tell you that."

"You're kidding, right?" Tammy asked. "We're not in any real trouble here. I don't think."

Bronwyn shrugged. "Okay. I guess I was exaggerating. I have three packs of cigs left, so I'll live."

"Until the cigarettes kill you," Griff said.

"Years from now I'll regret smoking. But right now, I regret nothing, as they say."

Ziggy kept looking out in the purple darkness. "I wonder if there's wolves."

"There aren't wolves," Josh said. "I don't think. Maybe coyotes. But we don't have to worry about them."

"Yeah, coyotes, rattlesnakes, big black scorpions the size of my wang," Griff said.

Josh made a sound in the back of his throat.

Griff shot him a look. "Yeah?"

"Your wang always seems to come up, if you'll pardon the expression."

Griff grinned. "The dongster needs a breath of fresh air now and then."

"Yuck," Bronwyn coughed.

Tammy laughed. "Oh, good grief, get a sense of humor, you guys. Hey, this is like Girl Scout camp."

"Time to make a few brownies, then," Griff said, heading off into the darkness to do his business.

"Damn, that reminds me," Bronwyn said. "Anybody bring toilet paper?"

"I have a ton of tissues in my backpack," Tammy said. "In the trunk."

"Good. I hope it's a ton that'll last all of us through tomorrow."

They all went silent for several minutes until Bronwyn said, "Wonder how far to the nearest town."

"Hey!" Josh said, leaning forward and sitting up. "*Naga*. That was the name of the town. We can't be more than, I don't know, ten or maybe fifteen miles. It was on the map."

"There was a map?" Tammy said. "I don't remember any map."

"The map you lost, you mean?" Bronwyn said.

"I didn't lose it," Josh said. "It fell out of my back pocket. Maybe when I fell on that little bastard."

Ziggy stared into the fire. "We could've bought a map at the Brakedown Palace."

"If this town is that close, why can't we see it?" Griff asked, returning from his duties, and apparently having overheard everything. "I mean, I don't see lights anywhere out there."

"I bet it's north of here. I bet we're south of where we thought we were. I bet it's over those hills." Josh pointed up to the ridge of hills that seemed to have an aura of indigo against the dimming sky.

"Maybe other cars will come by. Or truckers."

"Like Ely," Bronwyn said, remembering the truck driver who'd given them a lift.

"Yeah, you guys were lucky. He was cute," Tammy said.

"He was not cute," Griff said, coming back into the campfire circle. "He was a redneck."

"I hope you washed your hands," Tammy said.

"With sand." Griff grinned.

"Nope, Ely is high on the lustometer," Bronwyn said.

"God, I'm all out of brewsky." Griff finished the last of his beer.

"Lustometer?"

"Yep. Some guys are high on it."

"You got some weed to share, Zig?" Griff asked.

"I thought we said no pot," Josh said.

"Ziggy broke that rule at least two thousand miles ago. I bet you scored some in El Paso. Did you, Zig?"

Ziggy grinned. "Maybe. Maybe in Oklahoma."

"Oklahoma? They grow weed in Oklahoma?"

"Maybe somewhere along the road. We stopped in a lot of places. I ain't sayin'."

"I knew it!" Griff laughed, clapping his hands together. "Come on. We're all screwed here. Might as well enjoy it."

"I'm not into grass," Josh said.

"Tight-ass," Griff said.

"You don't have to smoke it," Bronwyn said. "Just make sure none of us gets too happy."

And then, they all got high. Josh eventually joined in, and kept saying, "I don't think this is right. I'm only doing it because of peer pressure," and he felt guilty about smoking dope and wondered if the cops were going to descend and arrest them all.

"I got a joke," Griff said. "Here's how it goes."

"You're awful with jokes!" Bronwyn shouted out.

"He's great at telling jokes. I love his jokes," Tammy said. "Tell it. Tell a good one, Griff."

"Okay. It is really, really good."

"So you say," Josh said.

"Okay. This guy goes into a restaurant. And the waitress, who is this hot little number with big tits and this great ass, says, 'What can I get you?' And the guy says, 'How about a quickie?' And the waitress says, 'You don't mean that. You mean—'"

Josh laughed, clapping his hand. "You're telling it all wrong. You're gonna give away the punch line."

Griff laughed. "Shit. Maybe I remembered it wrong."

"Okay, it's a stupid joke. It's really stupid," Josh said.

"Just let him tell it," Tammy said.

"No, I probably ruined it. You tell it," Griff said to Josh.

"Okay. But it's bad. Remember. It's bad and it's stupid. Okay. A guy walks into a restaurant. He sits down. The waitress comes over and says, 'What're you having?' and he says, 'How about a quickie?' And the waitress slaps him. Then she says, 'So tell me what you want, and none of this fresh stuff,' and he says, 'Well, I really want a quickie. I've never had one,' and she slaps him again and stomps off. And the guy across from him, he's been watching this and he leans over and says to the guy, 'It's pronounced quiche.'"

No one laughed.

"I told you it was bad."

"Man, you cannot tell a joke!" Griff laughed. "Man, you just can't." And he started butchering yet another joke.

And then, sometime around midnight, after they'd laughed at several nearly nonexistent jokes, and the girls had gotten them singing "Michael, Row the Boat Ashore," and "Kumbaya," and then, "Let It Be," Ziggy passed out on the blanket in front of the fire, and Bronwyn began talking about her plans for the future, while Griff and Tammy went off into the darkness in their too-frequent mating ritual.

Josh, less stoned than the others, heard the noise from the car first.

"WHAT WAS THAT?"

"What?" Bronwyn asked, sleepily, her eyes barely fluttering open.

"That noise."

"Probably a coyote. Don't worry," she said. "They don't get close to the fire."

"That was not a coyote," Josh said.

Then, the noise got louder.

"That's metal."

She sat up on her elbows. "Maybe. I don't know. Maybe it's something kinky that Griff and Tammy are doing."

"That was the scrape of metal, Bron. It came from over there." Josh pointed toward the Pimpmobile. Then, he noticed just how far away they were from the road. To get to the car would take more than a minute. For some reason, this bothered him. It wasn't exactly a quarter mile away, but the car was far enough off in the darkness that it bothered him.

As if he had never been passed out at all, Ziggy sat straight up so fast that it freaked Josh out.

"It's that little bastard."

"What?"

"Ziggy, don't be silly," Bronwyn said. "You're high. We're all a little stoned."

"Maybe," Josh said, weighing this as a possibility. He sniffed the air. It had a curious mix of the dusty road and mesquite to it. But there was something else. Something that reminded him of a church smell. He wasn't sure what that was, but he assumed it was in his head. All of it, in his head.

"I didn't hear anything," Bronwyn said. But she said it as if she were trying to deny something even to herself. "I mean, I heard something. Just not something that seemed strange. I bet it's because those two are going at it. They're probably breaking the seats. They're going at it in your car."

"I don't think so," Ziggy said. "It's that little bastard. That's what it is. It's that little rat bastard."

Bronwyn pulled her knees into her chest and looked at the fire. She puffed away at her cigarette, and didn't seem bothered by the noise.

It's because she doesn't want to think about them, Josh thought. *She doesn't want to think about Griff screwing Tammy. She loves Griff. There's no way around this. He hits girls. He's stupid. But he looks good and girls want that. They want to feel they got the football hero. They want to feel like they won some prize. Just like guys want pretty girls, no matter what the girl is on the inside.*

She's never going to look at me the way she looks at him. And he's a complete jerk. But she doesn't notice that. She just knows she wants him.

He scootched over in the dirt and sat next to her, crossing his legs in front of him.

"You okay?" he asked.

She shrugged, holding her cigarette aloft as if she could write in the sky with it.

"Life just sucks, that's all. Your basic existential angst. Each of us is all alone in the universe and all that jazz."

"I'm here for you," he said.

She turned her face toward him. "Don't cozy up if you just want something from me."

Ziggy pushed himself up from the rock on the other side of the fire. He stood there, beyond the crackling flame, a blanket wrapped around his shoulders. "What if it's all true? What if we brought that thing to life?" He balanced his weight on one foot and then another, and looked toward the car nervously. "It's dark over there. I can't see anything. But I heard that."

"Sit down, Zig," Bronwyn said. "It's okay. You're freaking me out. Just calm down, have a smoke or something. I promise you that Scratchy-poo isn't coming out of that trunk."

Josh laughed. "Scratchy-poo."

"Scratchy-poo," Ziggy repeated, but didn't laugh. He just kept watch in the direction of the car. "You know, I heard that sometimes these things have special powers. I mean, there are stones in England that Druids put together and they have ceremonies there still. And there's a place in France where there are these caves and they found these bones. It was some ancient religious thing. And I saw on *National Geographic* about this temple in India where there's this cult—"

"Zig," Bronwyn said. "What's your point?"

He looked at her, and the flickering from the firelight cast his face in a brilliant yellow and red shadow. "People believe in things. They do. And maybe if they believe in them bad enough, maybe those things can be real when they don't seem like they should."

"We should never have dragged you to *Texas Chainsaw Massacre* on Halloween," she said. Turning to Josh, she added, "He screamed like a baby the whole time."

"You never know what stuff is like until it happens to you," Ziggy said. "You never know. People go missing all the time. Bad things happen to people and no one can explain them. I heard in Oregon that two kids got lost in the woods and got torn up, and they thought it was a tiger only no one could see how tigers could be in Oregon."

Bronwyn raised her hand. "Oh, pick me. I know! I know!"

Josh cracked up, laughing.

"What's so funny? It happened. They said the woods were cursed. They got torn up," Ziggy said.

"Zig, it was because of marijuana farms. That same weed you smoke doesn't come from nice Midwestern farmers. Some of them use tigers and mountain lions on their property to scare off—or kill—intruders."

Ziggy looked at the joint in his hand.

"What, you think the marijuana is grown by Old

MacDonald? That the Feds don't raid the plantations in Hawaii and the Northwest? That nice people run them and everybody's stoned and happy? They're drug lords, Zig. You smoke that stuff—hell, so do I now and then— and we're ultimately supporting people who would be happy to cut our throats if we stole an ounce of their stash. I know about those kids. I read about it. They were hiking where they shouldn't have gone hiking," she said.

"You know everything, don't you?" Ziggy said, an edge to his voice that wasn't quite sarcasm but was close to it. "You know everything. Well, maybe we've gone where we shouldn't go hiking. I saw that thing. It's a sacred relic. I believe someone at that gas station stole it from where it was meant to rest. It's from some old religion that we can't even begin to understand. I believe people used to believe in it. And they died because of it. They laid down their lives in sacrifice. It freaks me out. It does. I think we're like those kids in the woods, off the path. And that thing is a tiger. Maybe a sleeping tiger. But sleeping tigers wake up. And when they wake up, they get hungry."

"Sit down," Bronwyn said. "It's the two sex fiends doing the nasty in the Pimpmobile."

GRIFF AND TAMMY hadn't made their way to the car until after they'd been up against a big flat rock they'd stumbled across in the dark. Griff had his shirt off fast, and then unbuttoned his shorts, which dropped to his ankles and he did what Tammy called his "penguin walk" over to her and nearly tore her top off to get to her breasts. Their lips locked, tongues tickling, and Tammy kept whispering things to him when they weren't kissing, and it all turned him on more. She had left the condoms in the backseat of the Pimpmobile, and so she had to disengage. "I'm all dirty," she said.

"I feel that way, too," he said, grabbing around her back to keep his fingers on the nipples of delight, but she peeled his fingers back.

"I mean dirty dirty," she said. "All this goddamn sand. Now let go for a sec. I do not intend to get pregnant just yet and unless we just fool around, that's a distinct possibility."

TAMMY JOGGED TO THE CAR, opening the back door. "My bag is in here somewhere. We just used them last night. Where'd I put those Trojans?" She kneeled on the seat, bending over to check the floor for her handbag.

"Maybe it's in the back," he said.

"The trunk?" she said. "Oh, maybe. Go pop it for me, okay?"

He wanted to pop more than the trunk, but he went around to the driver's side, opened the door and found what he hoped was the lever for the trunk.

It popped open slightly.

"I'll look," he said. He shut the door and went around to the back of the car and lifted the trunk up.

The light hadn't come on in the trunk, so he rooted around in things, and threw a couple of suitcases out on the dirt. He reached into a pile of clothes, but they felt funny. He wondered why they seemed so ragged.

Then, he touched the top of Scratch's head.

HE NEARLY JUMPED when he felt it.

It was bumpy, but he knew he was touching bone. He laughed to himself at the slight chill he got from the contact. It was kind of gross having a dead little guy in the back, even if it was about five hundred years old.

Then, he thought he found Tammy's little round suitcase, and as he reached for it, something grabbed him by the wrist.

It wasn't just a grab. It felt like razors on his skin.

For just a moment he thought he'd stuck his hand into one of the other guys' shaving kit, and somehow, someway their razor blades were all lying in a circle, like a bracelet on his wrist.

Then he felt a pain that shot from his hand up his elbow and finally ended at his jaw.

Something had scraped skin off his wrist.

He tried to bring his hand out, but whatever had it gripped it tight. It was like a bear trap on his wrist. His mind wasn't working right as he tried to see in the dark, among the piles of crap.

Then, the razors dug deeper and he screeched.

CHAPTER NINE

Tammy scrambled out of the car seat, and ran back to the trunk. She could make out Griff, but wasn't sure what she was really seeing. It looked like he was doing some kind of crazy fast dance. His arms were jerking around and his legs were all wobbly.

And then he began moving toward her, now slower, almost slow motion, and she saw something that looked almost like a small dog snapping at his heels.

"Griff?" she asked.

As he got closer to her, he whispered, "Help me. Help me. Get it off me."

She saw it, finally, as it scrambled up his back and perched on his shoulder, its teeth going into his neck.

She tried to scream, but her voice was gone. All she could do was whimper. She stood there, naked, watching Griff fall to the ground, to his knees, while something on top of him made the most awful sucking sound. A spray of blood hit Tammy across her face, along her breasts, and she tasted Griff's blood on her tongue.

And then her voice came back to her and she screamed loud and long.

❀

BEFORE THE THREE around the fire could register the scream, let alone get up and go running to them, Tammy remembered the gun. She tried to swallow the feeling of horror and shock inside her—*if you stop it gets you, move, girl, move and do something, don't just be scared, take action*—and she remembered Griff's gun. He kept it in his duffel bag. The duffel bag was in the trunk. If she could run around the other side of the car, she could get it. She knew she could. She had no other weapon. There was nothing else.

Quickly, she turned around and ran. She heard a strange almost animal whimper from Griff's throat, which would be the last thing she'd ever hear from him. Her mind spun a mile a minute as she tried to process what she had seen, what was happening, but her thoughts moved into a darker place where survival was more important than logic, and where nightmares could be faced. She reached into the trunk, and felt around the suitcases and the clothes and then, she found it. His duffel bag. She reached in, pulling out his dirty laundry. Her hand touched metal. The gun. She grabbed it. She wasn't even sure how to work it, but she knew it wasn't rocket science. Point, aim, pull trigger, fire.

She brought the gun up in the dark and pointed it at the thing. Her hands trembled so she kept both of them on the gun, holding it as steady as she could. She felt for the trigger. She tried to aim as best she could.

Griff fell completely to the earth, and that little thing was moving over him rapidly, its arms going up and then down on his body, and she saw what might be scraps of... skin? It was skinning him?

Oh my god oh my god oh my god, she thought as she closed her eyes and squeezed the trigger. But she hadn't squeezed hard enough. *Come on. It's a gun. You can do it. You've watched TV. You know how guns are shot.* She squeezed it again, this time using all her strength.

She heard an explosion that was momentarily deafening, and saw a bright light. For the barest second, she saw it—the bloody mass that was Griff, and that thing—that Scratch-thing—its claws going up and down like an expert chef as it skinned Griff, with blood pouring everywhere.

She hadn't hit it. She hadn't hit anything. She hadn't even aimed well.

Scratch made gurgling sounds as it moved rapidly around Griff's body.

Then, when a flashlight's beam hit its face—those turquoise eyes shiny green and alive in the light—it made a noise that was part growl and part shriek, and grabbed something and ran off into the darkness.

JOSH STOOD THERE, his flashlight focused on Griff's body.

Bronwyn came up behind him, holding a long stick that burned at one end, like a torch.

Then, he shined the light on Tammy. She pointed the gun at him. "Tammy," Josh said.

The gun went off.

Josh instinctively fell to the ground.

"Tammy!" Bronwyn shouted. "Put the gun down now!"

Josh hit Tammy with the flashlight beam. Tammy's naked body was covered with blood. Her eyes seemed wide and vacant as she stared at them. Then, she started screaming and wouldn't stop for the longest time.

ZIGGY WAS SHIVERING as if he'd been doused with ice-cold water. He kept the blanket wrapped tight around him, and he was standing as close to the fire as he could get without burning himself. He kept turning slowly around and around as if sure that someone or something would pounce at any second. He rolled the fattest doobie he could and lit it up and sucked in as much of the smoke as possible. The world turned into the blue haze of smoke with tongues of flames shooting up from the fire.

He saw something coming toward him in the dark—a low, thick shadow moving among the low scrub-brush.

"Heya, Zigster." It was Griff's voice, and as the thing moved into the aura of light from the fire, he saw the little bastard monster with bloody skin all over him, moving rapidly forward, claws clicking, waving the skin of Griff's arms and hands like too-long sleeves from its own arms, and on its large skull head, Griff's face-skin, with eyeholes that showed shimmering green.

Ziggy felt his heart in his throat, and his pulse grew rapid, and he took another toke and tried to get his feet to move, but something in the purple weed smoke seemed to make him feel safe. He was transfixed as the little bastard wearing Griff's skin moved around the fire, and came toward him.

"You ain't gonna get me," Ziggy said. "I'm high. I'm floatin'."

The little bastard scurried well around the fire, and Ziggy knew it was the fire itself that scared the creep. Ziggy reached in and picked up the end of a stick from the edge of the fire. He waved the burning stick in front of him, slashing at the air.

He saw the green eyes through the bloody skin. They seemed to be twitching. It was like the little bastard was thinking.

Ziggy took a step backward. He could run. He could either climb into the fire and burn up to protect himself from the little bastard, or he could run.

He stood a chance if he ran.

"What are you thinking, you dumb stoner?" Griff's voice came from the creature. "You can run from the Great and Omnipotent Flayer of Men? You can't. This thing can run, boy, let me tell you. It can run like a jaguar. It can leap real high. It can do all kinds of things. But Zig, it ain't so bad. It really ain't. Getting your skin all torn off ain't the worst thing. It feels pretty good. It's sweet. It's about giving your life to something bigger than you. Something eternal."

Ziggy held his breath, and tried to get as stoned as he could off his last hit of weed.

And then, the little bastard leapt through the air, discarding Griff's skin, which floated slowly down into the fire as the creature latched on to Ziggy's balls.

"WHAT IN THE world is that...stench?" Bronwyn asked. It was in the air—smoke from the fire off the road smelled like a barbecue gone bad. She and Josh and Tammy had been standing around the car, stunned. She had her arm over Tammy's shoulder. Tammy had finally calmed for a few seconds—enough time to lower the gun and quit shooting haphazardly.

Then, they heard Ziggy's choking scream.

"Shit!" Tammy shouted.

She went running down the road, her arms raised, gun in hand, no doubt terrified for her life.

Bronwyn began swearing, and Josh held his breath.

They both stood there one more second, and then Josh exhaled and said, "Ziggy."

CHAPTER TEN

Josh went running out on the desert, toward the fire. He felt he was moving too slow, and he saw Ziggy's red-lit face as he approached the fire, but it wasn't just the firelight—blood was spurting up from his body. Josh got there just in time to watch the creature tear open Ziggy from neck to bowels. His steamy entrails poured out in loops. Ziggy's eyes seemed to follow his body being ripped open, and Josh wondered for a second if he could see it.

Josh stopped at the opposite side of the fire and grabbed a stick from the flames. It was so hot that his hands felt as if they were burning, but he slashed it in the air, its trail of flame lighting up the night. As he got closer to the creature—now, scraping at Ziggy's skin and laughing gleefully in a voice that was too close to Griff's—Josh began slamming the burning stick down on the creature. It squealed and leapt up onto Ziggy's head, leaning over to scratch Ziggy's eyes out and hold them at the end of its black talons.

It stared at Josh, but it was nearly comical looking. Its turquoise eyes seemed to change from blue to green and back to blue again. Now it spoke first with Griff's voice and then with Ziggy's, alternating back and forth as if, in tearing out both their throats, it had stolen their voices.

"Get away!" it screamed. "You son-of-a-bitch, this is your old pal! Come on, boy, get the hell away!"

Then, as Josh brought the stick down to hit the creature's head, it leapt up as if it could fly, its claws spread wide, its arms impossibly long, and ran off into the night, letting out a shrill scream that sounded exactly the way Ziggy's scream had been one night in his sleep.

"OH MY GOD! OH MY GOD!" Tammy shouted while Bronwyn took a blanket and covered her. They had made it back to the fire without getting attacked. Josh stood on the other side, crouching over Ziggy's body.

Tammy's teeth were chattering so loud it was like some old typewriter noise, and she shivered as if she were freezing.

Josh stared at Bronwyn, who stared back at him. All three of them had tears streaming down their faces.

After several minutes, Josh said, "It's scared of fire."

Bronwyn, one arm still slung across Tammy's back, reached into her breast pocket and pulled out her Merits. She slid a cigarette between her lips, dropped the pack back in her pocket, withdrew her Bic lighter, flicked it, lit the cigarette, took the first puff and said, "What the fuck is that thing?"

"It's the Unspeakable Mystery," Tammy whimpered. "We let it out. We stole it. We're all gonna die! And not just die, we're all gonna get torn up just like Griff. Torn to itty-bitty pieces."

She hadn't actually seen Ziggy's body yet. Josh had laid a blanket over it, barely aware of his own actions.

Tammy looked around the campfire. "Where's Ziggy?"

Bronwyn raised her eyebrows to Josh, who went to the cooler and brought out a can of Pearl Beer. He tossed it to Bronwyn who missed it, but picked it up off the ground and dusted it off with her hand. She popped the top, and passed it to Tammy. "Take a sip. Come on. Take a sip," she said.

Too eagerly, Tammy grabbed the beer and chugged it down. When she was done, she dropped the can by her feet. "It got Ziggy, too?"

Josh nodded.

"What's the plan?" Bronwyn asked.

"I don't know."

"We've got to make a plan. We've got Scratch coming at us."

Tammy started giggling. She covered her mouth, but couldn't contain it.

"What's funny?" Bronwyn asked.

"It's not happening," Tammy said. "Don't you see? There's no way in hell this can happen. It's all a trick. Some kind of trick. Griff must be in on it."

Bronwyn petted the top of Tammy's head like she was a puppy. She leaned into her, touching her scalp to Tammy's cheek. "We'll get through this. Don't worry. Somehow."

Tammy guffawed, pulling away from Bron. "No, there's no way this is real. It can't be. There's no such thing as that…thing."

Josh went around the fire and sat next to Bronwyn. "What about each of us grabbing a log from the fire. We walk over to the car. If we set the car on fire. Maybe…"

Bronwyn said, "Maybe. Maybe not. Don't you have flares in the Pimpmobile?"

JOSH BROUGHT his flashlight into the trunk of the car, and shone it around the clothes and luggage. He pulled some of the suitcases out, and the bags of clothes.

Then, he reached down and drew something out.

Bronwyn and Tammy huddled together, each with a burning stick in their hands.

Josh held up a small cylindrical object. "One flare, coming up."

BACK AT THE CAMPFIRE, he had to wrangle with it a bit to get it to work, and then when he snapped it, it shot out into the air.

A brilliant, ragged orange-yellow streak of light. He set it down on the ground.

They all looked at it.

"No one's going to help us," Tammy said. "No one."

Bronwyn glanced at her watch. "It's almost midnight. Maybe six hours till daylight."

"What good's daylight," Tammy said. "We'll be dead by then."

"We could start walking along the road."

"Someone will see that flare," Josh said.

"No one is going to see that flare unless they're looking for us. That monster is going to come back," Tammy said. "It's going to cut us all up. It...it...it." She hiccupped this last part.

"We should go to the road. We should start walking," Bronwyn said. "We can keep lighting sticks, one after another, and then drop them when they burn out. We have the flashlight."

"What if we walk the wrong way?" Josh asked.

"I'm not sure there is a wrong way."

"What if it's there, out there on the road?"

"I think it's gone," Bronwyn said. "Let's assume that it's the Flesh-Scraper. Let's assume it got enough flesh. Let's assume that's all it wanted."

Josh wanted to go to her and hold her—she looked haunted now. She looked as if she'd gone from being a young woman of twenty to being fifty. She looked as if she had enormous sorrow at the center of her being, and he wanted to make it better for her somehow.

But he was scared shitless, only he didn't want to talk about it. Just looking between Bronwyn and Tammy, he wasn't sure what the hell he could do. He wanted to cry out to his father and mother to come get him. He wanted to find someone to protect him, but when he looked at the two of them, some other instinct came out within him. He wasn't sure what to call it, other than something more than the will to survive. It was something that seemed to wrestle deep inside his mind, that made him want to protect his two friends, although he wasn't sure that was possible. But another part of him just wanted to be safe himself, to get away from this place, to somehow wake up from this nightmare.

Tammy leaned forward and tapped Bronwyn to pass another beer over. "Please, I need it," she said. Bronwyn opened two, passed one to her, and began drinking one of the cans herself. Tammy chugged this one also, and let her blanket slip. Josh was so stunned by the night's events that he barely noticed Tammy's nakedness beneath the blanket.

Tammy wiped at the blood on her face as if it were water. "That thing talked. I heard it."

Josh nodded. "I did, too."

"This fries my brain," Bronwyn said, sipping the beer. "Am I the only one who feels as if everything I ever heard of in life was a lie?"

"Maybe this is what happens before you die," Tammy said. "I've been bad in my life. Real bad. Maybe that's the Devil. Maybe that thing is the Devil. It sounded just like Griff. Poor Griff."

"It's the ritual," Josh said. "When Griff pushed me over, and I fell on it, it got some of my blood and some of my skin. That's what the sign said. You turn it on that way. And now, it's skinning them."

They all said nothing for several minutes, each one looking out into the darkness beyond the flickering fire.

"Where'd it get Ziggy?" Tammy asked.

Finally, Bronwyn broke the silence. "He's over there." She pointed to the blanket at the edge of where the fire-light stretched, opposite them.

"We never knew his real name," Josh said. "Just Ziggy."

"James Wallace," Bronwyn said. "I heard it on the first day of one of our classes. That's his name."

"James Wallace," Josh said. "Rest in peace."

Tammy closed her eyes and began saying the Lord's Prayer aloud.

"Stop it," Bronwyn said.

Tammy opened her eyes and turned to her. "You got something better? I think we need to call on a higher power."

"If God gave a rat's ass about us," Bronwyn said, "he'd never have created that thing in the first place."

A strange and probably insane light seemed to brighten Tammy's eyes. "Maybe that's it. Maybe this is God's way of giving us purpose."

"Say what?"

"Maybe we're meant to undergo this. Like a trial. When I used to go to revivals, they talked about how God tested you. How the Devil tempted...and you need to believe in Jesus's power. That's what we need."

"Well, I guess being the Jew here, I'm outta luck," Bronwyn said.

"No, just accept Jesus," Tammy said. She had a weird little smile on her face that Bronwyn wanted to slap out of her. "If you accept Jesus in your heart, it'll be okay. We can get out of this. Through Jesus."

"Oh Christ," Bronwyn said. "Just keep drinking the beer, Tammy."

"It takes on the voices of whoever it skins," Josh said.

Bronwyn said, "I say we start walking."

She pushed herself up from the ground. "We have fire. We have what's left of that flashlight battery. If we walk fast, we can do more than three miles per hour. Tammy, you run cross-country."

She nodded.

"We could even try to run," Bronwyn said. "At least some of the way. Maybe Jesus will help you run."

"Do not tempt the savior," Tammy said.

"When did you get so religious?" Bronwyn asked.

"Since I saw that thing tear Griff open. Since all this," Tammy said, still with that weird light on her face that made Josh and Bronwyn both think of the movie *Song of Bernadette*.

"Scratch moves pretty fast," Josh said, then noticed Bronwyn's arched eyebrows. "We're on a first-name basis."

"It might not even want us. But if we walk that-a-way," Bronwyn pointed to the road, "maybe we stand a chance."

"Not if it gets us," Tammy said, keeping her eyes on the fire.

"It might be full," Josh said, and felt a little sick thinking of this. "I mean, if I remember right, it said on those signs that it drank the blood and wore the skins and used the meat for food. I mean, spiders, when they eat one fly, they don't always eat more."

"Yeah, but they wrap them up for later," Bronwyn chortled, and then covered her mouth. "I can't believe I'm making a joke."

"You feel that, too? That lightheadedness?" Josh whispered as if it were a dirty secret.

Bronwyn nodded. "Yup. It must be shock."

Then, he got up and went to the outer ring of light and vomited. He came back, popped a beer open, and guzzled it. "I'm talking like a nutcase. Maybe it's shock. Maybe it's just insanity. Loony tunies. I got the looney tunies."

"We all have them," Bronwyn said. "What do we do. Sit here until it comes back?"

"The car," Josh said. "It's like a tank. We put a ring of fire around it, and we wait. That thing didn't break out through the trunk. It can't do that. We're safest in the car. Then, someone will have seen the flare, and will see the ring of fire around the car. And they'll come."

SOMEONE HAD SEEN the flare out in the middle of that desert hellhole:

Billy Dunne.

CHAPTER ELEVEN

B illy Dunne and Dave Olshaker, whose ass still stung from rock-salt shot out of Charlie Goodrow's shotgun, were staying at a Motel 69 five miles out of a town called Naga, a good fifteen miles from the Pimpmobile, off the two-lane road that ventured off the highway that had ventured—via several other roads—off the main highway. Billy was just coming back from picking up some burgers and fries from a local drive-through, and as he drove down a desolate one-lane road back to the highway, he saw in the distance a strange orange light, briefly. Back at Motel 69, he told Dave, who was in bed already watching *Mork & Mindy.* Dave went out to the parking lot, and Billy pointed to the general direction.

"It's gotta be them," Dave said, wolfing down his hamburger, with its sauce and mayo dribbling down his chin. "I know they're up there. We know they're outta gas. We gotta go find 'em, Billy."

"What do we do with them?" Billy asked.

Dave snarled, "First, we just grab Tammy and get the hell out of there."

"It was smart to siphon their tank," Billy said.

"It was a stroke of genius if I do say so myself," Dave Olshaker said.

THEIR EVENING HAD BEEN none too pleasant.

When they'd arrived at the Brakedown Palace, Dave had gone in after Tammy, and had left instructions for Billy to empty the Pimpmobile's gas tank so they couldn't take off too fast. Then, inside, the place had been empty, so he followed the long corridor out into the long Quonset hut, along the creepy trail to the final room where, suddenly, all hell was breaking loose, and Charlie Goodrow had begun shooting at everybody, Dave included, and got him right in the left butt cheek with a powerful spray of rock salt. At first, he thought he'd been hit with a real bullet, but then, with the stinging, he knew exactly what it was.

While Tammy and her jerk friends took off in their car, he was stuck behind with Charlie Goodrow, who threatened to call the police.

"Go ahead and call 'em," Dave had said. "Send 'em after those assholes. They should be thrown in jail for everything they've done."

Charlie Goodrow had looked at him long and hard, and set down his shotgun. "You're not with them?"

"Not hardly," Dave said. He pointed to Billy Dunne.

"Me and him's been tracking them, because the snake with the blond hair stole my girl right out from under me."

"They stole my attraction," Charlie Goodrow said. "But...well, I guess I shouldn't call the police just yet."

"Call 'em," Dave said. "Please. They deserve arresting."

But Charlie Goodrow, for some reason Dave couldn't figure out, wouldn't call the cops. He said something about things being better left alone sometimes. Something about worse things coming when good went after bad.

Instead, Goodrow told Dave and Billy to get the hell out of his gas station before he pulled the shotgun out again.

Then, Dave and Billy had decided they'd lost them for good. They got the motel room and figured they'd better turn around that night. "You don't need her," Billy said, his arm over his buddy's shoulder. "You can do better than her."

"Yeah, she's a bitch," Dave said, shrugging off his friend's arm. He didn't feel comfortable like that. It felt wrong.

But now, looking out at the dark night, after midnight, the sting in his ass didn't feel quite so bad. He thought of what he'd do to her if he had her. If he got her. First, he'd tie her wrists to the bed, then he'd strip her, using his teeth to tear her clothes off. Then, he'd give her what she wanted most from him. He got hard, standing there, thinking about it.

Then, he said, "Billy, let's get on up to those hills up there. We gotta track 'em down."

BILLY DUNNE FELT like he was driving in circles for nearly an hour before Dave looked ahead in the dark and pointed to something off another road to the west. "Look, that must be them," he said. Billy glanced over and saw what looked like a fire off the road. "This is too easy," Dave said. "They're stranded. They got nothin'. My dream's coming true, Billy. Truer than true."

Billy swerved and made a U-turn, and went west on a slender, barely paved road and then went north. He nearly hit a coyote as he drove, and he thought for just a second that he felt Dave's hand on his knee.

CHAPTER TWELVE

J osh had just finished positioning some rocks and dry sticks about ten feet away from the Pimpmobile. Then, he helped Tammy arrange some on the other side. She'd dressed again, at first scared to reach into the trunk, but he'd used the flashlight to show her that no monsters lurked there. Then, they'd set to work, and in some respects, setting up the circle of fire as a perimeter around the Pimpmobile took all their minds off the terror that was somewhere out in the desert.

"Maybe it's over," Tammy said. She sat on the hood of the car, cross-legged. The fires comforted her.

"Could be," Josh said.

"Someone has to feed the fire," Bronwyn said.

"We'll take turns." Then, he noticed the doubtful look on Bronwyn's face. "Someone will see this. There's a town within twenty miles of here. The flare went up. Now we have a large fire."

"They may just think it's a fire. Nobody lives up here.

Nobody cares if there's a fire," Bronwyn said. "There's not enough to burn."

"That's not true," Josh said. "Fires on the desert can get out of control. It can be devastating if it spreads. Someone will see this from a distance. I bet you can see it for miles."

"We can't see a town. I'm not sure they can see us."

"Someone's driving out there. Someone's on the roads. They'll see it and stop somewhere and maybe call the police," he said. "You have to believe."

"I believe," Tammy said. "I believe that Jesus Christ is my personal savior and is the son of the everlasting God."

"Good for you," Josh said.

"I'll pray for all of us," Tammy said.

When Josh went around to make sure there was some dry brush to toss in one of the fires, Bronwyn followed him. "I didn't want to say this in front of her."

"What's that?"

"Josh. How can this be happening? Can you tell me?" She seemed like a little girl now, even with the cigarette hanging out of her mouth. "How is this humanly possible?"

"I guess it's not," he said.

She smoked some more, giving him a strange look that surprised him.

"Can you hold me?" she asked. "Right now. I know it's..."

She was about to say "weird," he was sure, but he didn't let her get to that word.

He went over to her and put his arms around her. She laid her head against his shoulder and began sobbing.

"We'll get through this," he whispered, smelling her hair and feeling weak and strong at the same time.

TAMMY WAS the first to get sleepy, and Josh promised her that he'd stand guard. Then, he told Bronwyn to go sleep for a bit, also. "We have the fire, we know it doesn't like fire. It's not going to cross over to the car. But if it did, you're inside a metal cage in that car. I doubt obsidian claws can even get through a car door," he said.

"Only if you sit in the car, too," she said. "I want you safe."

Tammy and Bronwyn lay together across the backseat, using blankets and rolled-up clothes as pillows. Josh sat up front, his one hand on the gun, his other on the Bic lighter as if this would help ward off Scratch. He kept looking around, feeling like he heard things. He didn't know what good it would do, but he locked the doors. Then, he felt sleepy, but fought it. All the beer had done a number on him, and he felt exhausted and drained on top of that—but he didn't want to sleep. Not that night. He was going to stay awake. He could sleep all day long if he had to, once they got to safety.

Then, suddenly, without even thinking he'd closed his eyes: He was on a waterbed that undulated with gentle waves, and Bronwyn and Tammy were there, too. They were both naked, kissing each other sweetly, nothing too dirty, and playing innocently with each other's breasts.

Then, Tammy reached over and grabbed his hand and brought it down between her legs. Then, they were not naked at all, nor were they the two women from his college. Instead, he was back home, and it was his mother and his aunt who took his hands and were taking him to school.

His aunt said, "You never told us that you didn't pass your Chemistry final."

"But I did," he said, or tried to, but no one seemed to hear him. His mother gave him a stern look and let go of his hand. Suddenly he was back in high school, but it wasn't even full of high school students—instead, the children looked as if they were nine or ten. He was in elementary school—he was sure of it. How had this happened? He tried to tell the teacher who came to get him that he was already in college, that he shouldn't have to go back to the fifth grade, but the teacher—Mrs. Raleigh, who had once humiliated him in school—told him he needed to mind his Ps and Qs.

"But this isn't right!" he shouted. "I'm almost twenty."

The other kids in the class ignored his shouts.

Then, he noticed something even worse:

He wore no pants. He sat there in his shirt, but no trousers, no underwear. Hanging out. And no one said anything. Why hadn't his mother noticed? How could she have let him leave the house without his pants on? Without something on? He tried to pull his shirt down over his balls, but it wouldn't go far enough.

Someone began banging at the window of the classroom. Someone yelled at him.

Josh opened his eyes, wrenched from the dream.

TAMMY HAD ALREADY BEGUN SCREAMING—NOT just screaming, it was like the sound cats made when they were in heat, it was a wail that barely sounded human. Bronwyn was up, and apparently had been shaking Josh.

"It's gonna get us!" Tammy screamed. "Oh my god, it's gonna kill us!"

But Josh saw headlights out the window. And then, like a nightmare come true, Dave Olshaker's face suddenly appeared against the windshield. "Hey, you losers! How's it hangin'?"

"GET OUT OF HERE!" Bronwyn shouted.

"How the hell did they get here?" Josh said, still wondering if this might be an extension of his dream.

Bronwyn had to slap Tammy to get her to stop the scream. Dave and his buddy were shaking the car up and down, trying the doors, running around the car.

"We should tell them," Bronwyn said.

"Are you crazy? Keep your doors locked. That guy's insane," Josh said. He had already dropped the gun on the floor of the Pimpmobile.

Dave was shouting, "Tammy! You're coming with me, baby! Do you understand?"

"Don't let him take me," Tammy said.

"They have a car," Josh said. "Oh my god. We can get out."

Bronwyn rolled her window down slightly. "Hey! Guys! We know you're mad. We know it. But there's some kind of..." She paused, unsure of what to say. "There's a killer out here. We need help."

"Griff is dead!" Tammy shouted. "Griff is dead!"

It probably was this cry that stopped Dave Olshaker in his tracks. He and Billy Dunne looked at each other for a second, then Dave started laughing.

"Oh my god," Bronwyn said. Josh looked back at her. She was looking up toward the headlights of the pickup truck. "They ruined part of our fire. Part of the ring we made."

"So?" He turned and saw the break in the circle of fire.

"What if it's been out there? Waiting? Just outside the fire?"

"No, it's not," Josh said.

But just as quickly, they all heard a woman's high-pitched scream, and Josh looked at Tammy but her mouth was closed.

It was Billy Dunne.

Or rather, it wasn't Billy Dunne.

He had been there, standing just in the headlights in front of the Pimpmobile, and suddenly, he was gone.

They heard a thud beneath the car.

Dave Olshaker glanced around the car, stepping back from it.

Inside the car, they were silent.

Then, Josh said, "Just go away. Just go."

"Billy?" Dave walked around the car. "Billy?"

"We've got to let him in," Josh said, leaning over to unlock the driver's-side door.

"No," Tammy said. "Don't let him in." She had a curious anger in her voice.

"Dave!" Josh shouted. "Dave, come around here, get in!"

But Dave Olshaker was looking around the car, crouching down as if checking under it.

"Don't let him in," Tammy said.

"Tammy?" Bronwyn asked, softly.

"He did something bad to me," she said. "Maybe this is what happens to bad people. Maybe…"

"Dave!" Josh said, rolling his window all the way down, signaling for Olshaker to get over there. He was about to open his door to pull Dave in, when suddenly they all heard it.

The voice from under the car.

"DAVY BABY," Billy Dunne's voice rasped. "Sweetie, come to Daddy. You know you love me, Davy, all hidden away inside you. I love you, too, we can love each other here, down here."

"What in God's name?" Dave said, still crouching.

"Don't let him in, Josh," Tammy spat. "Let it happen to him. Let it. Maybe bad people get what's coming to them."

"Shut up," Bronwyn said. "Just shut up."

"Dave! Get in this car right now! There's some kind of…some…that thing. That thing from the gas station. It's there. It's alive. It's…" But even as Josh said this, he knew it was too late.

He looked out his window. Dave, still crouching, glanced up at him, his eyes wide with an emotion that seemed to exist between fear and awe. Dave began stammering, and pointing underneath the car. It seemed to happen in slow motion, as Dave pointed and looked at Josh and his mouth began moving as if trying to get something out.

And then Scratch leapt out from beneath the car, its black hooks going to Dave's eyes. In the car, everyone was screaming, and Josh reached on the floor for the gun, hoping it would help, and then he tried to get his door open, but it was locked, and by the time he reached around for the lock, Dave's face had smushed up against Bronwyn's window. The two women screamed again as the bloody face slid down the window to the ground.

Then, Josh locked his door, rolled up his window.

And they waited. It was quiet for a long time.

The headlights from the pickup truck illuminated them as if it were nearly daylight.

They heard a thump or two beneath the car.

Tammy began praying softly, her hands pressed together, her eyes closed. Josh glanced at Bronwyn, but neither said anything.

And then, they saw something come out from under the front of the car that sent shivers down Josh's spine.

The creature emerged in the headlight's beam. Billy Dunne's face over its skull, his lips torn and flapping. It began a strange, slow dance that reminded Josh of an image he'd seen of Kali, the Indian goddess, who danced with skulls around her neck. The creature's arms went out at odd angles, and its legs moved around in wide arcs.

It's doing its dance, he thought. This is its ceremony. It

drinks the blood and wears the skin. It dances in the skin. It makes the sacrifice dance for the gods.

Josh felt Bronwyn's hand on his shoulder. It felt good, in the face of this. He needed her warmth.

They watched the strange, intricate, bizarre dance as the bloodied creature, wearing the tissue-thin skin of either Billy Dunne or Dave Olshaker, moved to the unheard music.

Then, it stopped.

It's watching us. It's waiting for us. Why? What is it waiting for?

A sound came from it. Not Dave's voice or Billy's voice or Griff's or even Ziggy's.

It was a sound that seemed more wild animal than human, yet it had a human cast to it. The creature began singing, raising its skin-hung arms in the air, skyward.

"Dear God," Tammy gasped. "Dear God."

The creature sang a tuneless melody that consisted of mainly open vowel sounds of ohs and ows, a slightly musical howl and shriek, but Josh was sure it was saying something.

"Why is it doing that?" Bronwyn asked as if any of them would know.

"It has a ceremony to fulfill," Josh said. "A ritual. It dances in their skins, and then it sings to its namesake god. That's what it said at the Brakedown Palace. On the signs. There's the sacrifice, then there's the ceremony."

And even as he said this, he thought he heard the god's name in the song, *Xipe Totec, Xipe Totec.*

What was it for? Why did it do this? For the first time, Josh wondered if there wasn't some insane logic to the creature's ritual. It wasn't just a monster from nowhere. It had been stolen from its resting place, somewhere in Mexico. It had been wrenched from its burial ground, and brought up here by some moron who decided to make a buck off it—or seventy-five cents—and forget that it was sacred.

He said it aloud. "Scratch is sacred."

"What?" Bronwyn asked, as if he were losing more marbles than he had moments before.

"That thing is a representation of a god. Xipe Totec. The Flayer of Men. We're seeing an ancient ceremony."

"Christ, you're starting to make sense."

"I don't know what good it does us unless you can remember what was on those signs. What else was written there," Josh said.

"We can make it to the pickup truck," Tammy said. "If we run. We can."

"No," Josh said. "We can't. It's too far. That thing is right there, Tammy."

"If all three of us go," Tammy said. "It'll only get one of us."

"Who will it be? You? Me? Bron? You can live with that?"

"Either that or we all die sitting here."

"We're safe here," Josh said. He reached back over his seat and touched her gently on the knee. "Tammy, just hang in there. I don't think it can get in the car. It may need darkness for its ritual. It may not be after us when the sun's out."

"Or maybe it just doesn't stop," Tammy said. "What about that? Maybe it'll be morning soon and that thing will still be waiting to get us. Or maybe it'll figure out how to scratch its way through the car. Maybe."

"Tammy, listen to Josh," Bronwyn said. "We've all been through a big shock. But it hasn't gotten to us here."

"The battery in that truck is going to die. Sometime in the next hour or two," Tammy said. "If we don't get out and make a run for it, we may never get out of here. We are already dead, if you think about it. We just haven't had our moment with that monster."

The singing in front of the car continued, and the creature they had all begun to think of as Scratch waved its claws to the sky as if talking directly to its god.

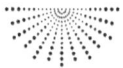

CHAPTER THIRTEEN

Perhaps an hour went by before the headlights of Dave Olshaker's truck flickered a bit. Then, they dimmed. Scratch had gone off into the darkness somewhere, and Josh guessed that it was either under the pickup or under the Pimpmobile.

"We can sit here and die, or..." Tammy said, after they'd all been too quiet and too tense and too watchful for too long. It was a surprise to hear her voice.

More of a surprise, she opened her door and jumped out in the dirt, slamming the door behind her.

Before they could say anything, she was running in the dimming headlights for the pickup truck. Josh held his breath, watching her, but he was sure he saw her open the driver's door and slam it again. He heard her shouts of joy. "I'm inside! I'm inside!"

And then, she flicked on the truck's interior light to see the layout of keys and pedals.

And Bronwyn said what Josh was thinking. "Oh shit. Oh shit!"

The truck was moving forward, toward them, and Tammy had a big grin on her face like all her prayers had been answered.

But Bronwyn and Josh both saw some little movement in the back of the cab of the truck.

It was in there, with her.

Josh opened his door, with Bronwyn shouting at him. He ran toward the truck. By the time he reached Tammy's side, Scratch had already begun throwing her around, and when Josh opened the door, it had dragged her out the opposite window, trailing blood.

The whole time, Tammy hadn't screamed. He was sure the last look on her face had been not one of terror, but of submission.

She hadn't even fought.

Perhaps she couldn't have fought.

He'd never know.

Then, twenty minutes later, out in the darkness, they heard Tammy's last shrill scream, although they couldn't be sure if it was Tammy, or simply Scratch imitating her voice.

Josh ran back to the Pimpmobile, and had to pull Bronwyn out of the backseat. "We can get out, let's go," he said. They ran back to the truck, climbing up, sat on the seat, and Josh put the truck in first gear, and it moved forward.

"It's over," Bronwyn said. "We can go. We can get help. Oh thank god."

But they got just about a mile past the ring of fire they'd created, and the pickup truck died.

"It's the battery," he said.

The headlights dimmed to nothingness. They rolled up both windows, locked the doors, checked to make sure everything in the cab was secure.

Exhausted, they folded into one another. Josh managed to close his eyes for a few minutes and not think of the horror.

Now and then, he awoke, because Scratch's claws raked around the side of the pickup truck. They had no light. He'd left the gun and flashlight back in the Pimpmobile. Maybe the Bic lighter was something, but he didn't want to waste it.

It was only two hours until dawn. He and Bronwyn sat up, and kept watch, but Bronwyn told him it might be better if they slept. "Maybe in our sleep, when it kills us, it won't be so bad."

"WHAT IF THIS IS IT?" Bronwyn asked. It was still dark—an endless night.

"It what?"

"It. Our last night on this earth. What if we don't get out. What if that thing kills us both?"

"You can't believe it. You can't. There's a way."

"I wonder if Griff thought that. Or Tammy. Or Ziggy." She lit what must've been her twentieth cigarette of the night. "It's like we're drowning in the ocean and there's a great white shark coming at us. Instead of water, all this desert. What if this is it?"

Then, she lowered the cigarette and leaned into him. Kissed him. Her lips were soft, dry, and yet somehow he felt moistened by them. She looked at him steadily. She no longer looked like a college girl. She no longer looked like a girl he was interested in. She looked like a woman who was preparing for something. And he knew what it was. Not death. But sex. Warmth. Lust.

Something human and animal, hot and cold at the same time, something nearly predatory, seemed to take over within him. He kissed her again, tasting the ashes of her smoky breath, and then he reached around and held her, pressing himself close, and she moved gently against him.

If his mind warned him against this, it somehow froze in silence, and his body took over. They wrapped around each other, and she pushed him backward. She was all over him, and he scrambled against her, and soon they were thrusting, and licking, as uncomfortable as the truck was, and it was like his dream: the two of them in a great green forest. He entered her body, he felt an intense, warm, wet embrace, and it shot the feeling up his spine right into his skull—a ripple of lightning—as she tossed and twisted her body to accommodate him and enjoy the breadth of his flesh. He kissed her neck as she twisted around so that he was now behind her, grasping her breasts in his hands, his lower body thrusting faster and faster, and she was moaning and whispering "yeah, oh, yeah, oh, oh," and then a slamming wave of thrusts ended as he reached his climax, as she reached hers, as they fell on top of each other, sweaty, burning, drained, full.

Afterward, he remembered too much, and drew back from her. Had it been a dream, after all? Had he dreamt that he'd made love to her? He wasn't sure. Was that what people did when monsters were after them? They took a break to mate? They bonded sexually so that they could face death more easily? He felt older than he wanted to feel. He felt as if he'd crossed some great chasm in life— and looking back at his life before that night, it had all seemed pampered and silly and wasteful. Life and death were too important to play around with now. Even college seemed ridiculous—another ceremonial dance like the one Scratch had done for them. It was nothing when compared to life and the struggle to survive one single night when faced with danger. He went to pull his clothes back on, and she came up behind him, kissing him on the neck. "I'm glad we did that," she said.

"Me, three," he joked.

"You love me, don't you?"

He didn't respond. Then, he thought better of it. "I don't know. Maybe."

"I'm sorry. It's not good to be in love at a time like this." Then, she laughed. "Oh my god, the sun!"

And it was true. To the east, a lighter purple came up, bringing with it a misty halo around the mesas and mountains.

"I don't want to die!" she shouted to the still-lingering dark blue sky.

"Me, neither!" he shouted.

"I want to live, goddamn it!"

"Me, too!"

"I want to get middle-aged and fat and watch bad TV and raise four kids into neurotic adults, and I want to see China and learn how to water ski!"

"I want to grow old and die in a nursing home!" he

shouted. "No, I want to die when I step off the curb in a
big city, and a crazy taxi driver comes out of nowhere and
hits me so that I bounce off the rest of the cars going too
fast through the yellow light!"

"I want to die with my head in a bowl of green pea
puree, with my Depends on, with only three teeth in my
mouth!" she shouted, laughing.

Then, they got quiet again.

He closed his eyes, and said a prayer.

"Know what?"

"What's that?"

"This is a bad dream," she said. "I bet that's all it is. I
bet I'm sleeping on the lawn, with you. Hungover. I bet
it's the Saturday we left campus. The bitch of it is trying to
wake up."

The day had officially begun, with the sun stretching
molten gold an hour later. Heat came up too suddenly.

Bronwyn took a drag off the cigarette. Rolled down
the window.

"Bron, it may still be out there," he said.

"It's a creature of the night, that's what the sign said,
'the Sun God is its enemy.'" She grinned, and then looked
a little grim. He practically could read her mind: it was
ridiculous to feel happy after the carnage. But they did.
Both of them did. They'd survived the night. She held her
cigarette up in the morning air. She leaned back and
looked up at the vague sun, melted as it was into a pure
yellow sky.

"If it's still out here, maybe it's sleeping."

"It doesn't sleep," she said. She puffed out dragon

breath. Sucked on the cigarette until it nearly disappeared between her lips. "I wonder what it's all about?"

"The creature?"

"No," she said, her voice carrying the quality of Ziggy when he was at his most stoned. She was ragged, and when he looked at her, he thought she was beautiful despite the circles around her eyes and the skin drawn tight around her lips. "No, you know how life is this thing? This thing that you grow up doing because you think one day…one day you'll get to this…I don't know…"

"Wisdom?"

"Yeah. Wisdom. Knowledge. You've known something because there's this key you turn, and you don't get the key or even know which door to go to when you're a kid. You assume grown-ups have it. You assume education brings it to you. Or experience. And then, here we are. You believe in God, don't you?"

"Sometimes."

"I don't. Not at all. I used to think all religion was just bullshit. But after last night, I started thinking that maybe people came up with God and religion to give us hope. That hope isn't a real thing, but people need it because otherwise… otherwise, life is just this jungle where you wait to see what ends up jumping out of nowhere and eating you. And you have God, you have order. You have a reason. You have hope."

"Sometimes when I'm not sure I believe in God, I think of goodness."

She glanced over at him.

"That's all God is. Goodness. A belief that there's a

goodness here. On Earth. That it's our job to find it. To create it. To keep it going. Like something you hold in your hand. If you want to. And it means fighting sometimes. It means standing up to darkness."

Bronwyn sat up, leaning forward. "On that note, I have to go take a leak," she said.

She opened the door, and slid down out of the truck.

He gasped for a second, his heart seeming to leap out of his chest. But nothing happened. No Scratch showed up suddenly, its claws extended.

Then, she squatted down beside the truck. "Don't see any monsters under here," she said. He looked the other way to give her a little privacy. He had to pee, too, so he got out and went around, peeing on a sagebrush.

Then, they found the cooler with Coke and even some Twinkies in the back of the truck. They devoured these like it was the finest meal in existence.

Then, they saw the siphon and the red plastic gas tank sitting at one end of the truck.

"Wow," he said.

"Wow is right," she added. "I guess we have Dave to thank for this."

"We're all to blame," he said. "All of us."

"WE'RE PROBABLY GOING TO DIE," she said, mid-Twinkie.

"Everybody dies."

They had begun walking back to the Pimpmobile to put what Josh had called "Plan B" into effect. He lugged the full plastic gas container, and she held the siphon and an extra Twinkie.

"Is that okay by you?" she asked.

"No. It's not okay. Today is not our day to die. That's all I know," Josh said. "This is not the day."

"They're all dead. All of them," she said.

"Maybe last night was their night. Maybe it was," Josh said. He swallowed a little dust, but felt better. Felt fear leaving his body as if through sheer force of will. "I'm not going to give in to this. We are alive now. We have some water. It can't be more than twenty miles out to the highway. Twenty miles is something we can do. Two gallons of gas will get us there."

"It's going to be hot as hell in an hour. Or less."

"So we'll get sunburnt."

"And it's going to find us."

"We don't know that. Are you just going to wait around, Bronwyn? Are you going to just sit there and let that thing tear you up like you were bait for a mountain lion? Think of it as a mountain lion. Don't get psyched by its claws. Or how we saw it at that gas station. We haven't seen it fly. It hasn't grown nine feet tall. It's little. Sure, it's fast. It's smart, maybe. Maybe not. But whatever you and I have, whatever is buried inside us that's going to come out someday…someday, years from now…I mean, what if you are destined to be a hero of life? What if I am? What if you go on to medical school and get into research and become the first doctor to cure cancer? What if I go on to write the book that changes lives? Is it worth us giving up now to this stupid little nasty monstrous…piece of shit? Are we going to let it win just because we're afraid? Are we?"

She stopped and took a step back, looking at him in a way that made him feel as if he were from another planet. "I've never seen you like this."

He sighed, but felt a steely resolve take him over. "I've never had to be like this."

Everything hurt inside him, every bit of him felt raw and raked, but he latched his mind onto the idea that this must be done no matter what.

Then, the Pimpmobile came into view.

Bronwyn dropped the siphon when she saw what had happened to it.

CHAPTER FOURTEEN

S cratch had been busy in the night. The Pimpmobile's doors were off their hinges. The trunk was open, and all the crap from it was spread out on the ground.

Worse, as they got closer, the interior was ripped to shreds, and wires had been pulled and cut.

And the keys were gone.

"You know," Bronwyn said. "I think we'd better start walking while we still have Twinkies in us."

Josh set down the gas, and sat on the shredded back-seat and began weeping like a baby. "It's all bullshit," he said. "We're no heroes. We're just fucked. That's all we are. Fucked."

Bronwyn put her arms around him and whispered, "Come on. Let's go. We'll get away from it. We have the whole day."

HE FELT BETTER on the walk. He kept apologizing for his

little breakdown, and she kept telling him to shut up about it.

"Okay, what do we know about it?" he asked.

"It skins people, " she said. "Oh, and it woke up because of your blood. "

"Yeah." Josh grimaced. "I hate thinking about that."

"What do you mean?"

"Nothing," he said.

"It's not nothing. Tell me."

"I think maybe...maybe it's connected to me now. Because of my blood."

"Bullshit."

"Maybe I'm wrong," he said.

THEY WALKED SIDE BY SIDE, Bronwyn with a slight limp, and she leaned on him now and then. She guesstimated a general southwesterly direction to the main highway, although all they could see for miles was more desert and mesas and arroyos and caverns and mountains in nearly every direction.

They stuck to the road.

"You studied the Aztecs, didn't you?" he asked.

"I read a book. I didn't exactly study them. I just don't remember the details," she said. "Anyway, I'm not sure this is some Aztec monster. It's easy to blame the Aztecs for everything. It's what history books do."

"Let's assume it's Aztec-ish, anyway."

"Okay."

"Remember. Force yourself to remember. You have to."

She stopped, closed her eyes.

"I can't."

"You can. What was on the cover?"

"An Aztec calendar."

"Good. So it was a round flat stone and had a face on it."

"Something like that."

"First page?"

"I don't think that thing is really from the ancient Aztecs," she said. "It's something else. They just made up all that stuff."

"Well, we know it hates the sun. And it loves the dark. And it skins people. And drinks blood."

"Oh I know," she said, "it's a vampire."

"I only wish," he said.

They continued walking, and he pointed out a snake moving along the edge of the road, so they stepped to the side, but kept walking.

"All right. It had a job. It skinned those who had been sacrificed. What about the ritual?"

"I just don't know."

"Try."

After another ten minutes, she said, "All right. Okay. It was an obsidian dagger. Used for the sacrificial victims. Tore their hearts out. The blood was like rain. They let the blood rain down because it was to encourage rain and the crops. The Flesh-Scraper was used to get the skin off."

"To wear it," Josh said, solemnly.

"Right."

"And somehow, it fed off Griff first. Was it blood?"

"I think so. I don't know."

"It'd make sense if it was blood."

"Wait," Bronwyn said. "Wait."

She stopped.

"Rain," she said. "Rain. Water. Liquid. It needs it. It's not just taking their skin. It drank them. It drained them. It needs water—water in the blood. It's a desert here. It needs water. It brings rain. That's its ritual."

"That was a rain dance? Last night? But why?"

"Maybe it doesn't like it too hot and dry," she said, shrugging her shoulders. "Its enemy *is* the Sun God."

"THIS ROAD IS ENDLESS," she said.

"Thank god," he said.

"Have we been walking for hours?"

"Feels like it."

"You thirsty?"

He nodded. "Mean thirsty."

"We must've gone twenty miles by now," she said.

"At least."

"Wrong direction," she said, too sadly. She pointed ahead.

He looked up—he'd been mainly watching the road for snakes and lizards.

The road ended in a dusty nothingness.

"We're not very bright," Josh said. He was soaked with sweat, exhausted, and had begun to wish he'd just stayed back at Dave Olshaker's pickup truck.

"Wait," she said. "Wait! Oh my god! Oh my god!" Bronwyn began jumping up and down. "Where the road ends! Oh my god, Josh! Josh!"

She was so gleeful he thought she'd gone insane for good.

Then, she began running to the west, across what looked like a well-beaten dirt path.

He looked in the direction where she'd run. Something shiny over the rise of land.

She stopped, turning around. She cupped her hands to her mouth and shouted, "Ely! He told us! He said he lives where the road ends! Do you hear it? I can. I can hear his ZZ Top records! He's playing them! Oh my god, Josh, we're safe! We're safe!"

Her enthusiasm lasted three more miles, and the closer they got, the more they glimpsed the hubcaps outside a large shack with a trailer behind it. ZZ Top's "Tush" played from within the house, and they went to the front door, rapping at it.

After a while, the truck driver—who had given them a lift to the Brakedown Palace—opened the door.

CHAPTER FIFTEEN

An hour later, something the entire town of Naga believed was a miracle occurred.

It began raining.

At first, it was a small trickle of rain, and then clouds swiftly overtook the fire of the sun. Thunder was heard in the mesas, and a bitter storm swept the desert.

Josh slept, his arms around Bronwyn, and when night came, he went out into the rain with Ely, who asked him what had happened to his friends. He lied. He wasn't ready to tell him about the night.

Bronwyn came out a bit later, standing beneath the eaves of the little house, watching the storm as it blew across the night sky.

"We can't leave it there," Josh said. "It's loose, now. You think the cops will believe us? You think anyone will?"

For just a moment, she looked empty. That was the best way he thought of it. She looked as if there was nothing to her at all. All she wanted to do was get away.

Even from him. She just wanted to run in the opposite direction, even if it meant Scratch would hunt others.

"Go on," he said. "You can call your dad. Get him to wire you money. Rent a car or catch a bus. And go on. But this creature's out there. I can't just go back to life and forget that. What if people go out and camp there? What if Scratch is just waiting for them?"

Her shoulders fell, slack. She looked down at her hands, then up to his face.

"Tomorrow morning, go," he said. "I don't blame you."

She didn't blink.

She wasn't going to stay behind; he saw it in her eyes.

"I think you should come, too. You are not obligated to deal with that thing. It's a monster, Josh. We can get help. We can…"

"Nope. I think there's a way to stop it. I think there's a way to end this. I need to try something."

"I don't want you…" she began. He knew how that sentence finished: *to die.*

"We all die, Bron. We die. Life is a short space of time. Some people die young, some die at middle age, some die old. We're lucky if it's swift. We're lucky if it's only seconds of pain. We're lucky if what's between when we're born and when we die is a powerful thing. A miraculous thing. I never believed in miracles. Before. I never believed that the goodness of the universe existed. But I know it does. I don't believe for a minute that we've gone through this night because life is horrible. Or because monsters rule. Or because we're meant to. I believe this is a test. This is a test, and to pass it, to find out who each of us truly is, we have to stand up to this thing. We have to stop it. Because not stopping it is just letting the bad things happen. For me, not stopping it is worse than getting killed."

"You're going to die out there. Please, Josh. Please. Don't be the next victim…"

"I am not going to sacrifice myself," he said. "I know I can stop it. I know it. Here's how I was living before this, Bron. I was living as if nothing mattered. As if life were a joke. As if it didn't matter if I was happy or sad or did nothing or did something. I was on disconnect. But last night showed me. Life is about something. We are about something. I am. And I know I can stop it."

"Please don't die," she said, quietly. Calmly. "Don't be some kind of hero."

"I am going to do what I know I have to do," he said. "We woke that thing up. My blood fed it. I have to put it back to sleep."

JOSH BOUGHT the little souvenir at a shop in downtown Naga.

Ely loaned him his busted-up Civic, and Josh drove around trying to gather what he thought might help. He went to the library in Naga and read a little in the reference section. He felt foolish and doomed, but something inside him—some engine—had begun to turn over. Something had changed within him from that one terrible night.

The rain continued into his second evening at Ely's. Bronwyn had already gotten on a bus headed for Los

Angeles, and although she told him she loved him, he knew now that it wasn't love. It was simply attraction and situation. Love was something else. He hoped to have it someday, but it wasn't a feeling you could hand over to someone. It was deeper than that. He wished her the best, kissed her goodbye, and he told her he would stop Scratch so that no one else would ever get hurt.

As he watched the bus disappear in the distance, he thought of that line from her poem: *The kiln of her skull explodes; a hundred broken memories burn.*

LATER, he sat down with Ely and told him everything except the truth. Josh refused to let another person who was either friend or foe die because they'd let Scratch out of its cage.

IN PRIVATE, he withdrew the item from the sack he'd bought the day before.

Probably not an authentic Native American design, but made to look like one.

Tourist crap, no doubt.

The stone was carved to a point.

An arrowhead.

Made out of obsidian.

Obsidian was the translucent dark stone used in the Aztec ritual.

The dagger went into the heart. Something like that.

He wasn't sure how it was done. But the heart was brought up, spraying blood.

The Flayer of Men, the Flesh-Scraper, then skinned the bodies.

And wore the skin.

Obsidian was sacred.

It had magical properties.

And even the avatar of Xipe Totec, Mr. Scratch, would have something resembling a heart.

Some engine that ran him.

Sure, he thought. Maybe it was all roadside attraction bullshit. Mystical babble that some asshole had written up to get tourist dollars off the highway.

He held the arrowhead in his hand. It felt cool against his hot skin.

Please. I don't believe in anything other than the goodness of the universe. Let it be here. Let it be with me now. Give me the strength to stop this abomination.

Without even knowing why, Josh fell to his knees, clutching the arrowhead. He closed his eyes.

Whatever I have in me. Whatever there is beside flesh and blood and molecules and nerves and bone. Let it come out in me. Let it come through me. In the name of Griff and Ziggy and Tammy and Dave. And that other guy.

Dave's friend.

In the name of them, and their memories. Their lives. Their life forces.

And my own.

Give me the power.

The knowledge.

The ability.

To stop this creature.

HE DROVE BACK up the road that ended, and found the Pimpmobile.

The rain had stopped hours before. The sun beat down on his scalp and the back of his neck. He got up after a bit, feeling slightly dizzy.

He went down and sat under a manzanilla tree—a gathering of bleached sticks more than a tree, but it provided a very slight shade.

He drew down one of the dried branches and began creating the weapon.

Within a few hours, it looked good.

The arrowhead was tied—stripped from his belt, which he'd shredded. The tree branch was smooth and white—an imperfect spear.

He tried throwing it, but his aim sucked. He felt weak, and sleepy, and knew he needed to rest if he were to fight in the darkness.

He slept, using his shirt and jeans as a makeshift tent, propped up between rocks and sticks and scrub.

It was boiling, but at least for a bit, the bright searing eye of the sun was not upon him.

Josh's dreams came fast and feverish—

They were dragging him up the long steps, up the pyramid. Only it wasn't a real pyramid. It was like a cartoon. It was like someone had made it up, and hastily drew the stones and the shadowy people who dragged him upward.

Then, they stood over him—Ziggy, Griff, and Tammy —and held him down against a wide stone bowl. Above him, the faces of Charlie Goodrow and Dave Olshaker. Their big greasy mugs looking down at him, while someone else raised a shiny black knife just over his head.

When it thrust down, he screamed, and Charlie Goodrow brought up a big mass of pulsating red, and crowed, "He's a gusher! Lookit that! The boy gushes like a goddamn sweet Texas oil field!"

Josh's blood sprayed up, peppering their faces, splashing their features until all of them were red. Josh thrashed, wanted his heart back, but felt no real pain.

Someone began playing a strange kind of reed instrument, and a drum began beating slowly. The voice of some unseen creature sang a strange, unmelodic song.

Although it was in another language, Josh possessed an understanding:

Flayer of Men
Bring us your rainfall
We give you blood
Bring us life!
We offer flesh for scraping
To you alone—
Flayer of Men
Dance in his skin
Dance so that children may be born!
Dance so that the crops will grow!
Dance so that the sun will not burn your people!
Dance and be reborn in blood and life, from your dark sleep!

JOSH SEEMED to float along the flat stone floor within the pyramid, lit by torches, and watched as the Flayer of Men scraped the skin, using long needle-like talons, carefully drawing the top layer of flesh from the meat, and pressing it, blood still dripping, against his shadowy face.

Josh drew closer to look at the eyes of the Scraper, but they were empty sockets, and Josh realized he was looking at his own skin, laid across the Flesh-Scraper's small body, wrapped and sewn together.

The Flayer began to move oddly, side to side—a dance of life and death, wearing the skin of the sacrifice. Its eyes became his eyes, its face, his face. The Flesh-Scraper began to look just like Josh himself.

Suddenly, Josh no longer watched this dance, but was inside, behind the skin, looking out.

CHAPTER SIXTEEN

J osh awoke.

It was night.

He sat up, feeling the dryness at his lips and the scaliness in his throat.

We are connected, he thought. *Me, with the Flayer of Men.*

By my blood.

It knows me.

HE WAITED A LONG TIME, until he heard the scraping sound.

The only light was the luminescence of the white sand of the desert, the enormous blue-faded moon in the sky, and the stars, which, as he looked up at them, seemed to him so far away as to be unconcerned with the problems of a man of nineteen, in the middle of a wasteland, waiting for a monster.

THE GASPING SOUND CAME FIRST, then the sound of something being dragged.

Then, against the whiteness, he saw a small dark form.

Running between bits of brush and clutches of cactus.

He felt a lump form in his throat. He wondered if a person could genuinely die of fright.

HE KNEW Scratch's hunting method, now. He knew the little mummy liked to get the scares going. It was its ritual. Get the scares going, make a big to-do, get people on the edge of their seats, and then, strike.

He felt his nerves jangling, and wondered if prey animals experienced this just before an eagle or owl swooped down, or a mountain lion neared.

He felt like prey, and it brought with it that strange sensation he'd felt before:

That somehow he was more alive now. That this monster, this evil, horrible thing, could make him more aware of every cell in his body, right down to his toes, and the electrical whirring beneath the skin of his fingers.

AS HE SAT THERE, thinking all this, feeling it, he felt the first scrape of talon along his ankle.

He reached back for his weapon.

The obsidian arrowhead, tied to the nearly smooth stick.

The hunt had begun.

A SECOND SCRAPE at his ankle took away an outer layer of skin. Bleeding. Hurt like hell. But he leapt up and circled around, feeling like a hunter in some ancient world, holding the spear up.

"Come on, Scratch," he said. His voice was raspy.

He could not see anything other than shapes against the earth.

He wasn't sure if he had begun imagining things, but it seemed like there were several shapes moving—shadows against shadows.

Shit, I'm losing it.

Make me a warrior. Make me a man. Make me the hero. Make me the one. It was like a chant in his head. *Fill me up with strength. Give me power over my enemies. I am good. I am just. I will overcome. I will defeat. I will be the victor.*

As he circled the car and then wandered a ways into the dark, holding the spear up, he felt...*tribal.* Connected. There was a welling up within him that convinced him he wasn't fighting some monster on the desert, but participating in an ancient rite of manhood—and he was meant to be here.

Gone were the trappings of home, university, as sense of the future and his hold on the past.

He was HUNTER.

He was HUNTER and this thing was his HUNTED.

I AM NOT PREY! I AM NOT PREY! You are rabbit. I am coyote. You are serpent, I am eagle! I AM THE HUNTER OF THE GODS OF DEATH!

A LIGHTENING of his being occurred—he no longer felt the small jabs of rock beneath his feet, nor did he experience the fear in the same way as he had, nor did the desert seem as dark.

He felt as if a weight had lifted from him to be cast off into shadows.

And there it was.

The Being.

The Creature.

The Flayer of Men.

He knew its name. Its ritual name.

Xipe Totec! You are under my foot!

Xipe Totec! You are the skin of the snake!

Xipe Totec! You have no power over me!

I am the PRIEST and the HUNTER of Death.

A small voice within him: *Am I mad? Is this insanity?*

But the larger voice within him—the voice of a man he barely recognized—said aloud, "I am here to destroy you!"

IT WAS HIS OWN VOICE, but it seemed to come from a different place inside. Something had been awakened.

THE CREATURE LEAPT AT HIM, and he lost his balance, falling backward. The spear went flying back, out of his reach.

He felt the claws dig in—Scratch was crawling up along his left leg. The pain was excruciating.

I'm not afraid of pain. I will not be afraid of pain. Pain is nothing. Pain is a scream to nowhere. Pain is meaningless.

He felt as if the veins of his legs were being ripped out, but he gritted his teeth and refused to accept the agony.

I AM THE PRIEST. I AM THE HUNTER.

IT TUGGED AT HIS LEGS, and began dragging him across the rocks and sand. His head hit the back of a rock, and he felt himself lose consciousness.

I AM THE PRIEST.
I AM.

HANG ON. Hang on. This is no dream. This is real. Wake up. Wake up.

Josh opened his eyes. He felt a pumping of blood within him. *I am alive. I will not die.* He pivoted on his hips as Scratch drew him across the dirt. Then he reached his hand out and dug his fingernails down into the earth. Pressed his fingers in. Held on.

The pain in his calves grew to a screaming pitch.

The talons had gone in deep. He wasn't sure how much blood he'd lost.

He dug his other hand into the dirt. Hurt like razors.

He groped in the dirt, and tugged himself back. Maybe a quarter inch. Glanced in the darkness. Manzanilla. Rocks. Car. He dragged himself further. Toward the spear. Toward the obsidian arrowhead.

He couldn't be certain, but he thought he saw the makeshift spear lying just out of his grasp.

Scratch was chewing on his left leg, but if he tried—if he took all he had—he could get the spear. Something was drawing him down into a dark maelstrom in his head, but he dragged himself forward.

Touched the edge of the spear. His hand went around it. He drew it back, and sat up.

He thought he saw the look on Scratch's face, as the turquoise eyes stared at him.

He brought the spear down into Scratch's jaw, and then pulled hard on it until he heard a crack. At first, he thought the spear had broken, but it was the creature's lower jaw that fell sideways, hanging by a small bit of gristle.

Then, he drew the spear out, putting his hand close to where the obsidian was wrapped around the base.

He plunged the arrowhead into the space beneath Scratch's breastbone.

Scratch's claws curled around his fingers.

"You can't kill me," Scratch said with Tammy's voice, but it was funny-sounding as its dangling jaw wagged.

"You know that. You know all about me, don't you? Give yourself to Xipe Totec! Heroes must be sacrificed."

But, in fact, just as Josh had suspected, the mummy had some kind of moist pulpy material within its ribcage: a beating heart, perhaps not like a human heart, but a heart nonetheless.

And the obsidian went into it.

The claws let go of his wrist.

He drew the arrowhead up.

At its tip, a mass of bloody tissue.

The great Flayer of Men lay still at his bloody legs.

At some point, Josh passed out.

CHAPTER SEVENTEEN

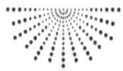

W hen Josh awoke, someone was pouring cool
water over him.

He opened his eyes.

Dawn light blinded him momentarily before his sight
adjusted.

A large, thickset man with a day's growth of beard sat
beside him. In his hand, a large bottle of water.

"Ely?"

Josh glanced around. Ely was carefully lifting him up
to get in the truck with him. "Hello, kid. I was pretty sure
you were a goner."

"My legs…"

"Yeah, I saw 'em. Torn up real bad. Mountain lion?"

Josh didn't respond.

"You're some kind of superman, kid. Lost a lot of
blood. I saw you just crawling by the road there. Let's get
you over to the hospital. They can patch you up. I suck at
it. Look, don't talk. We'll get there soon enough. Can you
hang on?"

Josh nodded. He took the bottle from Ely's hand and drank from it.

He felt the rumble of the truck start up.

"You kill the lion?" Ely asked.

"What?"

"The mountain lion. The one that attacked you. You kill it?"

"Not sure," Josh said. "I hurt it. I know that."

"Well, that's something," Ely said, and then got the truck in gear and pulled back out on the highway. "It's something to put a hurt back on a beast like that. When you're all better, I want you to tell me everything you didn't tell me before, okay?"

CHAPTER EIGHTEEN

All this happened in the late 1970s, before the new highway came in, before I moved permanently to Naga, Arizona, and before I began to understand my place in the world.

My name is Joshua, and I've grown to love this desert.

I WENT BACK, after I'd plunged the razor-sharp obsidian in that monster's heart.

After my legs healed up. After some time had passed and I could face it again.

I wanted to examine it before destroying it.

In size, it was four feet four inches tall, and while I didn't weigh it, I can guess it was about sixty pounds. The gauze on its body—what kept its bones wrapped—was not what I had expected. I had assumed it was some kind of cloth, but, instead, it was fine, thin layers of human skin, torn into strips, wrapped around the bone of the creature.

I held up one of its claws. Each talon was its own blade, and was razor-sharp.

I plucked the turquoise from its eyes, because I'd been reading about rituals by then.

It could be blinded. It could be incapacitated.

The more I looked at it, the more I began to feel for it. What is it in human life that does it? That holds a monster in its arms and feels something like kinship—an instinct to care and protect? A demon, sleeping, in my arms, seemed vulnerable and in need.

I placed it inside a leather-bound box that was lined with stone, closing it up inside it, its coffin. If no one fed it again, if no one let it out, surely, it could just sleep forever.

And in sleeping, what damage could this thing do?

ONE NIGHT, troubled by fears, I went out to the furthest mesa, and buried Scratch deep, the way I'd bury something toxic, something that no man should ever touch, ever know.

But the cities and towns are growing. They're taking over parts of the desert that were once vast wastelands, miles of nothing.

Now, years later, suburban homes are being built on the mesa, and the bulldozers dig down deep and carve out swimming pools. Scorpions swarm as they're sent from their nests. Rattlesnakes are killed by workmen who find them under nearly every rock.

I didn't mark the place where I buried Scratch. I didn't put a flag over it so I could find it.

I buried that little unspeakable mystery to end it, to forget it, to put the demon somewhere it would never be found.

But I was wrong. Everything can be found. All it takes is time.

They're digging all over that mesa. They'll bring him out. Maybe they already have.

A man and woman went missing a week ago. Their car was smashed up on the side of the road in the middle of nowhere. There was blood everywhere inside the car.

The Flayer of Men will dance again.

I'm certain of that.

Someone will feed it, probably by accident.

Someone will think it's cool when they find it, and the poor son-of-a-bitch won't know what hit him.

Maybe the couple in the car already fed him. Maybe they already woke him up.

It's been hot and dry for a hell of a long time, but I suspect a rainstorm's on the way.

The dreams have come back, too.

The ones at the pyramid.

I close my eyes and I can see the little bastard plain as day.

He's beginning to look more and more like me.

Scratch and me—we're connected by blood.

His voice, growing louder in my dreams:

Dance and be reborn in blood and life, from your dark sleep!

GET STUFF. STAY CONNECTED.
READ MORE.

Visit DouglasClegg.com

ABOUT THE AUTHOR

Douglas Clegg is the *New York Times* bestselling and award-winning author of *Neverland*, *The Priest of Blood*, *Afterlife*, and *The Hour Before Dark*, among many other novels, novellas and stories. His first collection, *The Nightmare Chronicles*, won both the Bram Stoker Award and the International Horror Guild Award. His work has been published by Simon & Schuster, Penguin/Berkley, Signet, Dorchester, Bantam Dell Doubleday, Cemetery Dance Publications, Subterranean Press, Alkemara Press and others.

A pioneer in the ebook world, his novel *Naomi* made international news when it was launched as the world's first ebook serial in early 1999 and was called "the first major work of fiction to originate in cyberspace" by *Publisher's Weekly*, covered in *Time* magazine, *Business Week*, *Business 2.0*, *BBC Radio*, *NPR*, *USA Today* and more. His book *Purity* was the first to be published via mobile phone in the U.S. in early 2001.

He is married, and lives and writes along the coast of New England.

Find the Author Online:
www.DouglasClegg.com

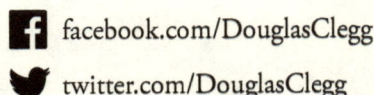 facebook.com/DouglasClegg

twitter.com/DouglasClegg